THE
BREASTPLATE
OF
FAITH AND LOVE

THE
BREASTPLATE
OF
FAITH AND LOVE

A Stafford Boyle Mystery

Paul McGoran

NEW PULP PRESS

Published by New Pulp Press, LLC, 926 Truman Avenue, Key West, Florida 33040, USA.

For information contact:
Publisher@NewPulpPress.com

ISBN-13: 978-1945734014 (New Pulp Press)
ISBN-10: 1945734019

THE
BREASTPLATE
OF
FAITH AND LOVE

PART I

AN OLD SCANDAL

CHAPTER 1

Claudia Chitworth sat in the enormous great room of Dismas Cottage and gazed out the floor-to-ceiling windows overlooking the mansion's manicured grounds and her beloved weeping beech trees. She didn't often come into this room. It was one of those showplace creations that certain super-rich Victorians fancied-crafted more for shock and awe than daily living. Today, however, she felt herself drawn to the windows and memories of family gatherings under those very same trees.

An old woman should not have worries like these, she thought. In just a little while, she would make her weekly call to San Francisco and her dear, dear niece Angela. Would this be the day she told Angela about young Sam? Probably not. No, she couldn't do that without telling her son Ivan—he would be angry if he weren't consulted.

But nearly two years had gone by, and it *must* be done very soon. What if Angela found out through some third party that she and Ivan had custody of a child by her dead husband's agency – a child she knew nothing about? Despite the awfulness of that man, Sam Porter, Claudia realized that her niece would feel a betrayal. Not his betrayal, but hers and Ivan's.

In death, Angela's forgiveness for that evil beast was total. She never spoke of him and never would, but Claudia knew her niece's mind. If she heard of young Sam's existence, she would insist on raising him with her own son Justin. This is what Claudia had to sort out. Would that indeed be the best thing for Sam ... or for Angela and Justin?

Oh dear, she thought, who could know such things? If only Kathy Dunnell had left the child with her own people, none of this would be a burden to Claudia in her final years. Evidently, the poor sick girl felt that Sam should have the advantages of their position and wealth.

When Kathy visited Newport the first time, Claudia warned Ivan not to get involved. But he hadn't listened. When do children ever listen? Later, in 2005, Kathy came back with Sam to grant them custody. She was very sick then, and there were tearful scenes. Claudia tried to remain adamant, but Ivan prevailed. He was sure he could assume the responsibilities of a parent.

"But what about your people, Kathy?" Claudia had asked. "Surely they want custody."

"My parents are dead, Mrs. Chitworth. My grandparents raised me. They're too old to bring up another child. They understand I want Sam to have this chance."

Now if they were too old, Claudia was as well. Ivan's promises notwithstanding, would he be able to raise a child by himself when she died? He would never marry—she had finally come to realize it. Angela, on the other hand, had married that wonderful Brad Styles. Together, they enjoyed all the resources necessary to raise two boys who were, after all, brothers. Well, half-brothers.

With a sigh, Claudia rose from the settee, walked into the foyer, and trudged up the stairs to her room off the second floor balcony. The bedroom was large, but cozy in the yellows and pinks she favored. Her bedspread, chair coverings, rugs, and wallpaper all incorporated those colors. The rich, glowing surfaces of her furniture grounded the colors and played against the honey pine floor with the mahogany stripe inside the apron. Her mood brightened here after a short time, and she sat down, picked up the old-fashioned landline telephone extension, and dialed her niece's number in San Francisco.

"Hello."

"Oh, Angela, it's you. Somehow I always expect your housekeeper to answer."

"Aunt Claudia! So nice to hear your voice. This is my cell phone, dear. You know that."

"Well, I should, but I cling to old notions so fiercely, I just never expect to hear you right off."

Claudia was delighted to hear Angela's rich, lovely laugh.

"Now tell me how Brad and Justin are doing," she said.

"Quite well, Aunt Claudia. You and Ivan are well, I trust?"

"Yes, Angela. Everything is fine here. Ivan is elusive, you know, he often disappears on me. But I can't expect him to let me know every time he goes out. He would exhaust himself just looking for me in this enormous old house. And I'm never alone, my maid is a comfort."

"Brad just walked by, Aunt Claudia, he says hello. He's off to a luncheon now. I probably won't see him until dinner. Justin has been sent to his room for a time out – I can't seem to stop him from acting up whenever he's told he won't be going out with one of us."

"Oh dear, the trials of youth."

"Yes, I suppose. He's really a wonderful child, but he does get moody and stubborn."

"Well, your sister Helena was like that, if you

remember."

Now why did she say that? Helena was Angela's *step*sister, unrelated by blood. Those weren't traits the child could have inherited—from Helena. She felt like a stupid old woman for saying such a thing. Thank heaven Angela ignored her gaffe.

"You're right. I remember how she clung to Dad in the old days when we spent the summer with you."

"Oh, how I loved those days, Angela. I was thinking of them just now, you know, staring at the beech trees from the windows in the great room. I am so nostalgic. It must be old age."

"Never. Not you, Auntie. I feel the same way about those times. Who wouldn't?"

"Well, I ... well, I'm glad everything is all right. Why don't I let you go now?"

"Are you sure? For a second there I thought you wanted to say something more, dear."

"No, no. I'm finished, Angela. I want to rest for a while. Give my love to Justin and Brad."

"I'll do that. And you give my best to Ivan."

"Certainly, dear."

"Good bye, Aunt Claudia. I love you."

"Thank you, Angela. You know I count on it."

As she hung up, Claudia thought about how close she came to broaching the subject of young Sam. But that would have been a mistake. Still, there *had* to be a way to get started, to work toward resolving the impasse. This wasn't about her feelings, she reminded herself. It was for Sam's sake and Ivan's, too. The boy's welfare might depend on it.

And suddenly she knew what that first step would be.

Sam had a right to know he had a brother his own age. She would tell him, and his questions would force both her and Ivan to a decision. The longer they waited, the harder it would be to explain. She wouldn't ask Ivan about this because he would stall, perhaps forever. She would never presume to tell Angela about Sam without Ivan's permission—but this she could do.

The boy would be in the little suite they still called the nursery—two adjoining rooms with bath that comprised his bedroom and a playroom. Maria, her maid, would be with him now.

Claudia's step was lighter as she walked out from her room and past the library to the nursery. She could hear Maria playing some counting game with Sam in Spanish. He was laughing as Claudia approached the open door.

~~~

Presents. So many, many presents with fantastic colored bows. And the tree in the big room covered with real snow! Not a Christmas tree, but something else, like a very tall round bush with a thick, raggedy trunk and layers and layers of palm fronds all shining with snow and icicles, right inside the house. The gift boxes were piled so high under the tree, Sam couldn't imagine having time to open them all in a single day. And every tag he looked at had his name on it! Oh, who had done this for him?

He would have to ask Ivan to tell him who to thank. Aunt Claudia said it was impolite not to thank for a gift. He was anxious to start tearing them open, yet he stood back for a minute to look at the tree and the room bathed in light from the hall. But the richness of the colored wrappings, the glint of foil, the soft silk and satin bows –

all of it was too much to resist. And he dived in.

He felt the first tug of disappointment when the snow and icicles began to melt, wetting his hair and dripping into his eyes. He swept the gifts within reach out of the way of the increasing torrent and yanked off their wilted bows.

Then the scene grew grim with the tree bare and all the presents wet, every one. He stripped the giftwrap off several boxes and lined them up. The tops were sealed with a little tape, forcing him to open them slowly. When the first box proved empty, he wasn't angry – there were so many more.

Oh, but the second one was empty too, and now he noticed how cool the room had gotten. He was wet, shivering and alone. And he knew all his gifts would be empty. It wasn't fair. There would be no one to thank and maybe no one to blame; but something was missing here and someone would have to put it right. As he turned back to look at the room one last time, the tree ... itself ... had changed.

Sam Dunnell woke up with a yell, writhing in his sweaty bedclothes. But he didn't cry. After sitting up and listening for a minute, he decided no one had heard him. He lay back down and thought for a long time about Justin. His half-brother, Aunt Claudia had said. Although he tried, he couldn't figure out what that really meant. Did they look alike, he wondered. Was he nice?

Aunt Claudia had wanted to know if he had questions, but he couldn't think of any. He just had this feeling something was missing. Missing before he knew about Justin, and missing still. It was like somebody had played a trick on him.

He already knew your life wasn't quite your own, and that parts of it could be stolen away. It had happened to him more than once – and he was only seven.

CHAPTER 2

It was May 1, a Tuesday. Stafford Boyle sat in his tiny home office, chewing over what Billy Moncton's wife had said. Everybody in Newport knew Billy, who had a reputation as an egotistical sonuvabitch. Even *before* he won a million bucks on that big-time reality show and started cheating on the missus.

Boyle's first meeting with Theresa Moncton had been four days ago, on Friday. He drove over from Newport to her place in nearby Middletown where she had agreed to meet him on her lunch break. Billy was supposed to be in Boston to meet with a reporter and to interview for a radio job, but she wasn't so sure about that.

"If not Boston, where do think your husband is, Mrs. Moncton?"

"Oh, he may be in Boston, but I don't think it has anything to do with reporters or a radio job. I think he's with another woman."

"What makes you think that?"

"Well ... I don't have proof, I just know something is wrong."

He could see she was tense from her body language and the strained expression on her face. She had folded her arms in front of her and was now crossing her left leg over the right. Suddenly, she reversed the leg cross, probably realizing how defensive it made her appear. And she had that tight-lipped look that told Boyle she might begin to cry any moment.

"Mrs. Moncton, may I have a glass of water? My throat's a little dry."

He said it to divert her attention and give her a chance to think about what she wanted to say. What she probably *didn't* want to tell him was that their sex life had dropped off. In Boyle's limited experience, that would be a factor she might be reluctant to broach to a stranger. If other patterns in her marriage had changed as well, Theresa Moncton's trip to the kitchen might jog her memory.

While she was gone, Boyle glanced at his notes. There were just two entries: Billy Moncton, Boston. In the background, he could hear the clink of ice in a glass and a faucet running. He hoped it had a filter.

Mrs. Moncton's round, pleasant face was flushed when she returned to the living room. She placed the glass of ice water on the mahogany coffee table just in front of Boyle, tucking a marble coaster with a cork center under it. She had regained her composure and was smiling. As she sat down, she smoothed her skirt under her thighs and made eye contact with him.

"My husband was a high school teacher before he went on *Castaways*, Mr. Boyle. When he returned from Australia, he went right back to work and his old routines. At that point, no one knew he was the winner. He didn't quit his job until after the big finale in New York. It was then things began to change. I didn't notice anything terribly wrong at first. It was gradual. But the publicity and money were complicating our life. There was this obsession about show business. And he was ... staying away from me, you know?"

"Show business?" Boyle didn't get that part.

"You'd have to know Billy. He was always a ham, so his push to find a job on television or radio wasn't a real stretch. But when his efforts fizzled, I expected him to ... step back and pursue something else. He didn't have to go back to teaching if he didn't want to."

She shifted her weight in the armchair and seemed to concentrate harder.

"What it amounted to," she said, "was that he was spending a lot of days away from home while I continued to work. The little trips made me suspicious. Last week a friend of mine spotted his car in Newport when he was supposed to be meeting with someone in New Bedford."

"Did you confront him about that?"

"No. I just asked him how things went. He told me he had the interview but wouldn't know anything until someone got back to him. Rather than confront him, I called you."

"Have there been unexplained telephone calls?"

"Not that I've noticed. He has his own cell phone. Still, I pay the bill, and I haven't seen anything out of the ordinary."

"When Billy goes on these trips, does he always take his car?"

"So far, yes."

"Any overnight stays?"

"No, none. I would definitely confront him over something like that, and he knows it."

"Okay, Mrs. Moncton. Why don't I tail your husband some morning soon and report back to you. And give me a call next time he says he's going out of town. That needs to be checked out too."

Boyle took a retainer for ten hours work. As he rose to leave, he glanced at the check she gave him and raised an eyebrow.

"Something wrong?" she asked.

"Well ... this is a joint checking account. Doesn't your husband look at the statements?"

"Oh, I see," she laughed. "No, he never even writes a check. He uses the debit card and I use the checkbook. Billy's not a math guy and he doesn't bother with the details."

"Have you noticed any changes in his spending habits?"

"We both spend more since the prize money. But it seems within reason to me."

Boyle nodded while his gaze took in all the new furniture the million-dollar prize had brought into the Monctons' home.

"Take a good look at my car when I leave," he said. "You may be seeing it from time to time. I wouldn't want you to call me saying there's a suspicious vehicle hanging around."

Mrs. Moncton showed him to the door. She was a nice lady. Boyle hoped she didn't mind that he never touched the ice water.

~~~

On Monday, he made his first move. Mrs. Moncton hadn't called, which meant Billy wouldn't be out of town today. By seven-thirty, Boyle intended to be in place to stake out their house on Kelso Street in Middletown. He left his condo in Berwind Lodge on Dixon Street, got into his silver-gray Honda Civic and drove down to lower Thames Street, stopping there to pick up a large coffee and cinnamon roll at Barry's Dandy Lunch.

Automatically, he checked out the slice of harbor front to his left as he passed by the diner's street-side windows. A light fog swirled over the patch of water visible between the low-slung waterfront buildings. Inside, the coffee smell was strong, the brew identifiably American. He couldn't stomach the brand at the more exclusive coffee shop or its knock-offs that were springing up all over. Coffee should taste like coffee, he figured.

The cinnamon bun was history by the time he parked at the end of Kelso Street and settled in. He pried the coffee container out of its holder and took a long toke through the sippy-cup opening in the cover. Through his windshield, he gazed out at an undistinguished suburban street. On the west side, a row of small ranch-style homes with a few split-levels interspersed. A nineteen-fifties to sixties development for sure. The east side was nearly all raised ranches – a follow-up development in the seventies, most likely. No sidewalks on either side. Indifferently trimmed lawns.

The Monctons' house was not quite so typical. It stood on the eastern half of the street about sixty yards down from where Boyle had parked on the opposite side. A slate blue garrison colonial with white trim surrounded by a picket fence – flowerbeds and lawn beautifully tended. The class of the street, Boyle thought.

At eight-thirty, he watched a white Beemer back out of the driveway at 57 Kelso Street. Billy Moncton's car. He followed as Billy drove to the nearest cross street and headed for West Main Road, pausing there for a traffic light. When Billy turned south at the light, it was evident he was headed for Newport.

Ten minutes later, Boyle grinned as Billy flew by Dixon Street on his way up Bellevue Avenue. Boyle was back where he started from just two hours ago.

They were in the mansion district now, and the little lawns and shoddy flower beds of suburban Middletown had given way to the majestic trees, manicured grounds and Victorian street lamps of fabled Bellevue Avenue. He had let Billy run pretty far ahead as traffic thinned out going up the avenue. But when he saw him make a left, Boyle hit the gas pedal to catch up.

Billy had turned in at Leroy Avenue. All mansions here. Old money homes owned by old money Newporters. The Beemer sprang into the driveway of an estate that Stafford Boyle knew by sight – Dismas Cottage, the Chitworth place. Some people called it Murder Mansion on account of the commotion back in 1999, the end of the infamous Shoo-fly case.

Boyle found himself gaping. My, my, he thought, what have we here?

In the end, what he had was not much. Billy Moncton went into Dismas Cottage and stayed for over two hours. Boyle felt stiff and crotchety by the time Billy came out and drove back home to Middletown. That was enough for one day's work, he decided.

~~~

Playing a hunch, Boyle skipped the ride out to Middletown on Wednesday, stationing himself instead on Leroy Avenue, too far away to be seen clearly by anyone pulling into the driveway at Dismas Cottage. Which is just what Billy's white Beemer did around eight forty-five.

Okay, he told himself, this is probably a regular thing.

No need to wait around and get leg cramps; just go find out who lives there. Especially the guy who opened the door for Billy Moncton. Boyle may have been too far away to be seen, but his binoculars gave him a clear view of a man in his late thirties who greeted Billy at the door.

He waited a few minutes longer when he saw a truck pull up alongside the mansion. A short, thickset man swung out of the cab and went to the rear of the truck to open the back doors. Driving slowly by, Boyle recognized Johnny Nunes, a groundskeeper he knew pretty well.

They chatted a minute before he got around to asking who was living there. Johnny smiled and cocked his head.

"Whatcha doin' Staff? Some sorta official inquiry, or you just got nose trouble?"

"Don't give me grief, my man. I'm curious about seeing Murder Mansion occupied. Car's in the driveway, after all."

"Ivan and old lady Chitworth are back year round again. But the Beemer don't belong to the Chitworths. Which of course you might of already figured."

He grinned and looked Boyle straight in the face. "Kinda early in the mornin' to be so curious, Staff. You gonna tell me about it?"

"Nothing to tell. Some days I do get up before noon, you know. Just to drive around and laugh at the working stiffs. See ya, Johnny."

"Screw you, Boyle!" Johnny's smile went ear to ear as Boyle eased away toward Bellevue Avenue.

CHAPTER 3

Newport, Rhode Island, is one of those ancient New England towns where long-time residents have no real secrets. Especially the upper crust. When they say the rich are different from you and me, what they mean is the poor bastards can never live like we do – in blissful anonymity. They are watched constantly.

Just figure for yourself – if you lived next to Angelina Jolie or Oprah, somebody that famous, everybody you know would be asking, on a daily basis, what she did last night, who came to see her, what's she like. It's human nature. You'd find yourself watching what went on more than you should and reporting back to all those curious relatives and friends.

So it didn't take much effort to find out a few things about the Chitworths. Boyle didn't have to ask if they were rich, that was common knowledge. Jeannie Somers, a woman he knew at the Preservation Society, filled him in on the rest. Jeannie was a real authority on Newport's social scene.

"Claudia Chitworth has spent her entire life between New York and Newport," she said. "She's one of the few remaining dowager queens from the old days."

"Who else lives at Dismas Cottage, Jeannie?"

"Just Ivan. He's her only son, born when she turned forty. Simon Chitworth was the husband. He died when Ivan was five years old."

"What does Ivan Chitworth do for a living?"

"Except for volunteer positions, I don't think work has ever been an option for him," she laughed. "Mainly, he plays a lot of tennis and golf with his social set. You know the type – a Newport trust fund baby."

"Anything else I should know?"

"Well, there's a little boy staying with them. I don't know how long he's been there. Someone said he's a distant relative from a southern state."

Boyle set that aside for now, it didn't figure into his case at all.

"Jeannie, one last thing. Was Ivan ever married?"

"You mean ... to account for the boy? Well, he did live in New York City for a number of years in the off-season. I can't really imagine my not hearing about a marriage, but who knows?"

Boyle decided he should meet Ivan somehow and size him up. He must be the guy who welcomed Billy to Dismas Cottage. Didn't Jeannie say that Ivan chaired a weekly writer's group at the Athenaeum, a private lending library? Why not focus on that?

After all, Boyle had often thought about writing a mystery novel. He had sure read enough of them. No reason he couldn't fake it through at least one meeting. But could he really churn out thousands of words in the form of a coherent story? Somehow, he always imagined big-time writers like Coben and Connelly just dictated their stuff to some lackey. If it wasn't like that ... he might not be cut out for the writing life.

~~~

On Thursday evening, Boyle left Berwind Lodge for the Athenaeum on Bellevue Avenue, a ten-minute walk. The weather was almost-summer mild. The trees along the avenue were filled out now, their leaves still in their first green freshness. The whole town had a newly scrubbed look, and the night air carried a lovely cool undertone.

He strolled up the bluestone walkway leading toward the front stairs and nodded to the bronze statue of Washington, circling round him to the building's side entrance on Redwood Street. Inside, portraits of colonial notables were hung high in the main hall. The young woman seated at the reception desk pointed out the function room where the writing group met. It was six-thirty, the group would meet at seven, and he expected to be the first arrival. Which he was.

Ten straight-back chairs surrounded an oblong conference table. Boyle sat toward the back of the room so he could face the doorway and watch the participants come in. He set out a mechanical pencil and a lined writing tablet on the table. Then he rested his hands in his lap and waited.

Before long, a middle-aged lady with a quiet tread and a quizzical expression walked in and sat in the chair nearest the door.

"I'm Stafford Boyle," he said, standing briefly and smiling.

"My name is Constance ... Constance Beaufort," she said in a timid voice. She pronounced her last name in the southern fashion—*Byoo*-fert — but without the southern accent.

Constance had long red hair with some frizzy gray mixed in. She wrote romance fiction, and her leather lawyer's satchel was brimming with paper. A man and woman, both young, both carrying briefcases, came in next, followed by Ivan Chitworth.

In a moment, the air was full of talk. The young man and woman jabbered with Ivan a full two minutes while they took seats and began pulling out papers and writing implements. Boyle kept his head up to intercept and respond to any remark or glance that might come his way, but none did. He noticed Constance kept her eyes on the table in front of her. The little group's social pecking order seemed obvious.

As the chatter began to subside, Ivan greeted Constance and looked toward Boyle, who smiled his best and introduced himself.

"Welcome to our little group, Mr. Boyle," said Ivan. "Let me introduce Trainor DeSales and Marilyn Rezendes. I guess you've already met Constance."

"Yes, I have."

Boyle nodded to the two young people, who gave him the briefest of glances before resuming their own conversation.

Ten minutes into the meeting, he realized everything here turned on genre. DeSales and Rezendes represented "mainstream" and "literary" fiction respectively. Ivan wrote historical non-fiction. All three of them were therefore a cut above. Ivan was not a snob about this, but the other two were insufferable. Because Constance and Boyle were identified with romance and mystery fiction – stuff people actually paid for and read – they were a lesser breed. Writers, perhaps; authors, never.

Ivan explained the usual format of their meetings was for one member to hand out copies of some pages – a chapter, say – read it aloud and ask for comments. This night, Constance held the floor. Boyle felt sorry for her at first, but he needn't have. She read nicely, he thought, and her chapter held his interest.

"Constance, that was lovely," Ivan said when she finished. "The story is really coming together now. I'm impressed."

She was beaming. "Thank you, Ivan. I was afraid the pace was too slow."

DeSales and Rezendes managed a condescending murmur.

As the newbie, Boyle didn't know whether he should comment, but he didn't hold back.

"I liked it a lot, Constance," he said. "Have you been published?"

Her rising color told him she took it as a compliment.

"No, but thank you," she said. "This is my very first novel."

Boyle saw he was in over his head, and that he'd have to get his business done tonight. There was no way he could come back to this group over a period of weeks. The thought of having to write something and read it, then lead a discussion of a writing topic—as Constance was doing now—was the stuff of nightmares.

When the meeting ended, he conversed with her a while, then hung around the main hall looking into a raised glass case at an exhibit of eighteenth-century diaries until DeSales and Rezendes left. They both said good night pleasantly. Had he been too judgmental about them?

He debated with himself about handling Ivan. For now, he decided to stay in character as someone interested in writing. This was only going to take a few minutes, he told himself. He already had an idea about Ivan Chitworth.

Boyle was standing by the front door when Ivan came out of the meeting room and walked toward him. "Mind if I tag along with you and talk for a minute, Ivan?" he asked.

"Of course not. How do you like our little group ... uh ... Stafford?"

As always, people had trouble with his first name. He figured Ivan couldn't decide whether to abbreviate it or not.

"Just call me 'Staff.'"

"Staph like the infection?" he laughed, his voice going way up at the end.

"No, Staff as in 'staff of life'," Boyle said, smiling.

Ivan's expression was smirky and his head seemed to bobble on his shoulders. He was definitely starting to flirt, and Boyle had his answer. Ivan Chitworth was gay. Nice enough guy, mind you, but no question about his orientation.

"Look, Ivan, I need to let you know I'm out of my league here. I won't be coming back. I'd just be wasting everybody's time."

"Well, I understand, if that's how you feel. But if you get something written and you want feedback, we'll be glad to help."

"Thanks."

"Anyway, it was nice to meet you."

"Same here. Take care."

They shook hands, and Boyle walked back down Redwood Street toward Bellevue Avenue. Behind him, he heard Ivan's car starting up.

~~~

When he thought it over, Boyle decided not to wrap the

case up just yet. No use outing anybody until he solved the mystery of Billy Moncton's little excursions. If he really was going on job interviews, the whole picture might change. For all he knew, Ivan was just an old buddy and Mr. Moncton was above reproach. Anyhow, he wouldn't need to tail him again unless and until Mrs. Moncton got back to him about some plan of Billy's to go out of town. So far, that left Boyle free for the weekend.

Even after five years of living in Newport, tooling around the island in spring was pure pleasure for Boyle. Which is what he planned to do Saturday. It sounded so good he'd do it alone if that pretty new waitress at McQuirk's had other plans. He called her to find out.

"Assunta, it's Staff." What a combination of first names, he thought. And what in hell would *her* nickname be?

"Hi Staff. Whazzup?"

Much younger than him, she was still way too old for 'whazzup.' He loved it anyhow.

"I have a totally unbeatable proposition. How would you like to spend tomorrow morning and afternoon with a handsome older gentleman known for his *savoir vivre*? An early breakfast, say, followed by a local expedition to little-known coves and sparkling vistas, and topped off by lunch in a nearby off-island community."

"Wow. Sounds practically—international. What's the catch?"

"The catch is I'm the guy."

"H-m-m-m. You know something? It still sounds good."

"Splendid, my lady! Pick you up around seven?"

"C'mon, Boyle! You have any idea how late I'll be working tonight? And how soft and warm my bed will be at seven tomorrow morning?"

"No, but I'm forming a very distinct mental picture."

"*Savoir vivre*, hunh? More like *savoir-jive-turkey*."

They agreed to meet at eight-thirty. This would be a follow-up date and he wanted it to come off just so. Casual and fun, but just so. He liked Assunta a lot and believed she felt the connection as well. Two weeks earlier he had taken her to a local theater production, and they had a nice time. After the play, they had a few drinks and shared a chaste goodnight kiss.

Boyle was a middle-aged man going after a thirty-year-old woman – yet *he* was the one who felt vulnerable. If Saturday worked out well, he'd try to see her again mid-week. Step up the old pace. Her waitress job precluded most evening dates, but that was all right – he kind of liked the idea of daytime romancing. Maybe it was the thought of ... what was that old song ... *Afternoon Delights?*

CHAPTER 4

Theresa Moncton called Boyle early Sunday evening while he was watching the Red Sox game. He used the remote to mute the sound but kept on watching as Theresa spoke.

"Billy's going to Boston tomorrow, Mr. Boyle."

"Did he say what time?"

"Eight a.m. bus from Newport. He has an appointment at ten-thirty with the program director at B-Bay Communications. That's with two capital B's."

"Gotcha."

From the camera angle on Boyle's television screen, it looked liked Ortiz had smashed another monstrous homer. Not knowing for sure, he was irritated – until the scoreboard display lit up to tell him he was right. Yes-s-s-s!

"Anything else I should know, Mrs. Moncton?"

"I can't think of anything."

"Okay. I assume he'll leave from the Gateway in Newport, but I'll be at your house tomorrow morning about ... ten minutes past seven. If he leaves home before that, call my cell. Otherwise, you'll see my car when you leave for work."

"Why don't you just go straight to the Gateway?"

"If the Boston trip is a ruse, he may not be headed that way."

"Oh, right," she laughed. "Good thing one of us is a detective. Will this be the first time you've followed him?"

"No. But we'll talk about that on Tuesday, after I see

where he goes tomorrow. May I call you at work?"

"Yes," she said, and gave him the number.

When he hung up, he un-muted the TV, then shut it down entirely. The Sox were comfortably ahead, and he needed to think.

He got out his notebook and looked up the page he started when he met with Theresa Moncton the first time. Under 'Moncton, Boston' he wrote 'Gateway, 8 a.m.,' as well as the date and Mrs. Moncton's telephone number at work. Mentally, he cobbled the things he already knew into a little scenario for presenting to his client. But his heart wasn't in it, and he closed the notebook.

He should think things through and formulate alternatives for tomorrow. If Billy wasn't headed for Boston, for instance, should he follow? He couldn't kid himself, however; he was damn sure he knew what was going to transpire. What was really on his mind was Assunta. Assunta the fair. He put the notebook away and let himself think about their date the previous day.

It had been raining early Saturday morning when he picked her up. She dashed from her apartment to his car as soon as he pulled into the driveway. He had dreaded bad weather, but she was laughing about it. And radiant. Which made him smile.

Moments later the sun burst through, and thinning clouds gave way to a blue spring sky. He kept her laughing through breakfast, until he was afraid he might be trying too hard. Afterwards, they lapsed into an easy silence on their drive through the other island towns of Middletown and Portsmouth.

Before long, they had a decision to make. Leaving the

island at this end meant taking a bridge to the north or another to the east.

"Bristol or Tiverton, Assunta. Which one?"

"Let's go to Tiverton and Little Compton, Staff. I haven't been that way in a while."

"To the east, then."

They flew over the Sakonnet River Bridge into Tiverton and stopped for a while at Four Corners, a village intersection with shops, a lovely stream, and ancient buildings. Assunta let Boyle hold her hand, which made him feel possessive and content at the same time.

"Blue moon this month, Staff," she said as they walked back to his Honda.

"What does that mean?"

"There was a huge full moon on Tuesday. Didn't you see it?"

"Nope. Stayed home."

"Well, there's two this month. The second one on the thirty-first will be the blue moon."

She paused, then looked at him smiling. "Stayed home doing what?"

"I needed to think."

"About ...?"

"About a girl I know."

"I'll bet. You are so outrageous!"

"But it's true. Don't you want to know who the girl was?"

"I'm gonna pretend you didn't ask."

If she had pulled her hand away just then, he would have worried about her saying that. But she didn't, so he drew her close and kissed her before they got in his car and drove down route 77 into Little Compton. The rest of the day flowed in that same easy way—through lunch at The Commons restaurant, walking the breakwater at Sakonnet Point, necking on the sofa at Assunta's place later. He couldn't wait to see her again come Tuesday.

And he found out her nickname. Sunta. Thank God for that. The alternative was unthinkable.

~~~

Boyle was at Kelso Street Monday morning at seven o'clock. No coffee, no cinnamon bun, just the aftertaste of pulpy orange juice with undertones of Shredded Wheat. He had quit smoking eight years ago, before leaving his last duty station in Norfolk, but on mornings like this the old urge came back.

He sighed and fidgeted his way through the next ten minutes, until Theresa Moncton backed out of her driveway and rolled slowly down Kelso Street. She gave him a little wave and a dim smile. Somehow that broke the tension, and he felt himself relax. Good, because he probably had twenty more minutes to sit through.

Billy Moncton came out of the house at seven thirty-five and zipped into Newport along the same route as last time, until he reached Marlborough Street. There he turned west and headed for the Gateway, a combination tourist information center and bus terminal.

Instead of following Billy into the public parking lot, Boyle found a metered space at nearby Long Wharf and jogged back. The eight o'clock to Boston via Fall River was just pulling in. It was almost ten minutes to eight. He wondered if he'd have to buy a ticket and tail Billy around Boston. He was betting against that, but if he were wrong,

26

it wouldn't be the only ticket he'd get today—that meter he just fed quarters to was going to expire in forty-five minutes.

The terminal portion of the Gateway had a mini Dunkin' Donuts franchise, a ticket counter, rest rooms and some benches. As he approached the glass entrance door, he saw Billy sit down next to one Ivan Chitworth, turn to him and smile. Ivan handed Billy a small paper item that appeared to be a ticket. Boyle retreated to an alcove at the corner of the building, staying within view of the bus. He waited until the boys boarded together and the coach left for Fall River and Boston.

Case closed, he thought.

CHAPTER 5

On Monday evening he was alone in his Berwind Lodge condo. He felt kind of poor-soulish because he had just eaten cereal for dinner. Technically, he supposed that would make it supper. Before he could dwell on this and make himself feel more of a loser, the phone rang.

"Mr. Boyle?"

"This is Stafford Boyle. What can I do for you?"

"I'd like you to locate somebody for me. My name is Guy Bosworth, and I'm calling from Tempe, Arizona. I found your name on the Internet."

"I see. Have you notified the police in Tempe, Mr. Bosworth?"

"I did that a long time ago. But Kathy disappeared in 2003 and there was no good reason to suspect foul play."

"Kathy?"

"Kathy Dunnell. We were going to be married."

"So the police lost interest along the way."

"They won't admit it, but that's what I say."

"Right. Well, what makes you think I can help you up here in Newport?"

"Kathy told me she was headed there when she left. She took her little boy with her and said she'd call me when she arrived. When I checked the address later on, it was a phony."

"Ever think she might not want to be found, sir?"

"Maybe, but I just won't accept that."

"What was her purpose in traveling to Newport?"

"She said there were people in Newport she considered family and things she had to settle before getting married. I didn't like it, but she was determined to go. She didn't even name these folks. You know ... I think about this all the time, Mr. Boyle. Everybody tells me to get over her, to move on. But it doesn't work."

Boyle heard the misery in this guy's voice and thought he understood him. He also understood that the police in Tempe would not have taken much trouble about a case that featured a grown woman leaving town under circumstances like those. He could hardly blame them. Since Bosworth had written down everything about Kathy Dunnell that might prove useful, Boyle had him fax a copy.

He hung up and switched the phone to fax mode right away. He only had the one landline. Sometimes he was ashamed he ran the business on a shoestring, but every extra bill he could avoid was another meal he could eat out or tank of gas he could buy. Of course, if he were more ambitious he'd have more clients, and money might cease to be an issue. Something to think about, that.

Not wanting to sit and stare at the fax machine, Boyle left the minuscule guest bedroom that served as his office and shuffled into the living room.

Coffee cups everywhere. Dust visible on every surface. He really had to get on top of the housework. Especially now that he might have a female friend to ask over from time to time. Wouldn't it be nice to see a foxy lady in his living room holding a drink maybe, and having a civilized conversation with him? Yeah, but not with the place looking like this.

What a dump.

The first order of business, even before checking the fax

out, was to type his report for Theresa Moncton. He looked at his notes and the checklist he used for surveillance reporting. Slowly, he began to run a narrative through his head. He decided not to commit the words "gay" or "homosexual" to paper about anybody. The report would be purely factual, although he was bound to give his client an honest impression of Ivan Chitworth. He could do that orally, in person.

Finessing the report was a little trickier than he bargained for. But it evolved into a two-page summary of events and observations that satisfied his professional sense. He placed it in a tan file folder and set it aside for his meeting with Mrs. Moncton.

Next, he examined the fax that had arrived from Guy Bosworth. One thing stuck out among a slew of mundane facts – Kathy was originally from Alabama and her grandparents lived there still. But Bosworth didn't know their first names and was never successful in finding a Dunnell family in Alabama who knew anything about her.

Now Bosworth said he found Boyle through an Internet search, so he must also have checked the usual on-line white pages data bases for all the Dunnell families in Alabama. No use going that route. What Bosworth probably didn't do was search for obituaries. He seemed too hopeful about finding Kathy to do that. Records from the years 2003, when she left Tempe, through 2005 might be archived, but they would all be accessible one way or another.

And there it was! Only three minutes worth of computer time, and Boyle knew that Kathy Dunnell died in Alabama in March 2005 "after a long illness." The family request for donations to the American Cancer Society in lieu of flowers gave him the illness. But there was no mention of a son. And the last name of the grandparents was Gore.

Why did that ring a bell? Let's see—Gore, ox-gored, Al Gore, Leslie Gore. No, no, something else. He flipped to a new page in his notebook and wrote the words "Bosworth," "Kathy Dunnell," and "Gore" with a question mark. Next to Kathy's name he wrote, "deceased 2005." Then he went back to the computer and found a telephone number for Anna Mae and Wilson Thomas Gore in Birmingham, Alabama.

At this point, he thought it best to wait for Guy Bosworth's check before committing more of his time. He had quoted his usual retainer for basic research without legwork and had done enough to get started. But what the hell, he had a telephone number and unlimited hours on his cell phone. And it still wasn't too late to call a presumably elderly couple about a few facts in an old death notice. Besides, with this out of the way, he could think about tomorrow—the meeting with Mrs. Moncton and his date with Sunta.

He flipped open his cell phone and punched in the numbers directly from the computer screen. While he waited for an answer, he added the query "name of son?" into his notes.

"Hello?" It was a sweet, elderly, southern voice.

"Mrs. Gore?"

"Yes. And who are you, sir?"

"My name is Stafford Boyle, Mrs. Gore, and I do investigative work in Newport, Rhode Island. I was asked to locate a Kathy Dunnell, who I believe was your granddaughter."

"You wait just a minute, Mr. Boyle. I want to put my husband on the other line, if you don't object."

"Certainly not, ma'am. Please go right ahead."

Boyle felt himself easing into her idiom, something he invariably did when speaking to Southerners. But why wouldn't she hear him out a little more before getting her husband on the line? That was odd.

"This is a Mister Boyle who wants to talk about ... Kathy. I want you on the other line, Wilson."

She made no effort to keep Boyle from hearing this as she spoke to her husband.

A stentorian male voice came on the line. "Hello? What is your name, sir?"

"Boyle, Mr. Gore, Stafford Boyle."

"I see ... two last names ... just like me. Ha! I'll never remember which is which."

"Perfectly all right, Mr. Gore. I'll answer to either one."

"Wilson, Mr. Boyle has some questions for us concerning our granddaughter."

"That's right," he said. "First I want to extend my sincere condolences. I just found out Kathy passed away in 2005. My client told me she was from Alabama and that you still lived there."

"What do you need to know, sir?" It was Mrs. Gore speaking.

"Was Dunnell her married name?"

There was a pause. Finally, Mr. Gore said, "Kathy wasn't married. Dunnell was just ... a name she used."

Mrs. Gore cut in. "Mr. Boyle, we would like to know whose business this is? Who is your client and why are you calling from Newport?"

"I wouldn't be able to reveal a client's name without permission, ma'am, but I can say he was planning to marry Kathy when she left Arizona. I'm calling from Newport because she told him she had family or close friends here."

"Good grief, Anna Mae, this is confusin' to me," said Mr. Gore.

"Well, sir, I was just curious about the name difference and I wanted to know why the death notice failed to mention Kathy was survived by a son. What's his name, now?"

"Sam," Mr. Gore said.

"Oh, Wilson!" Mrs. Gore was exasperated. "I'm sorry Mr. Boyle, but you'll simply have to excuse us now. And we'd be obliged if you didn't call us again."

Before he had a chance to object, the connection was gone. It didn't come clear right away for him, but gradually a picture formed and grew sharp. And Boyle was astounded. It was the old Shoo-fly sensation erupting again.

Yes, he remembered now ... Gore was the real last name of Kristi Darnell, the beautiful South Beach model who was Shoo-fly's girlfriend in Florida. So Kathy Dunnell was Kristi Darnell, who was originally Christy Gore.

And her boy Sam, whom the elder Gores didn't want to discuss, would be Samson "Shoo-fly" Porter's son, something no one knew about until right now. His second son, really, because his wife in San Francisco gave birth – probably around the same time.

Holy crap, a part-time P.I. in Newport doesn't need this, he thought. Shoo-fly had been the most notorious killer of the last ten years, and it looked like his saga wasn't over yet. The question now was whether Kristi actually came to Newport, and if so, why? Newport, where her sociopath lover was gunned down on Bellevue Avenue after one final murder at ... Dismas Cottage!

CHAPTER 6

When Michael Lester Cullion got out of San Quentin in late 2001, he had served a little more than two years for felony embezzlement. If he hadn't been very lucky, the charge might have been accessory to murder.

During the long months in prison, Cullion thought hard about his way of life. What tortured him at trial had been the District Attorney's insistence that he was a career criminal. Well, if that were true, he'd have to come to grips with it. He needed to understand himself and the things he had done.

Jim Hendrickson claimed to have an answer for him. He was a kind-faced preacher who came to the prison twice a month to conduct bible lessons. Cullion saw this as a way to start over, and he joined the group. But even with all Pastor Jim's help and mentoring, he couldn't claim to be born again. Still, he felt a commitment to Jesus, and he prayed daily for spiritual guidance. Unlike other men who attended Jim's classes, he didn't exult in his new-found belief; instead, he felt truly humble before his God.

And he had his share of problems. His proclivities for sin and crime hadn't disappeared; he only kept them in check as best he could. In a way, he was glad for his difficulties. How would he know he was a better person if the path was easy?

Maybe it had been a hard life, but he had a big share in making it that way. He remembered how his uncle stressed a man's being judged by the company he kept. Well, Shoo-fly Porter had been the worst possible company, yet he stayed with him for five years. Five years, because he had an unnatural attraction to the man; five years that ended in multiple murders and Cullion's own throat cut.

For the embezzlement from Sharples Communications that Shoo-fly had planned, Cullion went to prison — and yes, he deserved it. While he hadn't participated in those murders in Las Vegas and San Francisco, he did help Shoo-fly get rid of evidence. He admitted nothing to the authorities on that score, thus avoiding more serious jail time. This was another wrong, he realized, another sin to expiate. But he just could not have done years and years of hard time again. For this weakness, he hoped to be forgiven.

The important thing now and tomorrow was to live his life differently. In the short term, this meant two things: keeping his head on straight and staying out of San Francisco.

One way to keep his head straight was to insist on his own worth and dignity. He might be a little guy, but from now on he wouldn't respond to nicknames like Mickey and Weasel, tags he had been saddled with all his life. He was Michael now – or Mike, he supposed that would be okay.

Leaving San Francisco behind was important because of the terrible associations it had for him. He hated the town. Good thing he had permission to serve his parole in Idaho, where he grew up and where there was a job waiting for him on a grounds crew.

The landscaping work didn't last long when he got to Boise, but he soon found a job washing dishes and managed to scrape along from week to week. He kept his appointments with the parole officer and attended services regularly at an evangelical church. Still, the nights were hard. The spirit may be willing, he told himself, yet the flesh is eternally weak. He wasn't kidding himself, however; he knew it would be this way.

Four years passed. Then the letter came, filling him with hope and driving him to despair by turns. The sentiments were right, the situation was totally attractive – but he'd have to leave Boise and return to San Francisco. The town he swore he'd never set foot in again. It was Pastor Jim writing to tell him he had established a storefront church in the Mission district and could use his help.

Well, he sure was struggling to make ends meet in Boise. And here was Jim offering a place to stay – telling him he could take a full time job days and just help out weekends and evenings. This was a totally decent man whom he loved and admired, under whose tutelage he had come to Christ. So he said yes, saved for a bus ticket and left three weeks later. On the move again with no possessions, leaving behind even the second-hand color TV and the old Mr. Coffee that he thought of as his two luxuries.

~~~

Pastor Jim and his wife Betty were there at the bus terminal to meet him. They had warm smiles, and they each hugged him in turn. He hadn't met Betty before, but Jim had talked about her so often that he felt he knew her. Jim insisted on carrying Cullion's beat-up suitcase out to their car.

"Allow me, Michael," he laughed. "We're counting on your help, so we're determined to treat you like a prince from the get-go."

He watched them from his vantage point in the back

seat as Jim pulled out into traffic. They were old enough to be his parents – late sixties, he figured. Jim was tall and slim, but rangy and powerful looking behind that lively, open face and pleasant smile. By contrast, Betty was short and heavyset. Everything about her said housewife and mother from her pinned-up braided hair to her plain dress and deferential manner. Michael knew they had only one child, a girl who had died from leukemia at age six many years ago.

When they arrived at the Breastplate of Faith and Love Mission, he paused on the sidewalk and glanced in the direction of downtown. They weren't too far past Market Street. This was his neighborhood in 1999 when he worked at Sharples Communications. He sighed under the weight of a burdened memory.

The storefront church was a bit shabby outside, but he was sure he could help put that right. It was a small, two-story building sandwiched between decrepit apartment houses and had probably been built as a retail establishment of some sort. There were two large plate glass windows on either side of a recessed doorway.

Once inside, his spirits lifted. A second ground-level door to the right of the storefront accessed the Hendricksons' apartment. They walked into a narrow entrance way with a staircase to the second floor. Upstairs, the rooms were spacious and pleasantly, if sparely, appointed. Skylights filled the interior with sunshine. The ceilings were at least ten feet high.

When Jim and Betty showed him to his room, he was moved. It was evident they went through a great deal of trouble to make it nice for him. Jim seemed especially pleased to show him the separate entrance that led from the back of his room to the narrow alley between the building and the apartment house next door. It was his way of telling Michael that he could have as much privacy as he wanted.

Yes, he appreciated that. Jim handed him a set of keys and looked him in the eye.

"This is your home, Michael," he said. Betty was just behind him, looking on with a shy smile.

"Thanks, Jim," he said. "And thank you, Betty. Thanks a lot."

He stopped speaking then and turned into the room, not wanting them to see the tears that were springing to his eyes.

"You're welcome, son," Jim said. "Your suitcase is right here. We'll leave you now to get settled."

"We're having supper at five o'clock, Michael," Mrs. Hendrickson said, peeking around her husband. "We'd be pleased to have you join us."

He murmured his thanks again as the Hendricksons retreated, closing the door behind them.

~~~

For three days, he tramped all over the downtown area looking for messenger work or anything else he could do, but it wasn't happening. The one job offer that came his way was dishwasher in a restaurant on Market Street.

Same ol' shit, he thought. Why can't I rise a little higher than this? Still, he took it.

The red and blue neon sign with the coffee cup motif said Continental Diner. His boss was Theo, the elderly Greek who owned the place. Trying to keep things positive, he told himself this was a start. After all, he had a place to stay for free. Minimum wage wasn't so bad when it was mostly spending money.

It *won't* always be like this, he promised himself. He'd find something better so he wouldn't be living off the Hendricksons. For now, though, having a comfortable room and good people to share his life with gave him a sense of family for the first time ever.

Maybe it was a little suffocating, their daily concern for him and everything he did, but it was better than the dog-eat-dog scene he'd been through for so long. It was damn nice just to have a conversation without having to figure out the difference between what was said and what was meant. These folks said what they felt. Sometimes it made him stop and wonder – it was hard to shake the mental reservations, the cynicism that had been second nature for so long.

One Tuesday a few months later, Carlos, the Latino short order cook at the diner, walked off the job during lunch. He had been bickering with one of the waitresses for days and blew up when Theo called him on it. Cullion watched as the old Greek pulled out an apron from under the counter and took his position at the grill, heavy-lidded eyes scanning the orders propped on the stainless steel frame over the exhaust hood.

He had been at the other end of the counter, consolidating the cleared plates and cups into one plastic tub, when the drama took place. After a brief, stunned silence, the conversation level in the diner ratcheted up again. The patrons had seen and heard enough by now and were getting back to their meals. A tight, nervous feeling in his stomach told him to make a move. He could do that job, he knew he could.

Moving quickly with the tub of dishes, he tucked into the back room through the swinging doors. Except for this little batch, he was caught up. Putting the tub down, he wheeled around and walked out front.

"Theo," he said. "Gimme a chance, man, I can do this job for you."

"Grill man? You can do breakfast, lunch, sandwiches, the whole thing?" Theo looked pretty doubtful.

"If you could help me a little the first couple days getting used to the way the girls order, the way they write it down—I know I could."

"Mike, who's gonna wash dishes?"

"Right now I'm caught up. I'll do what comes back for lunch after the rush. Or you could spell me out here when it piles up. Ah, c'mon Theo!"

Theo was grimacing and shaking his head, but he turned and looked at him when he heard the urgency in his voice.

"So, you want a chance. Okay, take my apron. Here. Cook! You do good, I'll call the agency for a dishwasher tomorrow."

He already knew where everything was, no problem there. Theo stood with him the first day and read the orders until he got the hang of it. He didn't get panicky when the order slips piled up mid-lunch, but Theo stepped in anyway to do sandwiches and salads whenever he got behind. As he promised, he went back and did dishes after the rush, staying on with the second shift until they were caught up.

Although he went home with knots in his stomach that first day, he didn't stop to feel sorry for himself. All night, he kept thinking how he might do better. The first week had its ups and downs, but he got through it, learning technique quickly and staying in good temper. By week's end, Theo was smiling and saying "good boy, good boy" every time his shift ended. It was a producer's job and he had figured it out. He was proud of himself.

Contributing money to the Hendrickson household gave him the sense he was in control of his life for the first time ever. Jim and Betty listened to his stories each evening like parents happy for a son on his first job. The mission work was also going well. Evenings and weekends, Cullion did handyman work and helped Jim with newcomers, especially younger men who had criminal histories or involvement with alcohol and drugs. As often as not, those things went together.

Occasionally, he would even give witness about his life and how he had come to Jesus. However awkward it felt to speak out, he managed to convey his experience honestly, and Jim praised him for it. Of all the work he undertook, he was most at ease when painting. Sprucing up the storefront was a real pleasure. He loved the way the dark, rich blue color gave new life to the gold-tone lettering on the picture windows: Breastplate of Faith and Love Mission. He repeated the name over to himself. It was from Saint Paul, he thought.

Being busy was good. But he had ... feelings that never left. Sexual longings that plagued him. Maybe if he dated that waitress Julie—she was about his age, he knew she liked him. Would it work? He would need to master himself, would have to keep in mind how bad those old choices were for him.

If only he could talk to Jim Hendrickson about it. By

now, Jim knew everything about his past except for his attraction to men and how he had helped Shoo-fly after the Las Vegas murders. And there was no doubt Jim would listen and try to help. Except that he was afraid to hear Jim say he should go to the authorities and confess. Besides, how do you talk to a guy like that, someone with all the old-fashioned manly virtues, about your sex preferences? No, it wouldn't work. They'd be too embarrassed—both of them.

In the end, he found he needn't have troubled himself about it. And he shouldn't have come to rely so totally on his mentor's good opinion of him. It had all been a waste in some respects. Jim Hendrickson died suddenly, and a world of trouble opened up before Michael Cullion's eyes.

CHAPTER 7

Boyle was preparing himself to meet with Theresa Moncton. He picked up the folder with the report on Billy, slipped his bifocals on and read it carefully. There was nothing further to ponder, he knew it cold. When he called her at work, she suggested they meet at her office around twelve-thirty. He slid the folder into his briefcase and let himself think about Kathy Dunnell.

What he should say and not say to Guy Bosworth was a puzzlement. The man had asked him to find out what happened to Kathy—which he had done. But what should he tell him about her Kristi Darnell persona and the whole Shoo-fly mess? And her son Sam—would he have to go into that as well? Why didn't the obituary mention the boy? Did he live with his great-grandparents?

Well, first things first, he told himself. He snatched his keys from the kitchen counter, took up his briefcase and set out for the hospital. It was nearly eleven forty-five. As he drove through Courthouse Square to Broadway, he powered his window down halfway and felt the cool spring air wash over him.

He thought of Assunta and smiled to himself. They had a date at one-thirty, right after his meeting with Mrs. Moncton. They hadn't planned anything—for all he knew, she'd want to go grocery shopping. Nevertheless, he thought about things they might do in town. He had called her twice since their date on Saturday and thought she was happy to hear from him. His only reservation about their burgeoning friendship was the age thing.

Could he really expect this to go anywhere? He didn't want to be too eager and spoil what seemed a lovely interlude, but he felt the need to ask her some question or other in that direction. Okay, he said to himself, you can ask but don't louse it up. Two dates and a couple phone calls don't mean you can get all pushy.

So much for driving and thinking at the same time. He was two streets past the hospital before realizing it. No sweat—plenty of time. He managed a quick U-ey in sparse traffic to double back, then turned off Broadway for the hospital parking lot.

Theresa Moncton was on the hospital financial staff and had a small office in the administration wing. After signing in at the main entrance, Boyle acquired a visitor's pass and an escort. You could roam freely around the wards and outpatient facility, he thought, but God forbid you might be without strict surveillance in the land of the bureaucrat.

His guardian was a small, desiccated lady of uncertain years who said she volunteered two days a week. He thanked her as Mrs. Moncton stood up from behind her desk, taking official possession of him.

"How do you do, Mr. Boyle? Please have a seat."

"Good morning, Mrs. Moncton. Great weather we're having."

"Yes, it is. May I get you coffee ... or something?" There were anxious notes in her voice and gestures.

"Just water," he said. "Ice water if you have it."

She left to fetch his water while he relaxed and settled in. He noted that the office had a superannuated look: beat up file cabinets, stacks of reports and binders crammed into three sagging bookcases, a gray steel desk and chair that might have been standard issue in 1959.

There was a shortage of personal effects in the room, as well. A small plant garnished the desk, and a print on the wall commemorated an obscure film festival in Providence. Not even one personal photo on display. Wow, he thought, no better than an office in some boondocks duty station.

She came back and placed the ice water on the side of the desk nearest his chair. It was in a Styrofoam cup.

"I guess we can get started, Mr. Boyle," she said, taking her seat and leaning forward to listen.

Boyle already had the report out of his briefcase and held it in front of him. He fumbled into his jacket to retrieve his glasses and cleared his throat.

"I'm not going to read this report to you, Mrs. Moncton. It's yours and you can study it when I leave. I'll just hit the highlights and answer any questions you have."

"All right."

"Just one question before I get started. Are you acquainted with a local man named Ivan Chitworth?"

"The name rings a bell—society name, I believe. But I don't know him."

"I see. Well, I guess the pertinent thing is that your husband knows him. To start from the beginning, I followed Mr. Moncton on three occasions, twice last week and once yesterday. Last Tuesday, he left your home at eight-thirty and went directly into Newport, to a house on Leroy Avenue owned by a Mrs. Claudia Chitworth. A man answered the door. I was too far away to tell for sure, but I assume he was Ivan Chitworth, Mrs. Chitworth's son."

"Excuse me, are we talking about Dismas Cottage,

49

where the reporter was murdered a few years ago?"

"Yes, ma'am. Rupert McAllister was killed there. The Shoo-fly case."

"Go on, please."

"Your husband stayed there two hours, coming straight back to Kelso Street afterwards. On Wednesday, Mr. Moncton went to Dismas Cottage again in the morning. I don't know how long he stayed, but I can definitely say Ivan Chitworth greeted him at the door. Yesterday, I followed Mr. Moncton from your house to the Gateway, where he got on the eight o'clock bus to Boston with Mr. Chitworth."

"What do you know about this man?"

"I used a pretext to meet him last week. After observing him and speaking to him, it's my opinion the man is gay."

Theresa Moncton leaned back quickly in her chair and stiffened. When she spoke, there was an edge to her voice.

"And my husband, Mr. Boyle. What assumptions have you made about him?"

Boyle hesitated and sighed.

"This can't be about my assumptions, Mrs. Moncton. I don't know your husband. But I can tell you that I've investigated this as far as I care to. If I were to spend more time on it, you wouldn't be getting your money's worth."

Her apple-round face had turned red, and she appeared mystified for a moment. Then her expression cleared.

"I see what you're saying, Mr. Boyle. Yes, I think I can take it from here."

~~~

He hadn't anticipated feeling like crap when he drove over to Assunta's place in the North End. She lived in a huge Victorian house, converted decades ago into apartments.

Hers was on the second floor rear. Boyle parked on the street and sat for a moment, trying to get past the sour aftertaste of his meeting with Theresa Moncton.

Well, at least she didn't want him to keep at it. And if a divorce lawyer were to call in a few days asking him to find some hard evidence, he could just back off and refuse the case. No motel-lurking, camera-wielding detective work for him. Life was too damn short.

It was one-fifteen, and he hadn't had lunch yet, so he was glad when Assunta suggested they have a little something.

"Where do you want to go?" he asked. "How about Niko's pizzeria? They put out a nice calzone there."

"No, dopey. I can do something right here." She was peering into the fridge and checking out a couple of plasticware containers. "I'll put coffee on and give you, um, a meatloaf sandwich on whole wheat with lettuce and honey mustard. And a little pasta salad side order."

"Deal," he said.

"Sorry to twist your arm like that."

"Sometimes I'm a very willing twistee."

"So I've noticed."

"Have you also noticed I'm mad for your kisses?"

She cracked up. He came up from behind and cradled her while she worked at building the sandwiches.

"Assunta, you are so terrific," he said. "Do you think a decrepit ol' bear like me has any chance at all with a fine fox like you?"

Well, there it was. He had managed to get it out without introducing a negative vibe into the conversation. Since he was holding her, he would have noticed any tensing up when she responded.

"Ol' Bear will kindly back off while Fine Fox serves him a sandwich," she said.

There was no sign she took him seriously about this, and her voice was full of good humor. When the steaming coffee was served and they were both seated at her tiny kitchen table, she peeked over her sandwich and spoke.

"Look, Staff, I can't say I know you well, but I like you a lot. Seventeen years is quite a difference, but so far it hasn't made a difference. Know what I mean?"

She had put him at ease. He sure did appreciate it.

~~~

By five o'clock, he was home at Berwind Lodge. He pulled into his parking space, picked up the mail, and went directly to his office. Setting aside the advertisements, supermarket circulars, and bills, he gave his attention to an envelope with an Arizona postmark. Guy Bosworth's check was inside, which meant he owed him a call. Better not postpone it.

"Hello."

"Mr. Bosworth, this is Staff Boyle in Newport."

"Thanks for calling back."

"I'm hoping this might be a good time to follow up, if you have a minute. And thanks for the check, I received it today."

There was silence at the other end, and Boyle hoped Bosworth was sitting down and girding himself.

"I located Kathy Dunnell's grandparents in Alabama. The last name is Gore. Kathy's real name was Christy Gore."

"Really? Is she there with them in Alabama?"

"No, Mr. Bosworth. I'm afraid I have terrible news.

Kathy died a little over two years ago. She had cancer. I think she left Tempe knowing she was sick."

"What! No ... I can't believe that. Are you sure you have the right person?"

Bosworth's voice cracked and his breathing was strained. Boyle was breaking somebody's heart for the second time today. It made him angry and sick to his stomach.

"I'm afraid so. This has got to be an awful shock for you, I know. The obituary is still on line, you can read it at your leisure."

"I can't get my mind around this. I expected to hear she was living in Newport."

"I would venture a guess that she visited Newport, but I couldn't find any indication she was here any length of time."

"What about her son? Is Sam there in Alabama?"

He wished Bosworth had mentioned the boy's name before. Mrs. Gore might not have cut him off so quickly if he hadn't tricked Mr. Gore into revealing it.

"Well, you would think so, but the Gores wouldn't talk to me about him, and the obituary doesn't list him as a survivor."

"You don't think Sam is dead, too?"

"Please, Mr. Bosworth, I don't think anything of the sort. I just don't know where he is. Listen, why don't you wait for my report, think everything over and get back to me with any questions you have."

"I suppose you're right. I've got to sort this out. Can you fax me that report?" He gave him the number.

"Sure. I'll send it now."

Boyle knew that Guy Bosworth wasn't going to back off. But he wanted him to read the report first and reconcile himself to Kathy/Kristi's death. He rather expected a call tomorrow with instructions to investigate further.

Anticipating that Bosworth would want to call the Gores, he included their telephone number in the report. They might even be willing to open up to the man who wanted to marry their granddaughter. He had avoided any mention of the Shoo-fly scandal and the reasons for Kristi's multiple name changes. Time enough for that when Bosworth got back to him.

Later that evening, he thought to get his mind off work with some television. Clicking through channels with the remote, he kept alighting on trashy reality shows, angry news channel debaters, and educational snoozefests. Finally, he tried the classic movie station and got swept up into a crackling black and white thriller called *The Narrow Margin* with Charles McGraw and Marie Windsor, whom he recognized as a Vargas babe. Not a bad actress, either.

For Boyle, it was ninety minutes of pure pleasure, a B-movie for the ages. When McGraw knocked off the villain and escorted the endangered grand jury witness off the train in Los Angeles, the movie ended and Boyle went to bed satisfied.

At two o'clock in the morning, his eyes popped open. He sat up, punched his pillow, and turned to the bedside table to check the time. Something was making him uneasy. A sound sleeper, he didn't wake up like this for no reason. Suddenly, it hit him – the boy at the Chitworth estate. Who the hell was he? It must be all connected, he thought. The Billy Moncton case was over, sure, but Ivan Chitworth, Sam

Dunnell and Dismas Cottage were still in play.

~~~

In the morning, Boyle spent time contemplating what Guy Bosworth was likely to ask him. He'd certainly want to know more about Kathy's name changes, and there would be questions concerning the little boy. Would he wonder if Sam was Shoo-fly's son, something that had been carefully concealed until now? But Boyle had no reason to volunteer his suspicions about the child at Dismas Cottage. That would be totally irresponsible at this point. Then again, if Bosworth wanted him to confirm the boy's parentage or find out where he lived ... well, that might complicate matters.

Bosworth called early that afternoon. He was reconciled to his loss by then, but frustration was evident in his voice and in his silences. Boyle tried to be understanding. He saw his task now as lending a sympathetic ear, nothing more.

"I called her grandparents, Boyle. Nice people. I told them we were going to be married and how much I loved her. They were very kind, really."

"I'm glad you did that."

"They even apologized to me about being rude to you. But they wouldn't say much about Sam, only that he was well. Wouldn't even confirm or deny that he lived with them."

"Well, I guess they have their reasons."

"But I can't quite figure it. What do suppose those reasons are, Boyle?"

"Oh ... fear of publicity, I suppose."

"Hunh?"

"Kathy's name changes, Mr. Bosworth. Did they say anything about that?"

"Just that she was a model and had changed her name. But ... you're getting at something."

"Brace yourself for this one. Your Kathy Dunnell was originally Christy Gore, you know that now. But the name she went by as a model in Miami was Kristi Darnell. That's Kristi with a K. Ring a bell, Sir?"

"Uh, yeah, but ... what?"

"The big manhunt for Sam Porter several years ago, the one they called Shoo-fly. His girlfriend in South Beach was Kristi Darnell."

There was a grinding silence. Boyle closed his eyes while a very cruel truth dawned on Guy Bosworth, sitting there stunned probably, in Tempe, Arizona.

"Kathy and that guy? No, no ... oh, sweet Jesus. And Sam? Why would she name her son after that piece of shit?"

"I don't suppose we'll ever know that."

There wasn't much left to say. Bosworth had a ton of pain to deal with, and Boyle couldn't imagine his wanting to follow up. That left the whole thing about the little boy at Dismas Cottage up in the air. Although Boyle was curious, he wasn't the type of guy to take a baseball bat to a hornet's nest without a helluva good reason. No client, no investigation is what he figured.

CHAPTER 8

The funeral service for Pastor Jim in San Francisco was simple and brief. Cullion took two days off work and did everything he could for Mrs. Hendrickson, helping her arrange the cremation and details of the service. He was surprised at the cremation, figuring most Evangelicals frowned on it. But Betty knew her husband's wishes. The only thing he saw as a burden was her request that he give the scripture reading at the service. He stayed up half the night thumbing through the whispery pages of his bible, before hitting on a passage he thought Jim would appreciate.

At Betty's request, a friend of Jim's flew in from Minnesota to conduct the service. His name was Hugo Swanson, and he spoke of Jim's life in plain and heartfelt terms. The story of Betty and Jim's early bereavement over their daughter was especially touching.

Cullion was sitting in the front row with Mrs. Hendrickson. She had insisted Jim would be proud to see him there in the position a son might have taken. But he felt too small and stupid to fill those shoes. He thought everything about himself was inappropriate to the occasion, including the double-breasted blue suit he wore, which he had found at the thrift shop.

When it came time to get up in front of the congregation for the reading, he was terrified. He sat there fidgeting until he heard his name and saw the expectant look on Hugo's face. Betty gave him a gentle pat on the back as he rose to take the lecture stand. He placed his bible there, open to the passage from Acts, wet his lips and forced himself to look up. It made him feel better to see Theo in the back with Julie, a waitress from the diner. Nice of them to come, he thought.

The silence was beginning to feel oppressive when he finally spoke. His voice sounded reedy at first, although it improved as he went along.

"*And when they had eaten enough, they lightened the ship, and cast out the wheat into the sea. And when it was day, they knew not the coastline, but they discovered a certain creek with a shore, into the which they were minded, if it were possible, to thrust in the ship. And when they had taken up the anchors, they committed themselves unto the sea, and loosed the rudder bands, and hoisted up the mainsail to the wind, and made toward shore. And falling into a place where two seas met, they ran the ship aground, and the forepart stuck fast, and remained unmoveable, but the hinder part was broken with the violence of the waves. And the soldiers' counsel was to kill the prisoners, lest any of them should swim out, and escape. But the centurion, willing to save Paul, kept them from their purpose, and commanded that they which could swim should cast themselves first into the sea, and get to land: and the rest, some on boards, and some on broken pieces of the ship. And so it came to pass, that they escaped all safe to land.*"

~~~

Towards evening he took a long walk around the city, dropping in at the diner on the way back. Theo was sitting in a back booth, going through receipts and making notes on a yellow pad. Cullion slid into the bench opposite and waited until the older man looked up.

"I'll be in tomorrow, Theo. Thanks for coming today."

The old Greek nodded and pointed to the east.

"I been thinkin' all day, Michael. That was Saint Paul shipwrecked on Malta you was preachin' about this morning. I don't think I ever heard it in English before. It made me think how far I am away from home."

Cullion smiled. "Welcome to the club, Theo. I always feel that way."

"Julie was very proud wit' you. I could tell."

"I'll have to thank her for coming."

"You should ask her out, Michael."

"Really, now? You a matchmaker, Theo?"

"A-a-a-ay. Old people like to see young people together. They know it stinks to be alone."

~~~

Mrs. Hendrickson must have figured it stinks to be alone, too. A few weeks later, while showing him the monthly bills and collection receipts, she told him she needed to go home.

"That's good, Betty," he said. "You should take some time off."

"I ... don't think you understand me, Michael. My relatives in Minnesota want me to come live with them."

"Oh," he whispered. What else could he say?

"I know you can carry on Jim's work, Michael. He would have wanted that. You're needed here at the mission."

"Both of you showed a lot of faith in me. But I don't know, Betty. I want to keep my job at the diner. And I'm not a preacher."

"Keep the mission open, Michael. At first you could operate a couple of evenings and weekends. When you do find a preacher to help, you can resume a daily schedule. It will work out if you try."

Everybody was giving him advice lately, and they all meant well. Change was supposed to make you feel this way, right? Maybe he just lacked confidence. Remember those knots in your stomach, he thought, when you first took over the grill? You were determined then, and you got through it, didn't you? Sure, but running the mission, working full time, and trying to stay straight—could he really do all that?

It occurred to him that he had always been a follower and that he wanted to remain a follower. But now he was being challenged in another direction. Keep the job, get a girlfriend, run the mission. Be a man is what they were saying. Well, he'd pray on it, but all the prayers he could say would only help him make a decision. They wouldn't guarantee his decision was any damn good.

The first problem he needed to solve was making sense of the evening services. He pared down the format to just a reading, a theme, and some witnessing. The collection was pathetic at first. He was no Pastor Jim who attracted all kinds to the mission. Some guys and a few gals were coming, mostly alkies and druggies, mostly looking for a handout. And it was harder now to keep on top of the maintenance – he didn't always have the time.

But he had to admit it was rewarding; somehow he felt Jim's spirit at work in this place. The Breastplate of Faith and Love. He repeated it to himself often, like a mantra. The name and the image it evoked were his grounds for hope.

Cash flow, too, was a problem. The Hendricksons held a small mortgage on the building, and Betty agreed to let him forward a check to her every month in return for keeping the mission going. She could have sold the place at a profit, but Jim's work and memory were more important to her. Cullion figured he could swing it by renting the second floor apartment while keeping his own room. And it wasn't long before an immigrant couple with a young child took him up on the notice he posted at the mission. This was stopgap financing at best, but he was keeping his head above water.

When Julie Reyes starting coming to weekend services, he took the plunge and asked her out. She was so shy about accepting, he was afraid he had made a mistake. Later, she admitted that Theo had hounded her into making a move. Her shyness came from her fear that she had somehow trapped him into dating her.

He took her to a movie the first time, and they stayed out for coffee afterwards. When they walked back to her place, he held her hand. She was so petite and cute she made even a little guy feel like a big man. Gradually, they fell into a routine that had him going to her tiny apartment most evenings to chat and watch television.

He liked her, really liked her, and she was satisfied with him in bed. He wanted to feel good about that, but something was missing. The old desires still dogged him. And yet ... sex with Julie was better than celibacy, wasn't it? Change was tough – that's all he knew.

CHAPTER 9

To a great extent, San Francisco had forgotten the Shoo-fly scandal. After all, it happened in 1999, way back in the twentieth century. The new millennium had brought fresh problems and greater atrocities, especially the horror in New York on September 11. It wouldn't be right to say Shoo-fly wasn't remembered, but he had been eclipsed, papered over somehow.

No longer seen as tragic victims, Angela Sharples Porter and new husband Brad Styles had resumed their elevated status among the city's elite. They kept their own counsel, raised their son Justin in strictest privacy, and went back to their corporate concerns and numerous charities.

Justin, as the natural child of Sam Porter, would have attracted an unnatural amount of attention had they not been very rich and very careful. Their money, assiduity and connections kept his name out of the newspapers (they owned one of the largest) and the paparazzi at bay. Only one out of ten thousand could tell you the boy's first name. Far fewer could tell you that Brad adopted him shortly after marrying his mother.

Lately, Angela couldn't stop fretting about Justin. As she told her Aunt Claudia, the boy was sometimes stubborn and moody. She wasn't one to think back to his father every time a behavioral problem cropped up, but things were getting serious, and she had to wonder. The boy couldn't be trusted with pets, his tutor was asking for leeway to discipline him more strictly, and just yesterday he threw another tantrum when Brad explained he couldn't take him along to a business luncheon in town.

Right now was the first time Angela had strung those thoughts together into a single narrative, and it frightened her. She had no end of love for the boy, but he was occasionally ... unlovable. Mostly he was just a bundle of boyish energy, she had to remind herself. Mostly he was very responsive and showed his love generously.

Well, there was enough here to prompt a conversation with Brad. Perhaps he could allay her fears; after all, a man's perspective would be different. But if he couldn't? And if it wasn't?

Brad had just that second strolled out to the terrace. She had been waiting for him. It was morning, and coffee had been served. He pulled out the chair beside her, scraping it over the tiles, and sat down. She smiled and laid her hand on his as he leaned toward her for a kiss.

Brad's hand was warm to the touch. She realized how cool her small, pale hand must feel to him. He reacted by taking hers into both of his own, massaging it briskly while he beamed at her.

"G'morning, sweetheart," he said.

"Good morning, dear. Let me pour your coffee. Esther will be out in a moment with bagels. Are you going to want anything else?"

"No, I guess not. What I really want is sausage, bacon, ham, pancakes with syrup, three eggs, hash browns, sweet bread toast, jelly, and tons of butter dripping over everything. But ... a bagel is nice, especially plain, the way you like me to have it."

"No waffles with honey, dear?" she laughed.

"Only if you're having some."

"You know, I can't help it if I want you to last forever, Brad."

"And I will, I swear, but will it be a life worth living?"

He said it as a joke, but Angela took it hard. She tried to smile, but her face fell, and Brad was alarmed.

"Angela, honey, what's going on?"

"I've needed to talk to you about Justin, Brad. I've been postponing this because I've got to be wrong, but ... maybe ... maybe he has psychological problems."

Her eyes brimmed with tears, and her chin trembled. Brad reached out and stroked her face. He looked at her closely, puzzled.

"Is this about the tantrum he threw yesterday? One tantrum, Angela?"

"There have been others. But it's not just tantrums. You asked me last week what happened to his kitten, Chloe, and I told you she disappeared. She didn't, though. I took her away from him when I found her mewling in the garden during that rainstorm two weeks ago. He had tossed her out there in that awful weather because of a tiny scratch. He was far too rough with her anyway."

"I see. Are you ... holding back anything else?"

Angela glanced up at him and smiled wanly.

"Can't keep a thing from you, can I? Well, some of the play dates I arranged didn't turn out so well. He can be overly aggressive. I just don't feel I can deal with this alone anymore."

"I understand," he said. "We really should have talked sooner. But I just couldn't bring myself to be the first one ...."

"What do you mean? You've seen something else, haven't you?"

Brad sighed and looked toward the open French doors that gave into the house. Esther stepped onto the terrace, smiling, and brought a basket of toasted bagels to the table. She cleared the empty juice glasses and retreated. Brad spoke again when she was out of earshot.

"It's normal for a boy at seven to be interested in sex, but I think he may be too interested."

"What happened?"

"It's probably nothing. Don't get alarmed. I'm not even going to go into detail. Let's just say I've told him he's too old to be taking showers with me."

Angela's eyes were filling up again rapidly.

"No, Angela – no tears. Look, call Ray LaFreniere. Nobody in child psychology has a bigger reputation. At least not in this town. He'll be able to help, I'm sure."

She nodded. "You're right. I'll call him today."

~~~

He is all by himself in the midnight blue limousine. Like the ones that pull up to his house when his parents are having a party. But this one is his, he knows. He can't see the driver, who's up there in front, behind the smoked glass partition. If he knew how to use the console built into the seatback, he could signal him to go faster. But ... thinking about it works just as well. They pick up speed now, racing out of the circular drive and into the street.

Before long the roadway is a wonderful, wide boulevard as far ahead as he can see, and they're going faster yet, the wheels humming ever so smoothly over the blacktop. Signposts and old-fashioned streetlamps whip by on either side. Not a soul on the sidewalks and no other cars driving by, just his breakneck limousine rushing away to somewhere. Should he ask? Should he know?

Pretty houses and graceful brick buildings line the road on either side, but he knows from the vacant windows and featureless yards that they're more like buildings on a movie set. If you went behind, there'd be nothing. Like everything else, the movie set houses and buildings whip back from the car windows. It makes him laugh to know the whole spectacle is just for him, a kind of world of his own.

Soon they're speeding into the country, the sidewalks and streetlamps giving way to a vivid blur of trees, flowers and fields in earthy colors, with the wheels of the limousine still whirring soft over the endless road. When the countryside fades into sand, with golden dunes stretching out to an angry horizon, he begins to be afraid. It is, of course, a desert, dry and bleak.

Their headlong rush is immensely fast now, and the whirr of the wheels is a steady, vicious whine. At last, he sees where they're headed, far in the distance – just a dim vague pool at first, but growing, growing wide and filling the foreground while the limo becomes a bullet and the road ahead is a mere line leading to a fathomless gaping pit – dark unto blackness.

His eyes sprang open to the room and all its shadows. It wasn't the first time Justin had the dream. He woke up afraid, trying to roll it back to the beginning when it felt good to be in the limo alone on the movie set boulevard. He knew he wouldn't tell his mother and father about it. Not ever. Stuff like that didn't go over too big in his house. He was only seven, and maybe he was wrong, but he figured he was different from other kids, and people were watching him way too close.

CHAPTER 10

Doctor LaFreniere's office was in a new building not far from Union Square. Angela generally disliked modern buildings with their boxy shapes and flat surfaces – all glass, aluminum, and steel. They spoke to her of coolness and functionality versus warmth and humanity.

Walking through the lobby with Justin and waiting for the elevator, she noticed the same theme of sparseness wherever she looked: floors, ceilings, walls. Every office and stick of furniture she could see reflected it as well. Clean lines – the architects and designers always said that in favor of the style. Well, who had ever advocated dirty lines, for heaven's sake? They spoke as though geometry were synonymous with beauty.

When she reached the fifteenth floor and opened the double doors to Ray LaFreniere's suite, Angela and Justin were ushered into a very different world indeed. Red oak floors, rich paneled walls, crown moldings, archways and columns – all the elements of classic architectural detailing. Even the hermetically sealed windows had been altered from the inside with clever framing to suggest something more traditional. The colors and fabrics in use throughout the rooms were also suggestive of old world values.

In short, Angela was relieved. A place she could relax in was a place she could believe in. Doctor LaFreniere had created such a place, she thought.

The receptionist explained the format for the initial visit while an aide ushered Justin into a room that appeared to be part library, part playroom. She said it was monitored and that Dr. LaFreniere would begin to observe Justin from a screen in his office. Angela would join the doctor in a few moments, and they would talk as Justin continued to play by himself. After that, the aide would bring the child from the playroom to his office, where the three of them would get acquainted.

In future visits, the doctor would prefer to see the child alone each time. When he wished to consult with her or Brad, Justin would be taken to the playroom beforehand. The doctor was trying to instill in the child a sense that he was his only concern. He tried to avoid having any child wonder about the conspiracy between parent and caregiver. If the boy didn't see her walk into the office while he had to wait outside, that was less likely to happen.

"Hello, Angela. How are you?" Ray LaFreniere rose from behind his desk and rushed to meet her.

"Hi, Ray." I just love your office."

"Thanks. I'm glad you approve. It took a while for me to understand that an office can have a therapeutic effect. Not everybody likes it, but nearly all children do."

"Kids are smart," she said, nodding.

Angela knew Ray from charity functions, and Brad golfed with him when their schedules permitted. He was a nice-looking fellow, about forty-five, with sandy hair and a warm smile. But her social ease with him didn't make this any less difficult. He seemed to sense that and insisted they begin with a little chat about her and Brad. After a while, he looked back at the monitor screen and turned the sound on. Justin was playing quietly.

"Well there he is, your little boy. You wouldn't be here

if something weren't bothering you, so why don't you start out by telling me everything you want to. It might even help if you add in all the good stuff as well. Tell you what, Angela – don't even look over at me. Just watch Justin play and let it all out."

~~~

Angela had requested a morning appointment so they might meet Brad afterwards for lunch. She was pleased with the first visit, her confidence in Doctor LaFreniere soaring with his handling of her interview and his introduction to Justin. She told him absolutely everything that had been on her mind – it felt more like a transference of responsibility than a simple unburdening.

And now, as she understood it, she wouldn't meet personally with Ray until he had talked to Justin a few times. She mustn't ask Justin what he spoke about with the doctor. If the boy wanted to tell her, he would. She shouldn't pry.

Brad met them just after noon at Bistre, a little restaurant they favored on Powell Street. It was fashionable enough to be crowded most weekdays, but not so chic they wouldn't cater to the P B & J tastes of a little boy. With Brad managing the conversation, they had a pleasant time together and left about one-thirty. As always, Justin was good company in public – he never fidgeted in restaurants or stores. Today, his attention was taken by the duties of the busboys, waitresses and especially the chef, whom you could see across the open partition between the dining room and kitchen.

When they got home, Justin lingered a moment in the foyer with his mother before going off to his lessons with the tutor.

"Mommy?" he said, looking up at her.

"What dear?"

"Am I crazy?"

"Justin, honey, why would you think such a thing? Of *course* you're not crazy."

"Doctor LaFreniere is a psychiatrist, isn't he?"

"Yes he is. But psychiatrists talk to all kinds of people to help them understand themselves. Does that make sense to you?"

"I suppose so. Can he send me away?"

Angela knelt down to embrace Justin as they spoke. He kept her back a little with his hands against her shoulders, as if to signal that her answer was more important to him than her closeness.

"Honey, no one can send you away. No one. You're my son and I would never let that happen."

She was surprised at the way he searched her eyes to make sure she meant what she said.

"Okay. Thanks."

It seemed to her he said it somehow ... dispassionately. Like a slippery fish, he squirmed away from her and up the stairs to the second floor, calling his tutor's name at the top of his voice.

CHAPTER 11

Ray LaFreniere was recording his notes on Justin Styles. Naturally, he wouldn't be drawing any conclusions for a while, but he found Justin's case compelling. First, he was surprisingly analytical – an unusual attribute in a young boy. He wished he could say that was a positive thing. But when you combined it with his other salient trait – a kind of emotional distance from his surroundings – he was concerned for the child.

Suddenly he realized he said "emotional distance" because he didn't want to say "emotional deadness." That made him pause a moment and reflect on the things you could know and describe clinically, and the things you just couldn't. Still he kept on speaking into the mike, extemporizing in an elegiac tone that was unfamiliar and surprising to his own ears.

"What do little boys really think about? Despite the diplomas and citations on my office wall, I don't really have a clue. Oh, I know what they say, I know how to lead them in certain directions and let them talk, help them to open up. And I know how to listen and probe and how to make sure what they say isn't a fabrication.

"But have you ever caught a child staring at you and wondered what was really going on in that young mind? Because the words we formulate and use are only the aftermath of thought, not thought itself. And it's thought you should somehow get at in a patient.

"Thought isn't picture either. Not words and not

picture, but somehow surging emotion and action inchoate – or perhaps the lack of either – with maybe a few sketchy words and half-formed images thrown in just to confuse the issue. Can you see perhaps how little Freud and Jung and Eriksson mean to a practicing shrink?"

He chuckled to himself as he switched off the digital voice recorder. Where in the world had that come from? For now, he stifled the sense that Justin Styles had prompted all that philosophical noodling. He must have overcaffeinated himself this morning at Starbucks.

CHAPTER 12

Cullion watched the new guy slip into a back pew during a Thursday evening service. He was a rugged, good-looking man – mid-thirties, dressed in jeans, t-shirt and a brown leather bomber. He had a quiet, self-assured air as he looked around the hall. Jake Snider, he said to himself. He knew him from prison.

Luis, an elderly gent holding a patched and dog-eared bible, was reading a long passage from Job. You might have thought he *was* Job with his hangdog look and the plangent whine in his lightly accented English. But Cullion was always grateful when someone – anyone – volunteered to read. He was resting against a table to the side of the hall and listening to Luis when Snider walked in. Rather than be spotted there, he moved into the nearest pew and sat until Luis was finished and the witnessing had ended.

Julie always set up the Fellowship Hour, the euphemism Jim had concocted for donuts, coffee, and chat after the service. But tonight she was gone to Santa Rosa to help her sister, who had just had another baby. Before leaving, she promised Theo and Cullion she'd be back on Monday. So he had spent the necessary time setting things up tonight – brewing coffee in the big urn, making a run for donuts, and putting out chairs for anyone who might want to stay and talk when the service ended.

He knew it was just a self-conscious fantasy when people told you they could feel somebody staring at them from behind. In prison you got the feeling often, mainly because it was hard to keep your nose clean with all the warring factions. You were always on edge, or at least he was. Outside, the feeling gradually faded away.

But tonight, he swore he could tell where Jake was every second. And when he turned around to look – he was right. Even though he didn't catch him looking back, not once.

When he was set to close up, however, Jake walked over to him grinning, as if just realizing who he was.

"Hey, Mickey, this your gig?"

"Uh, my name's Michael, pal. What's yours?"

Jake looked at him, smiling still, and seemed to make a careful mental adjustment.

"Well, sure, it's been a long time. I'm Jake Snider."

His hand was out and Cullion shook it.

"Oh yeah, I remember you. Well, like I said, my name's Michael – Michael Cullion."

Jake paused another moment and held his look.

"No offense, man. Just thought I'd say hello. See you around ... Michael."

He watched Jake leave, satisfied that the guy respected him for bringing him up short. The man had been a notorious wolf in prison, although he hadn't ever hit on Cullion. Then again, "Mickey" Cullion's former prowess with a knife had helped keep the wolves away in San Quentin.

~~~

It was Sunday morning and Cullion felt terrific. For once the sun was out early and illuminated the street outside the diner's windows. He had walked over from his room at five o'clock to open up. Julie was still in Santa Rosa, but the other two waitresses – one a fill-in – came in on time, and things were ready to fly by six-thirty. Theo probably wouldn't get there until noon, when he would spell Cullion for the last hour and close the place around one o'clock. By then, he would be at the mission getting the Sunday service started.

Brenda unlocked the front door a little before seven when the first patron showed up, a regular who would want a short order of French toast with extra butter. The three slabs of bread were dipped and on the grill before the customer sat down in his usual booth by the entrance. Soon Cullion was deep into his routine. The place was filled, and the air was thick with customer chatter as well as the heavy diner smells of strong coffee and breakfast meat.

The first, brief slowdown occurred around ten-fifteen. The noise level dropped, orders were caught up, and Cullion had a chance to clean the grill before the next wave. Ready to take a breather now, he turned around to look out at the street and found himself staring directly into the eyes of Jake Snider, sitting hunched over a coffee at the counter just in front of him.

"Well, Reverend, you're a busy, busy man. Spiritual mentor, expert short-order cook ... any other talents I should know about?"

Jake was busting his chops and smiling good-naturedly. There seemed to be a hint there about something else, but that could be his defenses working overtime, he thought.

"First time I seen you in here, Jake. You in the working class now?" he asked, stripping a pair of latex gloves from his hands. He pointed to Jake's blue work clothes with the name patch sewn onto the shirt.

"Sad to say, bro, sad to say. I caught on part time with the maintenance crew at the Pinney Building across the way. Sundays I get the duty until one. I'm gettin' by, y'know?"

"Yeah, I guess I know how that feels."

"I saw your a-- ... I saw you there flipping jacks when I was walking by, so I figured I should say hi."

"Good, Jake. I'm glad you came in. Can I get you something to eat?"

"Uh, no. Truth be told, I'm a little short ... Michael."

The guy seemed to be on his best behavior, maybe even a little lonely.

Cullion stepped to the grill. "C'mon, Jake, name it. Bacon and eggs?"

"Okay, Mike, but I'll pay you back. Over easy, wheat toast. All right if I call you Mike?"

"Mike is fine. Bacon and eggs, over easy!"

At noon, Theo came in and relieved him right away. He ditched the apron, grabbed his windbreaker off the clothes tree next to the lockers and left by the rear entrance, coming out to Market Street through the alley.

While he walked over to the mission, he tried to organize his thoughts. Jake was big and damn hot-looking with the buzz cut and the dark beard. He had no idea if he could trust this guy, but he hadn't come on strong, and he seemed to have completely dropped the wise-guy routine Cullion remembered from stir. He didn't ask Jake where he lived, but after seeing him at the Breastplate and now at the diner, he figured he lived in the neighborhood somewhere.

Shit, I don't need this, he thought. It would tear down

everything he was trying to build if he got involved with this guy. Then again, what did he have really? A ton of responsibility, damn little free time, and a feeling he was just faking it, never making it. His love for the mission's work was real, and so was his commitment to Jesus. But his longings and his weaknesses were real, too. Best to admit it, he thought. And now that he had – how the hell was he going to deal with it?

As the service wound down around two o'clock, Jake walked in and slipped into the same back pew as on Thursday, dressed once again in jeans, t-shirt and leather bomber. If he had time to change from those work blues, Cullion thought, he was living nearby all right.

Why couldn't Julie be here today? That would have saved him, he figured. When the service was over and everybody was gone, he spied Jake outside the mission waiting for him. Even so, all he had to do was go out the back way, take the outside stairs, and go up to his room. Jake had no idea yet where he lived.

Instead, he walked outside, locked the mission door, and strolled over to where Jake stood. They spoke quietly for a few minutes and went up to his room, where they spent the afternoon.

~~~

Jake wouldn't be eligible to move out of the halfway house where he lived until he had a full-time job. That took some pressure off Cullion for the time being. It served to keep just a little distance between them, although Jake came around often.

Poor Julie, she thought it was nice he had a friend. She even asked him to bring Jake over to watch TV and have a beer, but he said no – he didn't think it was a good idea. So Julie and he still saw each other, even though their physical relationship had deteriorated. He wondered how long she was going to put up with that.

The very first thing he straightened out with Jake was his complete lack of interest in drugs or criminal activity.

"That stuff is behind me, pal. I can't live with those vibes, and I can't ever take another stretch in stir."

"Hey, I swear I don't want that either. First off, I gotta get out of the halfway joint. After that, I'm gonna try to make it straight. I'm not as sure of myself as you are, but day to day I'm doing what I have to."

Well, it was good enough for now. He figured Jake really *was* doing the best he could. Besides, the guy helped out with the maintenance chores at the mission. In fact, he did a lot of them now, no matter the mission's tight budget wouldn't let Cullion pay him more than a few bucks over materials' cost. Jake was a better plumber and electrician than he was, all of which gave him a little breathing space in his schedule for the first time since Jim's death.

He thought of Jim often. It was his own joke with himself that WWJD stood for What Would Jim Do. Hell, he knew Jim wouldn't be making time with no guy, especially an ex-con. One thing sure, though – Jim's old struggle with finances couldn't compare to what he was going through, the paycheck-to-paycheck crunch with absolutely no daylight. Jake's view, on the other hand, was that Cullion had practically made it to the middle class.

That was a hoot! Finances aside, the thought plagued him that he had traded away the spiritual basis for his life. And for what?

One evening when they had finished painting the hall, the last of the planned improvements, Jake asked him about Shoo-fly. It was a sore subject for him, and he hadn't discussed it in a long time, except with Jim Hendrickson. When he glanced over at Jake, he could see he was just cleaning a roller, and probably had no idea it was tough for him to talk about it.

"Ah, why do you wanna know, Jake?"

"Christ, it was a helluva big case. I'm just curious."

"The thing is, nobody here knows I was sent up for that. Theo doesn't know and neither does Julie. They know I stole money and served time, but that's all."

"Hey, I'll back off. I'll even forget I know you're connected. How's that?"

He shrugged. And then he started to talk. He must have needed to. And he didn't stop until he let it out, all the old fear and excitement and soul-sick misery. Jake stood slack-jawed, taking it all in.

"They called him Shoo-fly when we met in stir. Which he didn't like – his name was Sam Porter. After I got parole, we hooked up and landed in Vegas. Like a jerk, I helped him get rid of evidence and leave town when he butchered that gal Lana and her boyfriend. In San Francisco, he did it again – sliced up an old woman who guessed he was the killer.

"By then he was married to Angela Sharples, the society lady, and I was working for him – helping him take money from the company she owned. Any man should have been satisfied with Angela, she was gorgeous. But no, he had to be screwing her sister Helena too, a snotty bitch who wouldn't give you the time of day.

"Of course, I shoulda known my turn would come. He

cut my throat and left me for dead, probably figuring he was getting rid of the last person who could tie him to Vegas. It was a helluva mess, except that I wouldn't die. I even squeezed him for a payoff so I'd shut up and leave town. In the end, Helena turned on him, ratting him out when the police were closing in. Only Angela stuck by him. Without her help, he would never have gotten out of San Francisco.

"The press had a field day, especially this one reporter McAllister. He had it like Sam was Bundy and Cunanan and Dahmer all rolled into one. Anyway, he made it down to Florida under a different name, grew out his hair and a beard. Then McAllister runs a story that Helena left San Francisco and nobody knows where she was. But Sam must've remembered she had relatives up north.

"When he got to Newport and found her with McAllister, he had to be totally freaked out. He shot the guy's face off and went after Helena, even managed to put a cap in her. Before he could kill her, though, the cops took him down."

Jake shook his head as though he could hardly believe it. "Jesus, I know I never heard it like that!"

"Nobody has. Nobody. If the cops knew everything, I'd still be serving time and Helena would be in for a stretch besides. She delivered the payoff to shut me up. And a private dick told me he got money from Angela and Brad Styles, the guy she married later."

Cullion saw that Jake was stunned. Right away, he began to wonder if he had said too much. But when Jake didn't follow up with any questions, he felt easier. He had fallen for this guy, no doubt about it. And if you couldn't talk to your lover, who the hell could you talk to? At this pass in his life, he needed to confide in someone.

Neither of them spoke for a while. Cullion was kneeling by a ladder and folding drop cloths. When he finished cleaning the rollers, Jake pulled off his white coveralls and walked up to him, ruffling his hair and squatting down to meet him at eye level.

"Look, I gotta get back to the house early tonight. See you tomorrow."

"Oh. I thought we might go upstairs for a while."

"Yeah, I'd like that. But the house honcho told us to get back for a meeting at seven."

Cullion said he understood, although he had counted on Jake staying with him. He needed someone close, especially tonight. When he blew off Julie earlier in the day, he used the painting project for an excuse. She wasn't having any, and got all teary-eyed.

"Ah ... c'mon Julie," he groaned. "What's wrong now?"

"You don't love me!" she wailed. "I don't think you can even stand me anymore."

It was a bad scene and he was too embarrassed to defend himself. After letting him have it, she walked away. He should probably call her, but what would he say? He got red in the face just thinking about it.

CHAPTER 13

Jake left the mission because he was on to something and had to mull it over. Just when he thought Reverend Weasel had reached the end of his usefulness, a new wrinkle shows up. That stuff about the socialite dame playing bag woman for Shoo-fly had given him an idea. And maybe, just maybe, there was more to the story than that.

He remembered something about Angela Porter having a baby – that kid would be older now, say seven or eight years old. Those people were some of the richest in California, and you could bet they didn't like publicity. Yeah, there must be an angle or two here someplace.

All that crap from Cullion about "Michael" versus "Mickey" burned his ass. The only reason he hung around at all was he figured there was money to be had at the mission. But shit, weasel-boy was honesty itself nowadays. He'd probably call the police if a day's collection money ever disappeared.

Another thing – Cullion was getting way too sentimental about him. Hell, a little guy like that was okay when nothing else was available, but he wasn't his damn lover. And now that Cullion was neglecting Julie, he figured on making a move in that direction sooner or later. Some people couldn't see the forest for the trees, he thought. Well, that was okay. Advantage, Snider.

When he got back to the house, three of the guys were playing cards in the common room. There was no meeting, he made that up to get away. In his room, he flipped the overhead light on and sat thinking. Then he stripped, grabbed a towel, washcloth, and bar of soap, and headed to the bathroom.

As soon as the water began to run warm, he stepped into the shower stall and let it cascade down his chest. Slowly, he lathered himself – trunk first, then arms, then legs. Next he soaped up his washcloth and strung it across his back, shimmy fashion. Someone had left a sample bottle of shampoo on the inside shelf, so he worked a dollop into his scalp and beard. Finally, he let the water do its work, running freely until he was warm and lethargic, totally relaxed.

As he grew clean, an idea began to take shape. He was on the trail of something, maybe something big. Rushing now, he dried himself and pulled on his clothes. In a few minutes, hair still wet, he was racing downstairs to find a pen and paper in the common room.

"Writing home to the folks, Jake?" the counselor asked, grinning.

"Oh yes, professor," he deadpanned. "Father forgot to send my allowance this month."

The guys playing cards cracked up. The counselor shook his head and went back to his magazine.

When he thought further about it, Jake figured he might find everything at the library. They'd have computers there for one thing, and he might need to look at some old newspaper articles. Recalling what Cullion said, he wrote down the names and dates he was sure of. Then he read everything over carefully, underlining words as he went along: *Helena, Angela, child, tabloid story, $$.*

~~~

In the morning, Jake stopped at the library and signed up for computer time. While he waited for an opening, he asked a severe-looking Asian lady at the research desk about back copies of newspaper articles.

"You may need some old microfiche records for that," she explained. "Do you have the names of the newspapers and the exact date ranges you're interested in?"

"Not yet. I'll get back to you after I do some work online."

The Internet search went well; in an hour he had a couple pages of notes and decided that was enough. On a last minute hunch, he browsed in the stacks through the true crime section and found a book by Rupert McAllister – *From Las Vegas to Newport: The Shoo-fly Saga*. The dust jacket said the book was posthumous, taken from the reporter's extensive notes and interviews.

Now this is interesting, he thought. Maybe he could apply for a library card and come back for it later. But he didn't want a library card – and he didn't want to wait.

Deciding the library's security system could be based on embedding something in the book cover, he held the pages tight in one hand and yanked the cover free. Because it had a barcode strip and pocket, he ripped the first page off as well. Finally, he spotted a security strip on the spine and peeled that off. He slipped the remaining pages into his jacket, filed the cover where the book had been, and walked toward the exit. If he triggered an alarm despite his precautions, they'd have to chase him.

Reading McAllister's book later that night, Jake realized he had what he needed – he wouldn't be going back for microfiche records. It took him a week to outline the story and make a list of the things that only Cullion knew. He had to keep seeing him to flesh out the story. Not wanting to make him suspicious, he never asked more than one or two questions at a time.

Eventually, he put it all together. First, Mickey Cullion was accessory after the fact to the Las Vegas murders. Second, a private eye named Brunetti tried to blackmail Angela to hide what he had discovered about Shoo-fly. Brad Styles stopped that, but still gave Brunetti five grand to tell *him* the story. Third, Helena Swann carried a payoff to Cullion from Shoo-fly, which made her his bag woman and a possible accessory after the fact to the old lady's murder in San Francisco. Finally, McAllister never met with Cullion, like all the stories said. What really happened was Brunetti found him, got the whole story, and sold it to McAllister.

This stuff was dynamite; nobody had covered it before. And he figured it made Angela Styles vulnerable. She was rich and publicity shy. Most of the story involved her family, and it hit her sister pretty hard. Releasing it to the right news outlet would focus the spotlight on her and her little boy just when her life was back to normal.

It might be worth money to quash it, a lot of money. He thought the best approach was to write a story tabloid style and get it in front of her somehow with a demand for maybe twenty grand. Damn, he couldn't write for shit, but he'd have to give it a shot.

The newsstand in the building where he worked carried the kind of tabloid rags he needed to study. After reading a few, he saw why people bought the stuff. The stories were laid out quick and nasty, with a lot of insinuation. You might not believe all of it, but it was fun to read. And you nearly always got a real negative opinion about some big shot who should have known better. So that was what he had to do – give a real bad impression about Angela and her sister Helena in five hundred words or less. They wouldn't want to see themselves that way, and Angela would pay to prevent anyone else from reading it.

He spent anguished hours writing and rewriting the story. He knew it wasn't perfect; maybe it was no good at all. But he had gotten the point across. Angela Styles and Helena Swann would look like hell if this got published. Jake was proud of himself ... and ready to roll.

CHAPTER 14

He watched the ballroom fill up with ladies and gents in evening wear. A lot of these dudes must be on their second or third marriages, he thought. Lots of trophy wives around. Jake could swear the average age difference was twenty years or more. Sure, you could find couples with matching gray hair, but it was mostly salt and pepper – or half-bald – for the guys and blond for the gals. Even more characteristic was a paunch for him and pumped up boobs for her.

Nevertheless, the cut glass chandeliers sparkled alike on everyone, and dozens of amber-colored sconces spread a sweet honey glow wherever you looked. Outside the ballroom windows the whole city was lit up. This was a class affair. And why not? With Angela Sharples Porter Styles as the hostess, that was a foregone conclusion.

He had seen the notice in the newspaper she owned, the San Francisco Record. The annual Charity Ball and Dinner for Alzheimer's Research. And he would have passed right by the announcement if the name of her company, Sharples Communications, hadn't been displayed in bold letters. It was society page stuff, with Brad Styles's picture and hers – the perfect San Francisco power couple. A thousand-dollar-a-plate affair. Well, he figured the catering company would be looking for waiters. And he was right.

His uniform fit him nicely. Gray vest, black bow tie, white shirt, and black pants with a satin side stripe. Some of the waiters didn't look too professional in their black sneakers, but he was wearing a proper pair of leather pumps. He knew the sharpest looking guys would have a chance at the better tables, so he trimmed his beard carefully and made sure the outfit was spotless. He didn't expect an assignment to the head table, though. That would probably go to those with the most experience, the ones the maître d' felt he could trust.

It worked out pretty good. One of his tables was within fifteen feet of the place settings designated for Mr. And Mrs. Brad Styles. Close enough to scoot over at the right moment and hand the lady an envelope. At which point he would disappear from the hall. Half way through dinner, a hotel functionary approached Brad Styles and whispered something to him. Styles got up from the table, spoke to Angela a moment and walked away with the man. This was it. Jake delivered the drink he was holding, tugged the envelope out of his shirt pocket, and walked over to the head table – directly in front of Angela Styles.

Like Mickey said, the lady was a knockout. She smiled graciously as he stood before her and held out the unsealed envelope across the table. Slowly, her eyes shifted down to look at it.

"Yes? Who is this from?" she asked as her hand went out to take it.

"I wouldn't know him, ma'am. He said you'd want to read it right away."

"Very well," she said, her smile fading.

Jake backed away, walked quickly through the ballroom, then out to the caterer's staging area in back. In the hallway, he took the service elevator to the ground floor and left the hotel by the back entrance. He had pulled it off.

And he really doubted that she had looked at him close enough to describe him later.

They couldn't trace him because he gave a phony name and social security number. He wouldn't be looking to get paid anyway. Well ... not by the caterer.

~~~

Angela Styles pulled out two typewritten pages from the envelope the waiter handed her and set them aside while she retrieved a pair of glasses from her purse. As she began to read, the color rose to her face. It was as if a vicious tabloid story had been written by a fourth-grader with a rudimentary sense of spelling. In this case, however, the story was true.

Rather than read it a second time, she looked around to see where the waiter was who delivered it. Gone. She sighed and looked for Brad, spotting him with Cesar Beragon, a famous vintner and an old family friend. Anxious now, she folded the pages and stuffed them back into the envelope. Brad didn't have to see this, she thought, at least not right away.

It took all of her composure to get through the dinner, give her speech, and start the ball with Brad. She couldn't very well leave early, either; she would be the focal point of the receiving line at evening's end. In the meantime, the conviction grew that she must take care of this by herself. If it was the wrong thing to do, what in God's name was the right thing?

What she had in mind was certainly worth a try. There was no choice, really, when you thought about it. She had to keep that story out of the newspapers at all costs.

When Brad and she got home, Angela claimed

exhaustion, took a shower, and went to bed. It was after midnight, but she wasn't in the least sleepy. She was lying in bed thinking when Brad came into the darkened room, drew the covers back, and climbed in next to her. Probably assuming she was asleep, he put his hand on her shoulder and kissed her gently before turning to his side of the bed. Within five minutes, he was snoring.

Angela got up slowly, making her best effort not to disturb him. She took her robe from the chaise by the window and pulled it on. Watching Brad sleep for a moment, she suddenly thought of Justin and walked down the corridor to his room.

He lay there, small against the queen-size bed, a trickle of saliva running from his mouth to the pillow. As always when she checked on him at night, the bedclothes were in disarray, all but one leg uncovered. She stood by the bed, pulled the covers up, and tucked him in. Not wanting to disturb his sleep, she resisted the impulse to kiss him.

Instead of taking her evening bag upstairs when she came home, Angela had shoved it into the drawer of the huge drumtop foyer table. She knew she would come downstairs later to fetch it – precisely as she was doing now. As she passed into the library, the pink and translucent glass beads sewn onto the white satin bag glittered – struck by moonlight streaming into the foyer windows.

She sank into a wingback chair facing the fireplace and turned on the reading lamp. With a sigh, she pushed the heavy blond hair back from her face, opened the bag, slipped on her glasses, and reread that loathsome ... thing.

Infamous Shoo-fly Sequel

"It is said by many the case is closed. But we have found it is not. There is more to this tail of the society psycho path and his many loves. In the first instance, you may be surprised to know that Mickey Cullion was assessory in the Las Vegas killings for helping Samson "Shoo-fly" Porter burn evidence (his clothes) and getaway. He was only sent up for embezzlement, one of Shoo-fly's scams.

But the most shocking of all new facts is the involvement of those San Franciscans of great prominence. That would be Angela Sharples Porter (now Styles), Helena Swann, the sister, and Brad Styles, married now to Angela.

Did you know a private detective name of Pedro Brunetti tried to blackmail Angela for thirty grand? Well, you do now. Brad Styles got in the way of this development, but he still gave Brunetti five grand. Not a bribe maybe, but just to tell what he knew. Still, this was not published before.

The biggest news of all? Helena Swan was Shoo-fly's bag woman as well as his mistress. She carried a bribe from Shoo-fly to Mickey Cullion so he would not tell all. The big idea was to shut him up after Shoo-fly killed the old lady, Wanda Buckley. This makes her assessory too, because she must of known what the bribe was for.

One more thing. That reporter who made the case famous never interviewed Mickey Cullion like he said. It was the private detective Brunetti who found Cullion and sold the story to McAllister (who died too)."

To Mrs. Styles:

"I'm sure you would not like to see this all over the newspapers, on the front page. It doesn't have to happen either. All I want is twenty thousand dollars in twenties and fifties. We need to do this in a public place with no police or other people. I have a copy of this in a friend's email file, which gets sent by him/her to the Chronicle if I don't come back on time. This will hurt you and your family – just what you don't want, I'm sure.

Have the money in one or two big envelopes held in front of you Thursday at noon exactly, right by the entrance to the Cutliffe Building on Market Street. If you are not there or if anything happens to me, the email goes.

Do this right. I'll know you when I see you. You don't know me. I'll come near you and say Are those for me? And you'll hand them over."

This was no professional, she could see that. And whether that would prove better or worse for her, she couldn't know. But he wasn't asking for much and probably didn't have many resources for following up. The format of his blackmail letter was quite clever – but the execution! Still, she had to admit he had pulled a lot of information together and uncovered some embarrassing facts. And approaching her that way at the charity ball showed real ingenuity. Was the waiter her blackmailer, or was he only the messenger?

She had an idea that whoever it was could be cowed. If she gave him what *she* thought was reasonable and told him she'd involve the police next time, he'd probably leave well enough alone. But how would she get this message across? If he were going to snatch the package and run, there'd be no time for chat.

Well, she could put a note in the envelope, couldn't she? Just as he did. A note saying here's half of what you demanded, and you'd better be satisfied. If I hear from you again, my husband and I will work tirelessly to have you apprehended.

This was *not* about saving ten thousand dollars, she thought. It was about showing this creature who's boss. Besides, ten thousand was an amount she could pull together without making a bank withdrawal that would prove traceable later on.

Angela could be tough when she had to be. And she'd muddle through this, but ... was it true Helena worked with Sam as an accessory to Wanda Buckley's murder like it said in the note? The suspicions she had long repressed about Helena's relations with her first husband flared up. How that old hurt retained its power! She felt it like a half-healed wound opening up under pressure.

CHAPTER 15

Helena Sharples Swann was the figure people remembered most from the days of the old Shoo-fly scandal. She was Angela's racy stepsister who had devolved into the Black Widow, Sam Porter's femme fatale. Ultimately, she became his victim when he tracked her down in Newport and shot her, just before being taken down himself in the last scene of their sordid drama.

Now she was the lady in the wheelchair, victim of her own concupiscence, seldom seen but instantly recognized in San Francisco whenever she ventured out of the Marina district mansion. Putting aside all that had happened, Angela and Brad provided and cared for her in the very home she had disgraced.

Despite her paralyzed, useless legs, Helena kept up appearances. Her clothes were up to date, her makeup always fresh, her hair faultlessly cut and groomed. If she were a poodle, she'd be a champion. She sometimes felt like the family pet, in fact – the way she was stroked, fed treats, and encouraged to do little tricks for her mistress.

Oh, she supposed that was an exaggeration, the bitter spirit of a woman crippled at age twenty-nine. Conflicted feelings aside, she tried to be thankful for the life she led with Angela and Brad since returning to San Francisco. But there was a kind of watchful truce between her and them, especially between her and Angela.

The world saw her stepsister as goodness personified. She had always had a reputation for unaffected elegance, a kind of remote but admirable innocence. Of course, if Angela ever heard a description like that, she would have denied it, emphatically. Her self-image was one of probity and tenacity – unglamorous and old-fashioned.

Perhaps only Helena could reconcile these disparate portraits. Day after day, she sat in her wheelchair and observed them – Brad, her former fiancé; Justin, son of her heart's ruling passion; and Angela, queen of all she surveyed. She always loved her stepsister and still did. Yet there was a nagging tension between what Helena knew as fact and the resentment she felt about her own fall from grace. And it colored all her relations.

Today, however, was not a day to sit and brood over complicated relationships. It was Thursday, the day after the big charity ball, and she wanted to hear all the details. She had been invited, as always, but her presence at any society event was problematic. Photographers would show too much interest, and the best people would drift away with raised eyebrows and whispering God knows what.

Instead, she assisted Angela in planning the dinner and ball. Starting last Monday, she helped her rehearse her speech. Helena actively enjoyed these duties – they gave employment to her mind. In addition, they led to a proprietary feeling about the affair. She was anxious to hear all about it this morning.

But Angela didn't come down to breakfast.

"She left before seven," Brad said. "She woke me up at six-fifteen to say she was getting an early start – something about business in town and a breakfast with her committee."

"That was all?"

"I think so. I was so groggy I went right back to sleep. I suppose she'll call either or both of us later."

For now, there were just the three of them. Helena sipped her morning coffee and watched Justin devour a plate of blueberry pancakes. At eight-thirty, Brad left for work while Helena waited with her nephew for his tutor to arrive.

~ ~ ~

It had threatened to rain all morning, and the moody skies were just now letting a light drizzle sift through the cloud cover. Jake Snider stood on Market Street across from the Cutliffe building – close enough to watch the front entrance, yet far enough away to make it unlikely he would be spotted. As other pedestrians were doing, he stood near a bus stop under the awning of a retail store.

When he saw the blond lady in the pink raincoat take a position to the left of the Cutliffe's entrance, holding some kind of package, he flipped his cigarette into the gutter and walked to the nearest crosswalk. His heart was thudding in his chest while he waited for the traffic light to change.

He took deep, slow breaths to stay calm. If this went right, it would be his first decent score ever, and who knew what else might come of it. But don't get ahead of yourself, he thought. Stay focused, stay on target.

That morning, he had shaved his face clean. On his walk downtown, he put on sunglasses and one of those jokey baseball caps with an old man's fake gray ponytail sewn in.

Just before leaving the halfway house, he had taken somebody's cheap nylon windbreaker from its hook in the front hall. He was satisfied that no one would get a useful description of him, even if a camera caught his action.

Angela was gazing squint-eyed down the street as he drew near the building's entrance. He walked by her and into a soup and salad joint with a front door just beyond where she stood. The restaurant had a second entrance, he knew, that led directly into the main building's foyer. She'd be expecting him to approach her from the street, so he figured to come out of the building and surprise her. She'd have less time to study him that way.

Angela held the big envelope against her chest with her arms crossed in front. The sidewalk was clotted with noontime strollers. Jake walked up to her from behind and tapped her shoulder. She spun around, looking tense and uncertain.

In a curt voice, he said, "Are those for me?" and snatched the envelope from her, sprinting away into the flow of the crowd.

The next few seconds were crucial. His building was adjacent to the Cutliffe, right on the street corner. He turned there and raced to the service entrance, looking back to see that no one had followed before opening the big steel door.

Once inside among the ladders, trash barrels, and discarded boxes, he wrapped the windbreaker around the sunglasses and baseball cap and tucked it behind a row of paint cans on the top shelf of a metal cabinet to the left of the dumpster. From there, he stepped to the rear of the room and took the service elevator up one flight to the maintenance crew's locker room.

A buddy of his would have punched him in a half hour earlier, a favor he'd have to return some day. He was still breathing hard, but smiling, when he made it to his locker and changed into his work clothes. His leather jacket was there from yesterday, along with a duffel bag. He set the envelope down behind the bag, then closed the door and spun the combination lock. For punctuation, he rammed his fist into the metal door.

This was the best day of his life, he thought. He was golden.

~~~

Helena was on the terrace speaking to the housekeeper when Angela came home a little before one o'clock. Right away, Esther hurried off to assist her. Through the French doors, Helena watched as Esther took her sister's purse and raincoat. Angela looked toward Helena, but made no move to join her.

Sensing something gone wrong, Helena directed her scooter toward the entrance. But Angela raised her arm with a palm-out gesture, signaling her to stop. She walked onto the terrace, carefully closing the doors behind her, and passed Helena without looking. When she reached the glass and wrought iron patio table, she stopped and looked out at the bay.

While Helena remained speechless, Angela covered her face with her hands and began trembling. Her first tears fell soundlessly, until she had to gasp for air. After that, she wept freely.

"Angela, what's wrong? Tell me what happened."

Helena rolled up and reached for her hand, but Angela rebuffed her and turned away.

"It's starting over again," she said. "Someone is blackmailing me."

She had placed a small envelope on the table, which

Helena didn't notice at first. She picked it up now, pulled out the sheets of paper, and dropped them in Helena's lap.

"You'll want to read this," was all she said.

Right away, Helena felt the blood rise to her face. When she read the sentence that accused her of being an accessory to murder, she was furious.

"No!" she screamed. "No! Who is doing this? Who did you meet with today?"

Angela turned to her with a peevish look, her face flushed.

"Never mind that," she said sharply. "I took care of it. I gave him ten thousand dollars and a note to let him know there won't be any more. But your outrage won't do, Helena. What don't I know? What did you do with Sam that morning before he ran off?"

"Sam Porter? He wanted me dead, Angela, remember? I was the one who told you what he was. How can you think I would have helped him murder anyone?"

"It doesn't say that, exactly, does it? It says you carried a bribe to Mickey Cullion to help Sam. Is that part right? Well, is it?"

Helena had wheeled around sharply, away from Angela's gaze. She couldn't bring herself to speak again just yet.

"No answer," Angela said. "Oh, I wonder what that means. Have you ever been truthful to me about anything, Helena? What else don't I know?"

"You don't know the things you don't want to know, Angela. That has always been your way."

"Let me point out that I just asked you a question that I *do* want the answer to. And I'm waiting!"

Angela was pressing her close and Helena recognized that she wouldn't back off.

"Yes, all right! I never told you or anyone that Sam asked me to take a package to Mickey Cullion that morning. But that doesn't make me an accessory to murder!"

"What does it make you, Helena?"

"What are you getting at? Haven't I suffered as much or more than anyone because of Sam Porter?"

"I won't even try to answer that. We'd probably need a jury to decide. But you're stalling again. I want to know right now what you did that day and why!"

For the only time in her life that Helena could remember, Angela was implacable, relentless.

"I hated Mickey Cullion," she said, her voice weary. "You know I did. He called me up the day before to say that Sam had hurt him. He was demanding the money Sam owed him to shut up and go away. He said he'd tell all about Las Vegas otherwise. You know yourself we thought Sam was involved in casino fraud, not murder. That's why you thought Brunetti contacted you – and that's why I thought Cullion was contacting me. Sam gave me a package to deliver to him, and I did it. I didn't think you had to know. And I didn't tell the police because it looked too suspicious. I was terrified of a jail sentence."

Angela stared at Helena a moment longer, then turned and walked off into the house. The question she hadn't asked hung in the air. Were you sleeping with my husband? There it is, thought Helena, why don't you come out with it? Everyone one else has assumed it for eight years. But murder? How could you think I would help him with murder?

She powered her scooter into the kitchen and turned into the butler's pantry where a dumbwaiter shaft had been converted into an elevator. She was angry and sad – she supposed distraught was the word. Her thoughts were jumbled as she got off on the second floor and went toward her room.

Suddenly, one thought came clear. *Cullion*, she said to herself. Of course – the little bastard must be in San Francisco. Only he could pull something like this. He's the only one who knew.

Later, sitting in her room, she had to admit that Brunetti was also a possibility. But why would either of them implicate themselves like that in the letter, putting allegations about themselves in print that had legal ramifications? Still, they were the ones who knew these things. In the end, Mickey Cullion had to be her best bet. Was he really as illiterate as that blackmail note seemed to show? Or was that note the product of a mind more clever than she realized?

CHAPTER 16

His shift over, Jake punched his time card and went to his locker. He buried the fat manila envelope deep in his duffel bag and left the building. Once on the street, he walked around to the service entrance and retrieved the windbreaker with the sunglasses and baseball cap, jamming them into the inside pocket of his leather bomber.

A few blocks away, he broke the glasses and threw the two halves into different trash receptacles. In similar fashion, he ripped the ponytail out of the hat, discarding each part separately on his way to Cullion's place. The windbreaker he would keep until he could return later to the halfway house and hang it up where he had found it.

Jake had told Cullion he'd come over right after work. During the past couple of weeks, he had gone there every few days, setting things up for his score. Sure, Cullion could let him store a few things he needed to get out of the halfway house. No problem. Jake already had some stuff there, and now he'd bring over a duffel bag with some clothes inside and a lock on it. Only in the middle of the underwear and stolen towels would be a certain heavy envelope.

He was itching to count what was in it, but finding a safe place was more important right now. He couldn't bring it to the halfway house and expect nobody to see it. And just suppose there was a surprise search for drugs like they pulled from time to time. No, he could wait to look at it, count it, roll in it. Twenty grand was worth waiting for.

At the mission, he turned into the alley and climbed the

outside stairs. The door was open.

"Hi Mike," he said, walking in.

"Good to see you pal. What's that?"

"Duffel bag. I told you I wanted to leave it here, remember?"

"Yeah, sure, put it in the closet."

Jake saw Cullion had take-out for them, all set up on the little maple table by the room's one window over the alleyway. Playin' house again, he thought. This crap was getting hard to take. Still, he was hungry after his shift.

"Smells like Chinese," he said, looking toward the table.

"You got it. C'mon, sit down."

He opened the closet and tossed the bag onto the shelf above the clothes pole, pushing it to the left as far as it would go. Then he shut the door and walked over to the table.

"Whatcha got?" he asked.

"Moo-shu pork for you. Chicken lo mein for me."

"Aw-right!" Jake settled in and tore into the meal.

Cullion pointed at him with a quizzical look.

"Hey, you shaved off the face fuzz."

"Yeah, gonna start all over. Just a goatee an' mustache this time."

"Looks good to me now."

They were silent for a while as they concentrated on the take-out. But it was easy to see Cullion had something on his mind from the jittery way he kept looking up from his plate.

"How 'bout the job, Jake?" Cullion asked. "You goin' full-time soon?"

"Boss says I start next Monday. Forty hours. Got a

catch, though. I work Monday through Thursday, then off two days, then all day Sunday, for Chrissake."

"But you can leave the halfway house, right?"

"Well, I got to show a full-time paycheck first, so it'll take a week. Besides, I'll believe it next Monday when my time card says 'full-time'."

"You can move in here as soon as you're ready."

"I dunno, Mike. One room, you know? It's awful small."

"We can look for a bigger place, and I can get somebody to take this. With two paychecks we could handle it."

Jake grunted and let the moment pass. He hated all that 'we' stuff. Cullion was staring at him hopefully, but he wasn't going to tell him what he wanted to hear. Tonight he was supposed to stay until ten-thirty, then leave to make his curfew at eleven. And that meant getting cozy – ol' Mickey wasn't going to be talked into no movie tonight, he could tell.

Well, it won't be much longer, he thought.

Jake was already looking for a place he could afford on his own.

CHAPTER 17

When Helena woke up Friday morning, she decided not to go downstairs for breakfast with the family. As a result, she knew Angela would assume she was sulking. But that would be wrong. Helena wasn't sulking, she was angry and determined.

Determination was always her long suit. Yes, her personality was volatile – no one had to tell her that posed a problem. But she could focus and stay on course with the best of them when it was necessary. And today was one of those times. If Cullion were at the bottom of this, she was going to ferret him out of whatever hole he had found to hide in.

In the middle of Helena's tense reverie, the housekeeper came to check on her. Angela's doing, no doubt. It was eight-thirty.

"May I bring you breakfast, Mrs. Swann?"

Helena managed to smile. "Just orange juice and bran flakes, Esther."

"Is everything all right?"

"Yes, everything is fine. I have phone calls to make and some e-mail correspondence to take care of. I'm not sure whether I'll be down for lunch or not."

"Yes, ma'am. I'll check with you later."

"Oh, Esther? Tell Justin he may stop by during his break if he wants to."

For now, she sat up in bed and tried to concentrate. Cullion may have been released from jail by now, she thought, but he could be on probation still. When the police found him in 1999, he was in Idaho. Would he have gone back there? No matter – he would have been released in California, so his first parole officer would be here. That gave her a place to start, a way to begin checking up on him.

She remembered the name of someone who might help. Alfonso Bowers. He was the San Francisco police detective who ran the investigation and took her statement after Sam Porter ran away. She recalled his courtesy and his offer of help if she should ever need it. That surely meant official assistance on a police matter, but even so ....

Helena plucked her cell phone from the bedside table and scrolled through the emergency numbers she had programmed. After connecting to the police, she heard the typical series of useless menus, choices and announcements – the automated version of the bureaucratic runaround. Finally, she reached a bored male voice in the Investigations Bureau and asked to speak to Detective Sergeant Alfonso Bowers.

"That's Lieutenant Bowers, ma'am. He's Homicide. I'll forward you, but you'll probably get his voice mail."

"Sure," she sighed. "Why not?"

~~~

When he called back later, it was evident Bowers didn't want her poking around into the old case.

"Lieutenant, I'd like to know something for my piece of mind. Can you tell me whether Mickey Cullion is still in prison?"

"As I recall, Mrs. Swann, he was released in 2001, towards the end of the year."

"Would you put me in touch with the parole officer of

record?"

A chilly silence followed before he continued.

"Is there something wrong, ma'am?" he asked. "May I ask what's bothering you?"

"Well, if I knew where he was located, it might help. For instance, knowing that he went back to Idaho and stayed there would make me feel better."

"But why the concern right now? It's been ... lessee ... eight years since we closed the case and nearly six years since he was paroled."

"Lieutenant, I wouldn't have known when he was paroled."

"I suppose not, but it happened a long time ago, and I have this feeling there's something more you could tell me. Is there?"

Helena tried to think fast. It was obvious Bowers didn't want to nose around and locate a private citizen, one who had paid his debt, if he didn't have a legitimate reason. She could go to Brad, whose clout could be applied at the Police Commission, or she could tell Bowers just enough to enlist his sympathy and assistance. Not a real choice, she thought. Go for sympathy.

"This may be nothing, Lieutenant, so I didn't want to make an issue of it. I received a letter with some ... accusations. My sister has seen it, too. We're not willing to make it an official police matter. As a matter of fact, neither my brother-in-law nor my sister knows I'm making this call. I just remembered how kind you were to me and thought I might eliminate one cause for concern. It's probably just a crank letter anyway. We've certainly had others over the years."

"I understand, Mrs. Swann. Maybe I can help you out." He sounded much less wary now. "Let me call the parole boys and see what I can find out. In the meantime, don't worry about it. Most likely the letter's from a crank, like you said. One thing, though? If you receive another one you've got to come forward. All right?"

"Yes, Lieutenant. And thank you."

She was surprised when Bowers got back to her the same day. He downplayed the idea that Michael Cullion was the cause of her problem. The guy had an exemplary prison record and went back to Idaho soon after his release. His parole ended in 2005. Apparently, he worked at menial jobs there and had close contact with a local church group.

"So he's still in Idaho?" she asked.

"Well, no. But first I wanted you to know about his record. The parole officer up there was very positive about the guy. He told me Cullion left to become a kind of assistant to a respected clergyman."

"Oh. Can you tell me where he is?"

"Well, I will, Mrs. Swann. But if I'm ever asked, I'll deny it. I have no reason to follow up on this guy. He's absolutely clean right now."

"Honestly, Lieutenant, I'm glad to hear that."

"Michael Cullion runs a little storefront church here in San Francisco. They call it the Breastplate of Faith and Love. It's in the Mission district. Entirely legit and respectable, I understand."

~~~

In retrospect, Helena wished she hadn't called Cullion so soon after speaking to Bowers. A little more time and mental distance might have helped. But a sense of rage led her to search out the mission's telephone number right away.

She swung herself out of bed and into the scooter. At her desk, she found the number for The Breastplate of Faith and Love in a two-year old volume of the local white pages and punched it into her landline extension.

When Cullion answered, she lit into him. He didn't respond well to the sarcasm and anger in her voice, and he let her know it.

"Blackmail! What are you talking about, lady?"

"As if you didn't know! You're talking to me, Mickey, remember? I know what you're capable of."

"My name is Michael, Michael Cullion," he said with a certain dignity. "And if you think back, maybe you'll remember some of your own *capabilities* – the words that come to mind are some of the worst ones I know."

He had struck home, and she felt it. Before she could erupt, though, he attempted to placate her.

"Listen, this won't do any good. Why don't we both ease off and go to the cops with that letter. I'm not hiding anything."

But that was crazy, she thought. The letter says he's an accessory to murder. Unless ... unless he *doesn't* know about it. And when she probed about the money – he was totally baffled.

Was it Brunetti after all? How could it be? If it were, he wouldn't have accused himself of blackmailing Angela in the letter. Something was going on here, there was someone else in the mix. Someone they hadn't considered or didn't know about.

She wasn't willing to go to the police, of course, but

perhaps Cullion would meet with her and talk. If she saw him face to face, she'd be better able to judge him and his motives. But where? She could hardly have him over for drinks.

"You're right, we should figure this out," she said. "But before we get the police involved, I'd like to meet with you."

"I don't know. We never seem to ... communicate real well."

"Look, I shouldn't have said those things. But I believe you'll understand my reaction after seeing this letter."

He paused before responding.

"Well, I work at a diner on Market Street. We could meet there most any day."

He had probably forgotten she was crippled.

"Not too good. My car is equipped for me to drive, but if the diner isn't accessible ... "

"Oh, sorry. I suppose I could leave work for an hour or so some day."

"How about the grounds at the Palace of Fine Arts tomorrow? I can do that."

He agreed. They settled on meeting the next day, Saturday, at noon.

~~~

For the short drive to the Palace of Fine Arts, Helena left the motorized scooter behind and took a collapsible chair along that wasn't difficult to fold and store on the passenger side of her car. If she became tired, Cullion could wheel her around. Cruising past the Palace grounds, she spied him sitting on the lawn, silhouetted against the classical rotunda.

It was a sunny Saturday, and the park was full of area

residents and tourists. The complex was part of the Presidio and bordered on the Marina district. Whenever she came here, Helena recalled a scene from the movie *Vertigo* – Jimmy Stewart and Kim Novak strolling the walkways near the pond.

She finagled the chair out of the car, shifted herself into it, and pushed herself along until she found Cullion, who saw her and nodded. He's changed, she thought. He moves differently now – and that old shifty look of his is gone. He rose from the grass, brushing his chino slacks off while advancing towards her. Without blinking, he held her gaze.

"I like it here," he said.

"I used to come here often," she said. "But that was a long time ago. I don't get out much any more."

Cullion didn't reply. Instead, he got behind her to guide the wheelchair along the walk. They both remained silent for a time. When she saw a likely spot on the lawn near the pond's edge, she pointed and he wheeled her onto the grass and down, reaching level ground near some bushes. There was no one within thirty feet of them. A pair of swans glided by.

"We've never had much use for each other, have we?" she said, smiling.

"I've had my reasons."

"When all is said and done, though, Sam Porter was the problem – not us."

"Maybe so. But this isn't about him, is it?"

"In a way it is. Judge for yourself."

Helena pulled a copy of the letter from her purse, unfolded it, and handed it to Cullion. He took it, looked at her without expression, and sat on the ground by the side of her chair. As he read, she saw the anger and hurt play on his features. First Angela, then she, and now Michael Cullion – all three of them had the same smoldering reaction. When he handed the letter back to her, she spoke.

"Could this be Brunetti's work? Would he do something like this?"

"Nah. Nobody is less likely than Pedro Brunetti to give the law a chance to nail him."

"My thought exactly," she said.

He laughed. "But you thought I would?"

"Sorry. I did think it was you until we spoke."

"Y'know, I don't know how to say this," he started. "Sometimes you just gotta talk to somebody. There was an old guy helped me in prison – a preacher. I told him a lot of this stuff, like you would a priest. And there was someone else I trusted, too ... until now."

"Then you know who did this? Do you?"

Cullion sighed. "Probably. Did your sister give him the twenty grand?"

"No. Just ten."

He got to his feet and began wheeling her back to the walkway. She twisted around in the chair to look up at him.

"Can we do something about this?" she asked.

"Oh, I'm gonna take care of it," he said. "There won't be any follow up letters. I can't promise I'll get the money back, but I'll try. Can we keep the cops out of it?"

"The last thing we want is police involvement or anything that will cause publicity."

"Good. Then give me a chance to make it right."

~~~

Helena hadn't spoken to her sister since their awful

blowup. Poor Angela was distancing herself at the very moment she needed help and solace from someone. After doing what she could to mitigate any further blackmail attempt, she had to be in dread of what would come next. When Helena saw her late that afternoon, she hoped to ease her mind.

At first their talk was strained. Helena's attempt to make conversation centered on Justin – his lessons and his visits to Doctor LaFreniere. She was pleased to see Angela so much less worried about him now. Her sister's confidence in LaFreniere was very high.

"I unburdened myself to him," she said. "He's the type of doctor who makes it easy for you. And I have the feeling Justin will do the same."

"That *is* good news."

Angela managed a smile that quickly dimmed. When she spoke again, her tone was serious.

"I haven't wanted to talk about this, Helena, because the whole subject is stressful for me, but I'm sorry for the accusation I made. I know you weren't involved in Wanda Buckley's murder."

Helena was surprised, but grateful. Their argument had weighed on her mind.

"It hurt me, you know, hearing you say that. But when I thought about it ... I realized you had every reason to doubt me."

An awkward silence intervened. She wondered how best to let Angela know what she had done since yesterday. Finally, she forced herself to speak about her conversations with Lieutenant Bowers and Mickey Cullion.

Angela's eyes lit up with fear when Helena described

the meeting with Mickey.

"I can't believe you went to see him," she said, hands fluttering to her face.

"I was angry, and I had to find out. And I'm glad I confronted him, Angela. Mickey wants to set things right. He knows who's behind this and he's going to keep the blackmailer quiet."

"Did you find out who it is? His name, I mean?"

"No. I wanted to ask, but I thought it better not to know."

CHAPTER 18

The whole Michael Cullion thing is over, he thought. He was just plain ol' Mickey again, the low-life thief who gets led down the friggin' garden path by some good-looking creep. How did he let it happen? If his knowledge of the human heart had grown under Jim Hendrickson's tutelage, why hadn't his resistance to its weakness grown as well?

Standing in front of the dresser mirror, he stared hard at himself. He was thirty-nine years old and felt every day of it. People told him he looked much younger, but that was his size – a little guy always seems younger than his years.

He knew what to do to make this right, he thought, but where would he go from there? The thing with Julie was over, he had messed that up. And the whole fantasy he had built up around Jake? Just another self-delusion, one he seemed fated to repeat over and over.

Well, it stops here, he said to himself. He had spent much of his life so far trying to prove himself and his good intentions to other people.

From now on, let them prove themselves to me!

He found himself fiddling about in the dresser's top drawer, looking in at the socks and underwear neatly folded and stored there. Putting one hand underneath the stacks of clothing, he slid it along from right to left at the bottom of the drawer. The cheap, unfinished wood grazed his fingertips until he felt the resistance of a small box. He raised the box lid and stared for a long time at the articles inside before secreting one of them in his pants pocket.

Suddenly, he remembered the duffel bag. He had totally forgotten that Jake had asked to store it. Pulling open the closet door, Cullion spotted the olive drab bag with the zipper lock on the shelf to the far left. He yanked it down to look. The lock would be easy to break, but he couldn't bring himself to do it.

He'd just have to wait for Jake to show up. He still wanted to give him the benefit of the doubt, even though this was looking like the worst kind of betrayal.

What had he ever done to deserve it?

~~~

On Friday, Jake Snider had to sweat it out at the halfway house. He figured he might as well stay around in case the cops came calling. Not that he expected trouble, but if they were looking for him – well, here he would be, not hiding, not worried, and nothing to be found on the premises. Whenever he got too antsy, he would think about all those long, green Benjamins in the duffel bag at Cullion's place.

If no one saw him go into the service entrance after he took the package from Angela Styles, he could not be traced. No way. Even so, he couldn't help but replay every single detail of the caper – from the charity ball, to the drop off', to Thursday night with Cullion.

By nightfall, he felt at ease. More than twenty-four hours had passed and there was no newspaper story, no cops, no problem. He could even concentrate on the *Las Vegas* episode he was watching with the other guys in the common room.

Around two o'clock on Saturday, Jake walked past the

Breastplate of Faith and Love Mission and turned into the alley. He had a key to the back entrance now, and he figured on getting the duffel bag down from the closet shelf to check out his score. If Cullion wasn't around, that is. If he was – well, he'd have to wait until Monday. Despite what he had told Cullion, Jake already had permission to leave the halfway house, and Monday would be the day he took all his shit over to the new place he found just this morning.

Yeah, he thought, *no more mission, no more Mickey, no more "we."*

~~~

Cullion watched the back door open and stared at Jake when he walked in. He was sitting on the bed, trying to think what he wanted to say. But the words wouldn't form, and by now Jake was staring back with a puzzled look on his face.

"Hey, what's up? What's going on?"

"I gotta know something, Jake. I get the feeling lately I don't mean a damn thing to you. Is that right?"

"Whoa, Mike. Can it! You know I don't talk about stuff like that."

"You know what, Jake? You don't have to bother with Mike and Michael any more, it's just Mickey like it used to be. Nothing ever changes, huh?"

"What the fuck is this? You got some big dramatic scene in mind, play it yourself! I'm not havin' any!"

"Well, what *are* you havin'? Some blackmail maybe? Some score, some profit from things I talked about?"

Jake was quiet a moment. Cullion could practically see his brain cells groping to figure out what had gone wrong. He almost felt sorry for him.

"Ten grand is chump change, Jake. I can't believe you took all that risk for ten grand!"

Jake's mouth dropped open and his eyes started. He made a leap to the closet door, tore it open, pulled the duffel bag down and flung in on the bed. Quickly, he had his keys out, got the lock off, and was digging underwear and towels out of the bag to get at the envelope. Cullion looked on and shook his head.

When the package was open, you could see the stacks of bills had been augmented with newspaper to fill out the envelope. There was a note inside as well. Cullion watched anger darken the bigger man's eyes and twist his features as he read it. Then Jake jammed everything back into the bag, kicked it into the open closet, and slammed the door shut.

"C'mon Jake. Forget it, you know? Ten grand ain't worth it. We can make it right, see? Give it back and they'll never come after you. They don't want anybody to know!"

"Ten lousy grand! That cunt!"

Jake grabbed Cullion by the shirtfront and shook him. His lips were pulled back from his teeth, and his nostrils flared.

"How the hell did you know there's only ten grand in there?"

"Give the money back, Jake," Cullion pleaded. "We could still make it work!"

"Always with the goddamn '*we*' shit!" he yelled. "It was never '*we*,' you little fuckhole!"

Jake slapped him hard across the face, then pushed him over and knelt on his arms, pinning him to the floor. Cullion felt his nose break and his teeth loosen under a barrage of quick, sharp blows. Desperate, he used the limited freedom of his right arm to reach into his pocket and take out the knife he had found in the dresser drawer. The knife he had put away for good so long ago.

Cullion jerked free his arm, flicked the button and aimed true, right under the breastbone. He sliced, twisted, and pushed until he could feel his hand start to slide in with the blade.

Suddenly, Jake leaped away, reeling backwards. His hands flew in surprise to his open belly as he dropped to the bed. Cullion sat up on the floor and watched, covered in blood from his broken nose. Jake yelled out, screeched really, the pitch going high and weird, then trailing off as he ran out of breath.

When another scream filled the silence, Cullion turned his battered face to see the young immigrant couple who rented the apartment. They were standing immobile in the doorway of his room, faces horror-struck.

PART II

THE SISTERS

CHAPTER 19

When Detective Maynard Bennett took the call, he couldn't quite believe his ears. He had never heard of the victim, Jake Snider, but the name Michael Lester Cullion was all too familiar from the old Shoo-fly case. With his then partner Al Bowers, Bennett had investigated Wanda Buckley's murder eight years ago. They had subsequently taken it on the chin when Sam Porter eluded capture in San Francisco. The public was not pleased, and the Police Commission had a meltdown.

Despite having his throat cut by Porter, Cullion also got out of town before they could apprehend him. Sure, he was finally tracked down and did time, but it was a Las Vegas detective who found him up there in Idaho. In short, the Shoo-fly case had been nothing but humiliation and misery for San Francisco Homicide.

The first phase of the Snider investigation was quick, clean, and easy. Cullion was Mirandized and immediately confessed. And it was all videotaped. Now, some lawyer was bound to come along and try to have it thrown out, but that was just part of today's legal playscript. A professional like Bennett wasn't going to worry about stuff he couldn't control. For the present, everything was in order.

Except that he wasn't satisfied Cullion had given him a full picture. The murder had all the earmarks of a classic "homo-cide," but Cullion wasn't owning up to a sexual relationship. They had an argument, he admitted, but it was about some unspecified wrong Snider had done to a third party.

Cullion wouldn't say more because he didn't want to involve an innocent person. Supposedly, he did what he had to do in self-defense. Right now, that hardly mattered. Cullion's detailed description of the actual fight and murder was on record, and it matched the physical aspects of the scene perfectly.

Juan and Margarita Cansillo were on record also. Juan had called the police at Cullion's request. He and his wife had seen the immediate aftermath of the crime, and everything they said coincided with Cullion's confession. If he couldn't claim "case closed," Bennett was nevertheless happy to give his initial report to Al Bowers, who was his boss now.

Happy, that is, until the crime scene techs handed in the list of evidence found at the scene. And happy until Bowers came charging into the squad room with a real mystified look on his face. Bowers wasn't miffed at the list of evidence, even though it included a bombshell – the duffel bag with ten grand in it. He seemed to focus on the third party angle instead.

"Why the hell," he wanted to know, "haven't you found out Cullion's motive in more concrete terms, and who he's protecting?"

"Hey, Boss, this is day one of the investigation. Cut me some freakin' slack! I've got a confession, and it coincides with the known evidence. What more could you want in the first twenty-four hours?"

He had to agree with Bowers that the ten grand and the underlying reason for the fight were related. It sure didn't take a lot of brainpower to put that together. Cullion shrugged it off however, telling them he didn't know where the money came from. He claimed that Snider stored the bag in his closet, but that he, Cullion, had never looked inside. At that point he lawyered up, just like that.

"Okay," Bowers said. "When a public defender is appointed, let me know. We have enough for arraignment Monday anyway. That'll keep the brass happy for now. What about the press? Anybody sniff this one out yet?"

"So far it just smells like Mission district mayhem and murder, unless some old hand recognizes Cullion's name."

"That'll happen in no time, May."

"Yeah, I suppose you're right."

"Let's give some thought to that before I call the chief. I'd like to give him some suggestions for the public relations angle."

Bennett asked himself what the hell that was about. Why should he worry about public relations? That wasn't like Al Bowers at all.

"Oh, one thing more, May. Was there anything else in that duffel bag that could relate to this?"

"No. Just ... um ... towels, clothes, the money, some newspaper, and a large empty envelope. The money, newspaper, and envelope were kind of pushed in there, on top. The bag was locked when they found it, and the keys were in Snider's pocket."

"Were the Cansillos asked about the bag?"

"They were, yes. They never saw it. They couldn't be sure about the closet being closed, although they thought it was. Of course, they did leave Cullion in the room by himself when he asked them to call the police."

~~~

Angela Styles was at breakfast Tuesday morning when she saw the headline. Setting her coffee down, she felt confused and sickish all at once.

SHOO-FLY ACCOMPLICE SUSPECTED IN SNIDER SLAYING MICKEY 'WEASEL' CULLION IN CUSTODY

She read all their names in the first column under the banner – hers, Helena's, and Brad's – although there was nothing in the story to link them to this new atrocity. They were only mentioned in reference to the old scandal, thank God. And there was nothing about money!

Even though Cullion had confessed to the murder – disembowelment was the awful term the reporter used – the only reason he gave was self-defense. The photo of the arraignment showed that he had taken a terrible beating.

Was it possible all this had nothing to do with the blackmail attempt? Unless ... unless Helena had done something, paid or promised money to Cullion to ... get rid of the blackmailer.

Oh God, please no, she thought.

When Brad came downstairs, he was dressed for work and ready to leave.

"Don't go just yet, dear," she said. "Please stay to breakfast."

He frowned. "What's the matter, Angela?"

She raised an eyebrow and handed him the newspaper. When he had scanned the headline and read the first paragraph, he stopped, sat down, and looked at her.

"I can't believe it," he said. "Has Helena seen this yet?"

he asked.

"She hasn't been down. Read the whole article, Brad."

When he had, she could see him relax a little.

"Well, I guess that could have been worse," he said.

"So far, yes. But, darling ... I've something to tell you."

Brad listened quietly, although his face was tense and flushed. She told him about the charity ball, the waiter, the delivery of the money. After describing her angry scene with Helena, she pulled the blackmail note from her robe and gave it to him.

He sat down next to her at the kitchen island. Slowly, he read the note.

"Angela," he sighed, "this is awful, but I don't see any connection between the murder in the newspaper and this ... thing."

"I know. But Helena found out Cullion was in town. And she met with him on Saturday. He figured out who was blackmailing me, and he agreed to make sure it would stop."

Brad looked at her, baffled. She hesitated before speaking again.

"I ... can't help but wonder if she could have paid him to get rid of this man. Perhaps Snider was the blackmailer."

"Paid Cullion?" he asked. "To kill somebody? There was a time when I would have been quick to defend her against such a terrible accusation. But after everything that's happened ...."

"Well, I couldn't help wondering, but that doesn't make it true. Maybe we should just wait, Brad. We have no reason to accuse her of anything."

"I suppose you're right. Why ask for trouble?"

Brad said it so quietly, she looked up, wondering what

it meant. But he had turned away from her. After a moment, he spoke again.

"I'm worried about you, Angela. Why didn't you come to me? What could you have been thinking?" His face told her he was devastated.

She tried to blink back the tears. "Oh, honey, after everything you've been through with Helena and me, I wanted to protect you for once. I thought I could take care of it."

Brad stayed home with her until late morning.

~~~

Maynard Bennett had made a routine request for phone records and was looking through a list of incoming calls for the Breastplate of Faith and Love Mission. The physical telephone was a landline in Cullion's room. One number on the report stood out – and it belonged to Mr. and Mrs. Bradford Styles.

Damn, thought Bennett, this can't be happening. The last thing he ever expected in this case was a new link between Cullion and those people.

The call had come in at 4:35 p.m. on Friday, the day before the murder. Right away, Bennett left a message for Al Bowers and one for Angela Styles with her housekeeper. Mrs. Styles was the first to call back.

"What can I do for you, Detective?" she asked.

"Mrs. Styles, I'm sorry to disturb you. By now I'm sure you've seen the stories on the Mickey Cullion case, and I want you to know we think it's a shame the press has chosen to dredge up the old news."

"Yes, I've seen them. And thank you, but I suppose it was inevitable."

"One small thing has come up that I hope you can help me with."

"Oh?"

"Yes, a telephone call from your landline came in to the Breastplate of Faith and Love Mission last Friday. A three-minute phone call. Can you shed any light on this?"

"No, I can't. Are you sure about this, Detective?"

"Yes. I double-checked before calling you."

"Well, I had several guests on Friday. And there are the household members … and Esther, my employee. But I can't imagine anyone calling there. That's Culllion's church, isn't it?"

"Right."

"Well, I don't see how I can help you."

"If you would, ma'am, you could do just two things for us. Ask the members of your household about this. Someone might recall something. And help me make a list of everybody who was a guest at your house Friday."

"Detective, if there was a phone call from my home to that place, it *had* to be a mistake, some kind of misdial perhaps."

"I see what you're saying, Mrs. Styles. But it's something I need to follow through on. Could you help me put that list together, ma'am? It couldn't take long."

He knew he had handled this call as well or better than anyone else could have. But she wasn't having any.

"I'm sorry. I don't think I want to do that. No offense, Detective Bennett, but I think this request should be put in writing to my lawyer. I'm sure you remember him. He had to intervene the last time, when I thought some police requests were intrusive. Please don't take this personally.

You've been most kind. But I can't help you."

Checkmate, he said to himself. With her connections in the judiciary and among the very highest city brass, it would be months before they had a list. He knew it was still his case, but Al Bowers would have to take over the high society aspect. Good luck to him.

And now, he wondered, what was Cullion going to say about that phone call?

CHAPTER 20

Lieutenant Alfonso Bowers was proud of his career in the SFPD. When he was a kid, he thought he would become an army drill instructor like his dad. Somewhere along the way his fascination for military life wore off, but all the lessons he had absorbed on discipline and team building pushed him into law enforcement. And it suited him. He loved investigative work, despite the politics and social pressures you ran up against in a city like San Francisco.

So here he was, a middle-aged black man, a respected figure on the San Francisco police force, devoted husband and father to three kids – and, since last Friday, a guy with a problem. When he helped Helena Swann find Cullion, he did it out of respect – she had been very cooperative back in the day, during the Shoo-fly investigation in 1999. But he should never have done it. He hoped it wouldn't prove to be a case of – what was the saying? ... *no good deed ever goes unpunished*.

He felt sorry for Helena Swann; he saw her as ill-used. From his point of view, it was bizarre to think of her as the Black Widow while Mrs. Styles was Saint Angela to all and sundry. The heroism that Angela had showed in sticking by her husband, a vicious killer, was simply obstruction of justice to a policeman. However, he had to wonder if Mrs. Swann had manipulated him into a corner this time around. If so, he'd have to straighten that out.

When Bennett came to him about the telephone call

from the Styles residence to the Breastplate of Faith and Love, he was only too happy to take over that aspect of the investigation. Later in the day, they met to go over all of the evidence. There was a ton, and it all pointed in one direction. Mickey Cullion was going down, in spades.

"How did the arraignment go?" he asked Bennett.

"Held without bail, like we wanted. Judge Shafter barely listened to the public defender before making the decision."

"Great. Although I wouldn't want to be up on charges before a judge named Shafter," he chuckled.

Bennett seldom laughed at his jokes. This one was no exception.

"His lawyer entered the not guilty plea, like we figured, while Cullion stood there shaking his head."

"When you talked to him last time, what did Cullion say about the phone call?"

"He said he never got a phone call on Friday."

"Damn. Did you show him the list of calls?"

"Nah. I just asked if he got any calls. And I asked if he were sure when he said no. I handled it like you said."

"And the public defender?"

"She didn't pick up on it at all. You were right about that, too."

"Good, May, good. I want to keep the phone call quiet for now. Especially, I don't want anything in the news – but I don't want his lawyer in on it either. Not just yet, anyway."

"But Al, the discovery period? The defense?"

"If we find out it's exculpatory or even neutral, we'll give it to them, of course. For right now it's my decision that it's meaningless. If it remains that way, we'll *still* give it to them. But not while Cullion won't talk and we're still investigating."

"And the ten grand?"

"Keep it out of the press. As long as the defense doesn't know about the phone call, it'll be in their best interest to be quiet about the money."

"Well, you're checking on the phone call, so fine with me. But how am I supposed to keep on investigating the money? I have no where to go with it – there was no unusual activity in their bank accounts. We checked back three months."

"C'mon, don't give up, May. There must be twenty different ways people as rich as they are can pull ten grand together."

"Yeah, sure Al," he groaned. "Who are you going to see about the phone call?"

"Well, Mrs. Styles can't stop me from interviewing anyone who wants to talk. And I'm quite sure Helena Swann will see me. She's a household member who could have made the call. Right?"

"Interesting choice."

"Isn't it, though? And I see no reason not to ask her why she thinks Cullion had ten thousand bucks in his closet."

"You gotta be kidding, Al."

"Not at all. Just helping you check out the money angle."

~~~

Bowers was standing in Helena Swann's bedroom suite – boudoir, he supposed he should call it – which was nearly the size of his whole apartment in Pacific Heights. Which made it what – fifteen hundred square feet? Damn big anyway.

The waist-high paneling surrounding the room was finely crafted from gleaming walnut. Above the paneling, the walls were covered in a deep pink watered silk. Topping the room off was a twelve-foot high coffered ceiling.

Lord, what a lot to take in. There were two double-door entrances to the room, both of them featuring a kind of bull's eye mirror ensconced in an elaborate half-round transom panel above the fluted walnut doorframes. Drapery, chair fabrics and carpets in the room tended toward yellows and greens, except for the backdrop to the bed's canopy, which was a pleated material in royal blue.

The bed itself was relatively small, no larger than full-size, which he thought might relate to her disability somehow. He certainly couldn't tell antiques from reproductions, but he had no doubt the quality of each piece of furniture was high. The bed, chests, and dressers were made of crotch mahogany; other pieces appeared to be either walnut or tiger maple. The tabletops had the beautiful patterns and striations of fine veneers. Had Helena Swann ever even *heard* of Ikea?

Well, he had expected to be impressed. When he arranged the meeting, he wondered if Angela and Brad Styles would be there as well. From the peremptory way Mrs. Styles had treated Bennett, that would have been tantamount to letting him know his visit was futile. But Mrs. Swann had suggested a time when the Styleses would be out of the house. They would have the place nearly to themselves, she said. Except, of course, for Justin Styles and his tutor – and the housekeeper, who had just announced him.

After greeting him, Helena Swann shifted herself from the motorized scooter into an armless side chair, then gestured to a loveseat covered in pearl white damask. He sat down, adjusting his trousers to preserve the crease. She watched as he did this and smiled approvingly. The type of person, he thought, who notices every nuance of body language and assigns a value to it.

Bowers could see the opening gambit would be his. She would sit there serenely until he committed himself. If this were going to be a game of cat and mouse, he had no doubt she intended to be the cat.

"Your suite is lovely, Mrs. Swann. Words fail me," he said.

"I spend so much time here, I'm afraid I fuss over it a great deal."

"The result is ... beyond charming. It's perfect."

"How nice of you to say that!"

He couldn't think of a good transition, so he waded in.

"Mrs. Swann, when you called me last week about Mickey Cullion .... "

She interrupted. "But Lieutenant, we both know that never happened. Remember what you said?"

Whoa, he thought, she wants to hold that over me and take control of the interview.

"I said I'd deny telling you where Cullion was. For now we can let that lie, Mrs. Swann. But denial won't work if it bumps up against my responsibilities. I'm sure you understand."

He had made her stop and think.

"Yes, perhaps I do," she said. "As you see it, where does that leave us?"

"I'm only interested in your honest responses to three questions, ma'am."

"I see. What are they?"

"When you called me, you mentioned a letter you received that contained certain accusations. May I see it?"

"I'm sorry, Lieutenant Bowers, but I told you I wasn't willing to turn that into a police matter."

"What were the accusations?"

"Just the ravings of a crank. I won't talk about this any further."

Bowers sighed.

"My second question is about a phone call." He placed the report on the table between them and pointed to the entry with Brad and Angela's landline number. "Did you make this call to the Breastplate of Faith and Love Mission last Friday, Mrs. Swann?"

"I did not."

"I see," he nodded. "Let me put that another way. Did you make a call to Michael Cullion about an hour after we spoke last Friday?"

This time she hesitated before smiling and responding.

"If I'm not mistaken, a Detective Bennett spoke to my sister about that phone call. I think you should follow her advice and contact her lawyer about it."

He knew he was glowering now; he couldn't help it. She had no intention to be forthcoming. But he needed to press on.

"Well then, on to my final question. What do you know about a large sum of money found in Cullion's possession?"

She remained cool, but her eyes told him the question startled her. Why would that be? She either knew about the money or she didn't. Which was it?

"Absolutely nothing. How much did he have?"

He decided to ignore her question and wait for a further reaction. It wasn't long in coming.

"Lieutenant, you've asked your three questions. May I show you out? I'm sure we both have a lot to do this afternoon."

Again he ignored her. "I wonder," he said.

"You wonder ...?"

"I wonder if Jake Snider did something to make you pay Cullion to get rid of him for you."

"How dare you accuse me of such a thing!"

"Ah, Mrs. Swann, I'm afraid you misunderstand me," he said, rising to go. "I accuse no one, I was just wondering."

He had spoken softly, with a smile. And he forced himself to remain smiling as he left. On the stairway to the first floor, he saw a young boy staring at him. This must be Angela Styles's son, he thought, the child she had by Sam Porter.

~~~

It might not have been wise to telegraph his suspicions and the direction of his investigation to Helena Swann. But with both sisters stonewalling, he needed to shake things up. And the shake up wouldn't stop there, he thought.

At headquarters, he called in his friend Bennett and told him he was taking over as lead investigator. You didn't often catch May Bennett showing his anger, but he let him have it this time.

"You bigfooting me, Al? What the fuck for?"

"Whoa, May, easy! It's the Sharples family. The phone call and the money point their way. You gave them to me, remember?"

"Yeah, I remember all right. I also remember I'm the guy who took Cullion's confession, for Chrissake! We already have the murderer and the evidence to convict him, and that was on my watch!"

"Look, you know you're not satisfied with Cullion's story. If the defense had the phone call as well as the money right now, they'd be making hay in the press and we'd never get Angela Styles or Helena Swann to loosen up."

Bowers didn't blame Bennett for being pissed. He couldn't tell him yet, but part of his motivation was selfish – protecting his own ass from the mistake of helping Helena Swann to begin with. He'd make sure to tie Bennett in to the next important step he had to take: a meeting with the police chief and the president of the Police Commission.

Important, but grueling. There was nothing in the world he dreaded more than getting those two together to discuss an investigation they assumed to be closed. The chief, Dan Cinzano, would understand where he was coming from; Bowers would approach him first and lay out the problem. But the power and influence represented by Sharples Communications was a wild card, and he'd need to ask the chief to call in Hilary Saunders, president of the Police Commission. Together, the three of them would have to decide how to approach the remaining evidence.

Those were the political realities Bowers had to face. The problem would be Saunders. In a city of ultra-liberals, she stood out as the most recalcitrant cop-hater of them all. Every use of force was occasion for another blistering attack through the media and another call for investigations and special reporting. The only cop who passed muster with her was the cop who took the social worker approach to police work, thus avoiding pursuit and danger at all costs.

And yet, she had the connections that could make things happen in San Francisco. If she would get behind them, folks like Angela Styles and Helena Swann might open up and begin to cooperate.

The thing that stuck most sharply in his craw was the possibility he would have to admit his error. If it struck her as useful politically, Hilary Saunders might choose to give Bowers a public spanking that would hurt him career-wise and be personally humiliating. No matter how he diced and sliced that one, his ego would take a terrific beating. Well, he thought, set it to rest for now: no use buying trouble in advance.

~~~

Chief Cinzano called the meeting for ten o'clock the next morning. For her part, Ms. Saunders insisted they meet at her office; she needed to prepare for a presentation at noon and couldn't leave. Otherwise, they'd have to schedule it another day.

Bowers suspected the jockeying had more to do with turf and power issues than any practical consideration. Both officials worked at 850 Bryant Street, so it didn't matter in the least to him whose office he sat in, as long as it happened real soon.

When the four of them gathered in her spaces at ten, Hilary Saunders spent the first five minutes on her phone, discussing audio-visual equipment and the physical set-up for her presentation. When she hung up, she turned to the three men without apology and peered at them over her glasses.

"Well, fellas, what can I do for you today?" she said brightly.

Cinzano introduced Bennett. Saunders and Bowers had already met. The chief went on to explain the circumstances that brought them to her. It was their belief she could smooth the way to a productive meeting with Angela Styles and Helena Swann about the telephone call and the ten thousand dollars.

"Let me get a few things straight first," she said with some asperity. "From the newspaper accounts, I thought Bennett here was in charge, but you're telling me Bowers has taken over. What's that about?"

Bowers spoke up. "It was my judgment, Commissioner, that Detective Bennett had no way to pursue the telephone call or the money evidence after being stonewalled by Mrs. Styles."

"And so you took over and got stonewalled by Helena Swann. Where'd that get us?"

"Hilary," Cinzano interrupted, "the assignment and reassignment of detectives is my concern, not yours. You know that. Let's get on with this."

"Well excuse me, Dan," she said, "but it seems to me Detective Bennett secured the evidence, arrested the suspect and took his confession. Assuming he didn't manufacture the evidence or use coercion to obtain the confession – always a concern of mine with your boys – he should get a commendation. What do *you* say about this, Detective Bennett?"

"What I say, Ms. Saunders, is that you seem more interested in giving us grief than in helping us. Why is that?"

Bowers couldn't believe Maynard Bennett had it in him to fence like that with somebody in power. He glanced over at Cinzano, only to see him looking straight ahead and smirking. After staring coldly at Bennett for a few moments, Hilary Saunders burst out laughing.

"Bravo, Detective Bennett, bravo! But you see, I have to listen to the citizens of San Francisco every day. They complain to me on a depressingly regular basis about the grief given to them by your colleagues on the force. So it's fitting that the grief comes full circle, don't you think?"

Bennett opened his mouth to reply, but Chief Cinzano stepped in.

"No, we're not going to play this game, gentlemen. Hilary is either going to help us ... or not. We can go to the press ourselves right now about the telephone call and the ten thousand dollars, and let them connect the dots to Angela Styles and Helena Swann."

The chief paused then and turned to Saunders with a wide-eyed look.

"Oh ... but they're friends of yours, aren't they, Hilary?"

"Very good, Dan," she said. "Well played. And now that you've put both your cards and mine on the table, what is it you need from me?"

"We want you to arrange a meeting with Angela and Brad Styles about the phone call to Cullion's church. We think Helena Swann should be there too. You would host the meeting, Bowers and I would attend."

"What about representation from the D.A.'s office?"

"I don't see that you need that. We're just asking a few questions about a three-minute phone call, Hilary."

"What's the reason we want Helena Swann to attend?

The phone line isn't in her name."

"No, but she lives with them and she knows Cullion. And we want to see how they react – all of them – to questions about the money."

Saunders pushed back in her chair and crossed her arms.

"No, I don't think so. You told me you have no evidence that links these people to the money. I'm not at all sure I want to bring it up. I'll play that one by ear."

"Where does that leave us?" asked Cinzano. He wasn't looking at Saunders any longer, and his jaw was pushed out.

"Helena Swann won't be attending, and no one will ask questions about the money ... unless I do."

It was like pulling teeth, but they had their meeting.

~~~

Brad Styles reserved the boardroom at Sharples Communications for them. He and Mrs. Styles were there when Bowers and Dan Cinzano arrived. Hilary Saunders came late, sweeping into the room with greetings and apologies for her tardiness.

Bowers knew that Ms. Saunders was on the board of directors at Sharples Communications and that she and Angela Styles were board members for the San Francisco Repertory Company, a non-profit theater group. Their social lives and professional lives crisscrossed any number of times a year and in any number of ways. And even though she never said so, Bowers knew she had been a close childhood friend of Helena Swann. He wondered if relations among the elite in other cities were as incestuous as these.

The boardroom was an enormous affair at the top of the

Tremont building downtown. It managed to be modern and pompous without having a great deal of distinction. A series of interlocking rosewood sections formed themselves into one giant conference table nearly forty feet long. As many as two dozen gray leather chairs surrounded the table. The room and its amenities seemed to overwhelm the little party of five.

Brad Styles's administrative assistant served coffee. A silver tray with fresh pastries from a nearby bakery sat on a credenza under the windows. Bowers coveted one of these, but held back when everyone else declined.

At first, Hilary Saunders chatted easily with Brad and Angela Styles, making no effort to bring the chief or Bowers into the conversation. This seemed to embarrass Brad and Angela, who would at least look their way and smile from time to time. Finally, Saunders made sure everyone had been introduced and began to talk about the telephone call.

"Angela, we wanted to question anyone who might have made the call from your house to Cullion's mission, but you objected to making a list of everyone who was in the house that Friday. Is that about right?"

"Yes, I asked Detective Bennett to pursue it with my lawyer."

"All right, I understand. There is a problem you should be aware of, though. The phone call is a piece of evidence to us. While we are still investigating, we can control access to evidence to a certain extent."

"We understand that, Hilary." It was Brad speaking.

"Good, good. You're probably also aware that we sometimes share evidence with the press when we think it will help us ascertain a fuller picture of a crime."

Saunders let that sink in for a moment. Then she continued.

"The other thing that happens with evidence is generally out of our control. When the defense receives evidence as part of the discovery process, they may look at it and think of ways to present it as a smoking gun. And they often leak it, or even just present it outright to the press with a theory that it tends to exonerate their client and point to someone else."

Bowers realized that Hilary Saunders had done a nice job of putting the Styleses on the spot without squeezing them overtly. Angela Styles looked downcast, but Brad smiled and began to chuckle.

"Chief, based on Hilary's scenario here, why don't we rescind that silly demand of ours about the lawyer."

"Of course, Mr. Styles, we'd be happy to have your cooperation."

"Perhaps you won't mind if we personally ask everyone about the phone call before turning a list over to you. That would make it go down a lot easier, I'm sure."

"Certainly."

Everyone was smiling now, even Angela Styles, but Bowers wasn't satisfied. It had gone so well, he knew Saunders would not be inclined to ask about the ten grand. It was time, though, and he had to know.

"There's one other thing to discuss," he said. "When Michael Cullion was apprehended, we found ten thousand dollars in his room."

Hilary Saunders had an angry look on her face and was signaling for him to stop. He was sure Dan Cinzano was horrified, although he just stared. Bowers went on without a pause.

"I'm bringing this up because of a serious lapse in judgment I made a day before the murder. Your sister called me, Mrs. Styles, and asked me to help her locate Mickey Cullion. She said she received a threatening letter and she wanted to make sure he wasn't in town. I went ahead and checked, figuring I could allay her concerns. Mrs. Swann wouldn't share the letter, claiming it was probably from a crank. What I found out was that Cullion was running a legitimate church in town. I shouldn't have told her where he was, but I did. And the next day, Cullion killed Jake Snider. In light of all this, the ten thousand dollars becomes doubly significant. Where did that money come from? And what was it for?"

"Lieutenant Bowers, surely you don't expect Brad or Angela to know the answer to that!" Hilary Saunders was livid, and she wasn't making the slightest effort to hide her fury or her contempt.

"No, Ms. Saunders, but I'd like them to reflect on it and get back to me if they think of something that might help."

Screw her, he thought. At least he'd be able to look at himself in the mirror when this was over. If he still had a mirror, that is.

CHAPTER 21

Angela had been devastated by Lieutenant Bowers's revelation at the meeting with Hilary Saunders. So they knew about the money all along, she thought. Yet it was all so confusing. If Jake Snider had been the blackmailer, why did the money wind up in Cullion's room? Did they have an argument over splitting the money, or was Cullion telling the truth when he said the fight was over something Snider had done to a third person – namely, her? As often as she looked at the newspaper articles and the old mug shot they ran of Snider, she couldn't positively identify him as the man she had seen. She couldn't even tell if the man at the charity ball was the same man who took the envelope from her on Market St.

And her note – the note she put into the envelope to warn the blackmailer against further contact – why hadn't Bowers mentioned that? If it was gone, who got rid of it? Was Cullion covering up for her? Helena said she told him about the blackmail and the money, and he was supposed to try to get the money back. Was that true?

Or did Helena's involvement go deeper? Could she have encouraged Cullion to kill Snider and keep the money, despite what she said? That might put an entirely different face on what Cullion was doing. Once again, she found herself doubting her sister's reasons for acting as she did.

The salient feature of that blackmail letter, the most damaging allegation that it contained, after all, was that Helena had been an accomplice to a murder committed eight years ago. That was a powerful motive for acting to harm the blackmailer. Brad would have to help her sort this out. She knew he would be supportive, although she wasn't so sure he would give Helena the benefit of the doubt.

Around five o'clock Esther fed Justin and left for the night. Angela took him up to his room then, where they talked about his lessons. He seemed anxious to play computer games, so she didn't linger long. She greeted Brad in the foyer when he got in at six o'clock, and they decided on a quiet supper together. While they sat at the big kitchen island with soft drinks and the burgers she had just grilled, Angela confided her fears to him.

Brad was quietly thoughtful until they had cleaned up and stacked the dishes. "Let's go into the library and talk this out," he suggested, draping his arm around her shoulders.

He was being very good-natured about this, but she wondered if he might be considering why he ever got himself involved with two sisters who could *not* seem to keep their affairs private. Whatever he thought, she was gratified when he summarized the dilemma for her more simply than she would have thought possible.

"Honey, let's figure out what the right thing to do would be if Helena's telling the truth," he said. "She'd have to disclose her contacts with Cullion, right?"

"I guess so."

"Okay. That would release him to corroborate the story. And you'd have to disclose the blackmail letter and tell how you delivered the money. Then the police would ask Cullion about the note you included and whether he got rid of it."

"I see what you mean."

"If that's what happened, his story about protecting a third party – you, I guess – and his claim of self-defense would become credible. And the charges against him would likely be reduced to manslaughter."

For a moment, Angela's expression brightened. Then she frowned. "On the other hand, what if Helena was looking to harm the blackmailer. What if she paid Cullion?"

"I can't see how she would ever admit that."

"How am I going to find out?"

"Well, you could put it to her with the best face on it – tell her you believe what she said and that you both have to go to the police. What she says at that point will reveal a lot."

"She'll say that we're exposing her to the accessory charge."

"Yes, but since she claims it isn't true, she has to do the right thing. Mickey Cullion shouldn't go to jail for second-degree murder because telling the truth would be inconvenient for Helena."

~~~

The thought that a man was willing to incur a second-degree murder conviction rather than expose her to some ugly publicity determined Angela to go after the truth. In doing so, she hadn't forgotten the ties Cullion had to her first husband.

Before this, she had thought of him as "that terrible little man." But the little man had sought redemption in prison and was trying to work out his salvation in a cheesy little storefront church. She had the sense now that he wasn't such a little man after all.

It was eight o'clock when Angela knocked softly on

Helena's door. Brad had suggested putting it off until tomorrow; but if she did, she knew she wouldn't sleep tonight. He stood by her, holding her hand and waiting for Helena to answer.

"Come in!" she called.

"Brad's with me, Helena. I hope we're not disturbing you," Angela said as they walked into the suite.

Helena was sitting in the motorized scooter and aiming her remote at the television in the armoire.

"There, that's off. I was watching that awful local show, the one that shows all sleaze, all the time."

"You mean FriscoTales?" Brad asked. "Our very own biography channel."

"Clever, Brad. Yes, that's the one. Whenever I forget my name is 'Helena Swann, the Black Widow,' I turn it on to remind myself."

Angela laughed. "I swear people who haven't met me think I have three last names," she said. "I'm always Angela Styles-Prominent-Socialite."

Helena moved towards the grouping of chairs in the middle of the suite. She never received guests while sitting in the scooter, so she shifted herself into an armchair and waited for Brad and Angela to get settled on the couch.

"I'd love to think we're just going to get cozy and chat," she said. "But somehow ...," she let it trail off.

Brad spoke up.

"Hilary Saunders asked to meet with us this morning, Helena."

"Ah. I can't tell you how long it's been since I've seen Hilary."

"The Chief of Police and Lieutenant Bowers were there as well."

"How very ominous. What did they want?"

"It was about your telephone call mostly. They want us to ask you about it. That part wasn't a surprise."

"There's something else, isn't there?"

"Yes, something very unexpected happened. We could tell Hilary was surprised too. Lieutenant Bowers came clean about helping you locate Cullion just before Snider was murdered. And he wants us to think about why Cullion had ten thousand dollars in his room."

"I see. What did you say?"

Brad shrugged.

"We're thinking about it, as he requested."

"Well, that's your business, of course. Just don't expect me to talk to any of them about the phone call."

"Helena," Angela said, "as soon as Cullion's lawyer knows about the call, it will be in the press. They'll hound us day and night about it."

"Let them! I don't care! What good will it do to talk about it?"

Brad spread his hands, trying to look conciliatory. But his words came out with an edge.

"It could be the difference between murder and manslaughter to Mickey Cullion. Angela will have to tell them about the blackmail letter and the money as well. I'm positive Cullion has been covering up for both of you."

"In what way is he covering up for me? I only called him to find out who was blackmailing Angela."

"We're afraid the defense could claim you ... promised him something if he got rid of Jake Snider."

"You mean that's what *you two* think! Accessory to murder?"

"Helena, please!" Brad begged. "We're not accusing you

of anything. We just want to do what's right."

"What's right for Mickey Cullion, you mean. Why are you so focused on him? Think of the awful publicity for Angela. And think of me! That letter claims I was an accessory to murder eight years ago. That would make twice! I might as well declare it my occupation!"

"But you know it isn't true, Helena."

Angela watched the color drain from Brad's face. Her breathing felt constricted.

"Isn't my existence miserable enough?" Helena moaned. "Why can't you leave well enough alone? If you want to get rid of me, tell me to go. Kick me out and be done with it! But don't condemn me to Chowchilla so Mickey Cullion can serve two years instead of ten."

"That about does it for me," Brad said, rising from the couch.

"Sure Brad, go. Just as you did the last time I really needed you."

"Helena, don't," Angela said. "This is too embarrassing. You've no right!"

"Oh, haven't I?"

Brad had drawn himself up to his full height and Angela could see he was trying hard to control himself.

"Yes, we had a relationship once and I ended it," he said. "I ended it when you nearly destroyed me. Angela won't admit it, but you nearly destroyed her as well. Do you honestly find it exceptional that we took solace in each other after that ... catastrophe?"

Helena turned her head aside in anger, hands trembling in her lap. In a teary blur, Angela saw Brad stride out of the room. She wiped her eyes, then rushed out to follow him. He hadn't waited for her.

CHAPTER 22

Even though he was a powerful executive in a large organization, Brad Styles was able to maintain his reputation as a nice guy. He was bred to values like politeness and consideration, and it showed. Over the years, many people had peeked behind the scenes at Sharples to find out who *really* ran things – the reporters and competitors who took Brad's measure just couldn't reconcile the fellow they met with the success of his organization.

Brad wouldn't even assume the high-falutin' titles of his colleagues in the industry. He remained satisfied with his fifteen-year-old job description as Executive Director. In the company organization chart, he reported to his wife Angela, who was president. Her title was mainly a fiction, but Brad insisted she keep it. The reasons were partly sentimental – her father Sam Sharples founded the company – and partly pragmatic, because her name and heritage carried a long way in the business and social worlds of San Francisco.

As nice a guy as Brad Styles was, however, he could be pushed too far. And Helena had pushed especially hard when he and Angela tried to convince her to reveal her contact with Mickey Cullion. After the emotional scene in Helena's suite, he stormed out into the corridor and disappeared.

Angela followed a few moments later and headed downstairs, most likely thinking Brad would retreat there to the library in search of privacy. Instead, he was upstairs pacing their bedroom. He heard her, on the staircase probably, calling his name. Rather than answer, he took the opportunity to be quiet. She would find him soon enough, he figured.

He kicked off his shoes, removed his polo shirt and Dockers, then looked into his massive chest of drawers for something comfortable. Finding a black tee and tan shorts, he pulled them on and padded barefoot over to the right of the French doors that gave out onto the balcony above the garden. There he opened the oak armoire that housed a mini-office he used from time to time.

Brad flipped open his laptop and booted up. While waiting, he took deep breaths: four counts inhale, four counts hold, four counts exhale. By the time Angela opened the bedroom door and peeked in, he had logged on and accessed the Internet.

"Well, there you are," she said. "I thought you had taken a walk when I couldn't find you downstairs."

"I heard you call me, but I had to cool off before I spoke again. I would have started yelling and God knows what would have come out. Helena has an extraordinary capacity for evil at times. Right now I feel outright hatred for her."

"Brad, don't be hard."

"Maybe I am. But it's true, Angela. I felt my heart harden towards her. I hate to lay down ultimatums, dear, but she can no longer live in this house."

"This is her home, Brad. Please don't . . ."

"It's either hers or mine, it can't be both any longer."

"But she's my *sister*, Brad."

"Yes. She always will be. I wouldn't try to keep you from

seeing her, Angela. I just don't want her around me anymore. And I'd prefer it if Justin only saw her in your company."

"Brad, please give her time. I think she'll finally do the right thing."

"She may, I suppose. And you may be surprised to know I believe her now. But that doesn't alter my conviction that she'd rather see a man sent up for murder than inconvenience her precious ass. It doesn't lessen the bitterness in her heart over every perceived injustice the world has inflicted on her. And it won't change the way I feel. I've had enough of Helena Swann for a lifetime."

"I believe her too, and yet I know you're right. I never thought it would come to this ... but I'll do it ... I'll tell her soon."

Brad had come over to where Angela sat on the bed. He drew her close and buried his face in her fresh smelling, honey-colored hair.

~ ~ ~

Overnight, Angela had grown used to the idea that Helena needed to establish her own life apart from them. It weighed on her to think she was throwing a disabled woman out of the home she had known for nearly ten years, and she felt bound to help her in every way possible. But she couldn't reconcile herself to making the further demand that Helena speak to the police about contacting Mickey Cullion and meeting with him.

Perhaps I could take that on myself, she thought. She was already prepared to give them the blackmail letter and relate what subsequently happened. Why not admit to a telephone call and a meeting with Cullion, just as if they had been her actions instead of Helena's? It seemed to make perfect sense.

And yet she realized that the letter's charge of culpability in the murder of Wanda Buckley still accrued to Helena. She couldn't change that.

How could she go back to her on this point? That thought was much on her mind the following morning. Helena hadn't come down for breakfast, and she supposed she wouldn't see her all day unless she made it a point to invade her suite.

When Brad strolled into the kitchen for coffee, she told him her plan.

"Honey, what courage you have," he said, shaking his head. "But I don't see how it could work. You were busy that Saturday – people could be found to testify you were elsewhere. And Cullion could burst your bubble at any moment by saying it's not true."

"I hadn't thought of that. You're right."

"You know, yesterday you said that Helena would do the right thing eventually. We're not so pressed for time that we can't wait a little for that to happen."

"But she can be awfully stubborn. After last night, she won't think about doing the right thing for days and days."

Brad laughed.

"Yes, I think I made sure of that." he said. "Tell you what. Now that I've cooled off, I believe Helena and I need to have a long chat. She won't be expecting that, so it just might be the right tack at the right time."

"What could you possibly have left to say to each other?"

"Lots of things, really. We can clear the air and go from

there."

"Brad, you amaze me."

"Bullshit, Angela. I never amaze anyone."

"You're not going to tell her to leave, are you? Not today?"

"That's a thought. Who knows?"

~~~

Brad kept turning over in his mind what he would say to Helena and how she might reply. In the end, it didn't help him very much to go through all that. They had accumulated so much baggage during the past twenty years he was at a loss to predict how they would interact. It might go very nicely, or it could end in threats and nasty recriminations. With Helena who could tell?

In college, they had been lovers, which didn't last. A product of Helena's ambitions getting in the way. When her attempts at a career in New York fizzled, she returned home and married Jeremy Swann. Brad also was married by then. Five years later, they were both single again and lonely.

He was already in charge of the Sharples empire when Helena came home. Naturally, he saw both sisters often – he was practically one of the family. And once again he fell. Steady, studious, reliable Brad in love with the dark-haired belle of every ball. She was witty and poised and even a little dangerous. When they became engaged, he was the happiest man he knew.

Then the ugly saga of Shoo-fly put an end to his illusions, and his happiness. Every aspect of their lives was subject to exploitation for months. He still regarded reporters as piranha or worse. When everything settled down, he had become Angela's ally and protector, finally her husband. When he saw he had to help integrate Helena into his new life with Angela, he accepted the burden willingly. He did it because his wife's magnanimity and forgiveness was an unparalleled example of goodness to him.

Night was falling as he ascended the staircase to the second floor and walked along the corridor to Helena's suite. He knocked twice and waited.

"Come in!" she called.

She was in the motorized chair looking out the large windows over the circular drive. Her back was to him as he walked in. How well he remembered the long, wavy hair, still as dark and glossy today as ever. He stopped a few paces into the room and paused. He was smiling at her as she turned to greet him.

"Brad ... I never expected to see you today."

"I guess I'm surprised myself. But when you think and think, and you can't get things out of your mind, it's best to turn to someone who knows you well."

"Do we know each other well, Brad? I'm not sure I feel that way any longer. Although I certainly did once."

"I think we do. I know we remind each other of some very unpleasant facts of life, but can you name a single person in San Francisco who is better qualified to write your biography than I am?"

Helena smiled and nodded.

"That's so," she said. "But don't you dare! And I'll promise not to write yours."

"Such a dull affair by comparison," he answered.

"Not dull, no. You would look far too trusting and ... easy at times perhaps, but ultimately heroic. Whereas I ... I would be glamorous and evil by turns, and ultimately pathetic."

"Pathetic? How I disagree. And evil? You must be feeling a bit sorry for yourself tonight."

"Yes. I guess I am. Brad, I'm glad you came to see me. Tell me what it is you want to say."

"What I hope to get across is that we're going to get through this, Helena. You and Angela are going to get through it, and so am I. We've had more difficult things to handle, and we managed. We don't have to be afraid if we do it together."

Helena's right hand went to her platinum neck chain as she looked Brad full in the face.

"You're right. It's the same thing you said yesterday, but everything got in the way. My strength is brittle, Brad. I don't always make good decisions, but I can stand on my rights until the cows come home. When you were here with Angela last night, I suddenly wanted to hurt both of you. Whatever was right for you couldn't be right for me, you know?"

Regret was in her voice. "Sometimes I feel like a bitter old woman."

"Don't, Helena. There's no need. I'm even glad you balked last night. I think I've found a way out that works for both of us. We just have to ... get rid of something."

He could see her face change from doubt and sadness to conspiratorial anticipation and outright glee. What an incredible creature she is, he thought.

CHAPTER 23

Shonda Wallace was Cullion's public defender. She was a big black gal with her hair in cornrows and heavy gold hoops in her ears. Cullion liked her — she was aggressive and smart. They joked with each other about their odd couple appearance: the little white dude with the enormous black female defender.

"You know, Michael," she deadpanned, "when I get you off, I'm gonna dress you up and install you as my pimp."

"How 'bout I take the tricks you don't like and do them for you?"

They laughed, but with his prospects so grim, the light moments between them were short and few. Nearly every day, she asked him to go over his story. Why wouldn't he talk about the third party he was trying to protect? Where did Jake get ten thousand dollars? Was he *sure* the fight wasn't about the money or some other guy?

Hell, she had to know he didn't *want* to be charged with second-degree murder.

"Why won't the jury believe that I acted in self-defense?" he asked.

"Maybe they will and maybe they won't," she said. "Michael, when a guy slugs you and you rip his guts out with a knife, a jury is inclined to think you're a badder dude than he was."

She tried hard to convince him to give her the name of the person he was trying to shield. His best bet was a plea bargain, which was impossible without a name, somebody to corroborate his story.

"Is it that Julie Reyes who comes to see you?" she asked.

"No," he said, "not Julie."

Today was different, though. Shonda wasn't full of questions today. When she sat down with him, he could tell she was anxious about something.

"We're going to a meeting today, Michael."

"Both of us?"

"Yeah, you too. No leg chains, but you'll be cuffed in front. I've got your clothes, you won't have to go in the jumpsuit."

"So? What's it all about?"

"Michael, I wish I could tell you. I threw one big ass fit, but it didn't help. All they would say is that it could be to your advantage."

"Sounds good, no? Who is 'they,' anyway?"

"They is one hell of a lineup. The president of the Police Commission, the chief of police, and the D.A."

"Heavy, Shonda."

"Heavy, yes. So I wish your story wasn't such a lightweight, know what I'm sayin'?"

"It is what it is, Shonda. I can't help it."

"Oh yes you can, dammit!" she said. "I know you can!"

~~~

Around two o'clock Shonda and Cullion were escorted into a conference room at 850 Bryant Street. The sheriff guarding him was asked to wait outside. The lady who identified herself as president of the Police Commission introduced the police chief and the D.A. Cullion didn't catch anybody's name. He felt self-conscious about the handcuffs and tried to keep his arms off the table.

He remembered Shonda saying the commissioner was Ms. Saunders, a well-known liberal activist she admired. Anyway, this lady was saying something about private citizens volunteering information – and all of a sudden the conference room door opened again. Shonda tensed up and put her hand on his forearm as Angela Styles walked into the room followed by Brad Styles wheeling Helena Swann.

Oh man, he thought, what way was this gonna go?

Ms. Saunders was speaking again. "Mr. Cullion, I understand you know Mrs. Swann."

"Yes, I do," he said, while Shonda turned to him – mouth open and eyes bugged out.

"And Mr. and Mrs. Styles? Do you know them?"

"I know who they are."

Cullion was embarrassed listening to Angela Styles tell what happened at the charity ball and the next day when she made the payoff to Jake. The poor woman's voice shook so bad he had to look away. He guessed that Brad Styles was there to help his wife get through it all.

When her turn came, Helena looked right at him as she spoke about their meeting. He got the feeling she was daring him to contradict her. But that wasn't necessary; she told it pretty straight.

The District Attorney asked him if he had anything to add. Before he could reply, Shonda cut in.

"Excuse me, please. I'll see if my client has anything to say in just a moment. Right now we'd like to see the blackmail note Mrs. Styles mentioned."

"Mrs. Styles informs us she destroyed the letter." It was Ms. Saunders speaking.

Cullion saw the D.A. nodding in agreement.

"I see," said Shonda. "But the copy? Mrs. Swann said she made a copy to show my client when they met."

Helena spoke up. "When my sister told me she destroyed the original, I disposed of the copy also. We were afraid it would be published eventually if we turned it over."

"And what about the note Mrs. Styles included with the money?"

The D.A. cleared his throat to speak. "It was never recovered," he said. "We don't know what happened to it."

Shonda's hands flew up. "There's no proof, so we just take their word for all this? How convenient!"

"Does your client dispute any of this, Ms. Wallace?"

Shonda leaned in and whispered to Cullion.

"This is bullshit, Michael. Don't say anything for now. We're already down to manslaughter, and you may not even do time. Tell me what was in the blackmail letter. They're covering something up."

She had that nailed down. The sisters got rid of the blackmail letter because it pointed to Helena as an accessory to murder. If he shut up and talked it over with Shonda, he'd be in the driver's seat. His conscience told him that backing up Angela Styles with that story about her note to Jake was the right thing to do. Still, if the tables were turned, what would any of these people do for *him?*

Cullion exhaled and shook his head. "Thanks, Shonda. It's okay," he said. "There's something I need to say for Mrs. Styles here."

"No, Michael, don't!" she whispered furiously. "It's in your best interest to hold back. Say nothing!"

He looked her in the eye a moment while he fussed with his handcuffs. Her passion for his cause made him waver.

Then he cleared his throat and looked out to the expectant faces around the table.

"Yeah, I got something I wanna say. When it was all over and Jake was dead, I thought about the note Mrs. Styles put in with the money. Jake was real mad when he read it, so I went and got it out of the bag to figure out why. It didn't say much except she'd never give him more money, but she *signed* it, you know? I thought that would get her in deep. So I tore it up and flushed it down the toilet. Then I went through Jake's pockets, got his keys and locked the duffel bag. Before the cops got there, I put the keys back."

Like a gush of air let out of an overfilled balloon, the tension in the room dissipated as Cullion spoke. If Shonda was uptight still, everyone else had relaxed. The D.A. turned off the recorder and stepped outside to signal the sheriff. Cullion and Shonda were escorted out of the building.

Chapter 24

When Dan Cinzano got back from the big meeting, Al Bowers was waiting for him. He had a feeling his career was on the line, and he had to be the first to know. If necessary, he was prepared to resign. Cinzano lumbered into his office and flopped in his chair. Bowers couldn't read his expression. His boss looked straight at him, nodded, then yanked his tie off.

"C'mon Chief, talk!" Bowers said.

"It's all politics, Al, you know that? Politics ... advantage ... and power."

"Dan, please ...."

The Chief was smiling, toying with him. He settled in at his desk, cleared his throat, and explained how Angela Styles and Helena Swann figured into the case with Cullion. Then he looked up at Bowers and grimaced, as if he were still puzzled about something.

"Lessee now ... after the meeting, Brad Styles cornered me, the D.A., and Hilary. Styles had a 'concern' about any further press coverage. He announced Mrs. Styles wants to donate the recovered ten grand, which he'll match, to the Police Athletic League or other charity we choose – *as soon as the case is closed*. 'No Publicity' writ large ... is what I got out of it. The D. A. and Hilary will hafta try to rein in Shonda Wallace. Styles never said so, but there'll be no check for twenty grand if his wife and sister-in-law come to grief in the press."

"What'll happen to Cullion, Chief?"

"The D. A. will reduce the charge to manslaughter. With his priors, though, he'll do some time. Maybe a year."

Bowers was shaking his head. "So ... no publicity for Angela Styles or Helena Swann, no public spanking for me, and no second-degree murder charge for Mickey Cullion. Man, what's it all about, Chief? What was it Jake Snider put in the blackmail letter that made it turn out this way?"

"That's what everybody wants to know. No doubt he had something on one of our socialite buddies."

It seemed to Bowers that Brad Styles must be some kind of genius for engineering the whole wrap-up. In the end, the folks with the most to lose had made it to port safely. The ones who wouldn't get their payoff would be the media and the part of the public that salivates over scandal. He began to laugh, quietly at first, then louder until Cinzano pushed away from his desk and glared at him.

"You can laugh, Al, but it's Hilary Saunders who winds up in the catbird seat. That bitch put me on notice the twenty grand will go to *her* favorite charities, while I have to be content that my Homicide Detail isn't dragged through the mud for compromising the case. 'Screw the Police Athletic League' were her exact words, I believe."

Bowers made a coughing sound to cut his laughter short. He realized he owed his boss big time for screwing up with Helena Swann.

CHAPTER 25

Stafford Boyle thought the headlines and news articles from San Francisco about Mickey Cullion lacked the pizzazz of the Shoo-fly stories back in 1999, even though all the old references and names were there. That's what comes of recycling old villains in the news, he figured.

The details of the new murder were murky, but the suggestion was unmistakable that Cullion and Jake Snider had something going on. The religious angle was played up, too – sex and religion was hearty fare for public consumption. Of course, sex-religion-and-*murder* made for an even tastier stew.

Newporters probably had more curiosity about the story than anyone save San Franciscans. And Boyle was the most curious of Newporters after hunting down one of the principals of the old scandal and finding out she had died in her Alabama hometown under the name Kathy Dunnell.

Until the headlines from the left coast petered out a few weeks later, it seemed there was a major Shoo-fly revival going on. Still, he felt there was precious tabloid ore waiting to be mined right here in Newport. In short, he couldn't get the boy at Dismas Cottage out of his mind.

Just by asking around, he found out the little guy was enrolled at a private parochial school on Brenton Road run by the Cluny Sisters. Maria Torres, Claudia Chitworth's maid, drove him to the school in the morning, and Ivan Chitworth picked him up when school let out. No one had mentioned the boy's last name, and he hadn't asked.

Because he had absolutely no reason to involve himself in Ivan's business, Boyle didn't intend to probe any further.

Until Guy Bosworth called him back, that is. Guy had read all the news stories coming out of California and wanted him to look into something for him.

"All I keep thinking about is Kathy and what she went through," he said. "Her son deserves the chance she wanted him to have. I intend to adopt him, like I promised."

"He may have been adopted or have a legal guardian already, Mr. Bosworth."

"Then find out for me. I've got to know."

"All right. I'll get on it."

"One other thing, Boyle. I want proof that he's Sam Porter's son like the boy in San Francisco."

"Well ... proof. I dunno about proof. I can't see me getting a DNA sample, you know."

"A birth certificate might do."

"Sure. But getting a document like that legally ... "

"What *can* you do?"

"Let me check around and see what I can find. We'll take it one step at a time."

Why exactly he didn't tell Guy Bosworth his suspicions about the young boy living at Dismas Cottage, he couldn't say. Except that he felt he'd be piling on by making the Chitworths the focus of yet another investigation. First, he'd look for some evidence that Kathy's child was Shoo-fly's son. That would keep him occupied while he chewed over his reluctance to mess any further with the Chitworths. Shoot, why couldn't he just go where the money was like other investigators?

The first, mechanical steps were the easy ones. He

started with a map of the U.S. to orient himself. Then he checked birth records on the Internet in the South and Southwest, the two regions most closely associated with Christy Gore/Kristi Darnell/Kathy Dunnell.

With all those names, that gal was a real shape-shifter. Because Kathy Dunnell was the name she escaped *to* after her tough times in Florida, he started checking under that one. An hour into his search, he struck pay dirt in Texas.

Sam Dunnell was born in Greenville, Texas at Presbyterian Hospital on May 3, 2000. If it was a full-term birth, that would put the child's conception in early August 1999, when his mother was living with Sam Porter in Miami Beach. Q.E.D, as far as Boyle was concerned. Later that day, Guy Bosworth accepted his logic and asked him again to locate the boy.

When he got off the phone with Bosworth, Boyle walked out of his condo and strolled down Dixon Street toward Thames. Dixon was little more than an alleyway between Bellevue Avenue and Spring Street. On one side of the street was the elegant dressed limestone wall of the Elms mansion. On the other side was the more rudimentary stuccoed wall of Oakwood, an estate that fronted one block to the south on nearby Narragansett Street. Boyle walked smack in the middle of the roadway, little concerned that a car might come by until he reached the first cross street.

It was just after Memorial Day and the air was warm, the sky blue and cloudless. Nearing Thames Street, he heard the background noise of tourism and traffic rise sharply. Thames was busy with cars and foot traffic, even down here in the fifth ward, the old Irish ethnic neighborhood just south of downtown.

As he strolled northward, the crowd thickened, especially so when he crossed Memorial Boulevard and stepped onto the cobblestones of upper Thames Street. Tourists ruled here from the harborside shops and wharves of America's Cup Avenue on the west to the older establishments on the east side of Thames.

Natives never did this, he said to himself. They never walk downtown in the high season. And who could blame them. But today he found it strangely calming to follow the herd. You had only to step on the treadmill with the other tourist lemmings and put one foot in front of the other. Before you knew it, your mind was cleared of the stuff you'd rather not think about.

And when you tired of the endless crush of folks in too-short shorts and loud shirts, all you had to do was step off onto a side street up Historic Hill or walk a little farther north into the Point section. Like magic, the tourist noise abated just a few yards away, where you were among houses and streetscapes hundreds of years old. Except for the hardy few, most visitors never followed – it was just too easy to stay on the downtown tourist treadmill.

By the time Boyle was ready to start back home, a little plan had begun to infiltrate his gray matter. The beauty of it was he hadn't even tried to think about Guy Bosworth or Ivan Chitworth or Sam Dunnell. No, the tourist treadmill had done all the work. And his restless feet, he figured – without them he'd still be sitting at home, stymied over what to do next.

He was rounding Thames Street onto Washington Square when he began to put it into words for himself. First off, he knew the kid at Dismas Cottage was Sam Dunnell.

He had to be. The logical next step was to speak with Ivan Chitworth confidentially. He could approach him Thursday at the writer's group. How would Ivan react when he brought the subject up?

~~~

Thursday dawned warm and fair. Boyle skipped his usual breakfast of cereal and juice and decided this was a coffee and cinnamon roll morning. After a long shower, he threw on a pair of tan shorts and a navy blue pocket tee, walked out the door and down to the Dandy Lunch through the narrow streets of the fifth ward.

He was early, and it was quiet in the diner. Georgette, the counter waitress, poured his coffee and served up the roll steaming from the grill. There were four pads of butter on the side, which he spread lovingly over the top and poked into the whorls of frosting and braided pastry.

"Sure you couldn't get more butter on there?" she asked.

"Well, I could, but that's all you gave me," he replied.

"Never saw anybody use them all like that."

"In that case, why put them out?"

"It looks good to give you more than you need."

"Do you give your husband more than he needs?"

"Don't get fresh. That pig gets more than he deserves!"

"Damn. Now I've lost my appetite."

"Serves you right," she said, walking off with a smile.

Georgette was like the cover of an old Mickey Spillane paperback – lurid and to the point. Boyle figured there wasn't a Starbucks in the world with waitresses like Georgette.

Twenty minutes later he finished his second cup of

coffee and licked the last remnant of cinnamon-flecked frosting from his fingers. He wiped his hands with a skimpy paper napkin, left five bucks on the counter and walked back up the hill towards Bellevue Avenue.

Tonight he'd try to catch up with Ivan at the writer's group. In his mind, their chat would be a simple one, something he could handle in a very straightforward manner. The only thing he had to reconcile was Ivan's image of him as an aspiring writer with his real occupation. Well, what's so unusual about a part-time P.I. who thinks he wants to write a mystery novel? It wasn't even a lie, not really.

Right now though, his mind was on Assunta. They had fallen into a routine of getting together three or four times a week and he looked forward to each and every meeting. The only odd thing about their affair was its domesticity. Because they met during the day, a lot of the things they did together involved markets, shopping and errands, stuff like that.

Not that it bothered him, he loved any kind of activity with her. But he worried that she might harbor a yen for the romantic atmosphere of candlelit dinners and dance clubs. It was the age thing, he knew. Why the hell did he have to agonize over it, though? She wasn't complaining, after all. And there was certainly no lack of passion between them.

He was afraid, he supposed, because he wanted to tell her he loved her and he couldn't bring himself to do it. Fear of rejection, probably. If they were the same age, he might have asked her to be his girl. But at forty-seven he'd sound and feel like a moron trying to get the words out. For God's sake, why did these things have to be so complicated?

Despite his cerebrations on their relationship, he had a terrific time that afternoon. They wolfed down chowder and clam cakes at Flo's, took a long walk at the nature conservancy at Sachuest Point and spent a pleasant two hours at her place watching a romantic comedy she got in the mail from Netflix.

They were holding hands when the movie ended, sitting close on her old couch with the floral slipcover. He cleared his throat awkwardly and spoke up just as the long skein of credits was reeling up through the sappy music.

"I love you, Assunta," he said.

Her jaw trembled and she looked up at him, blinking and dewy-eyed.

"Wow. You just took my breath away."

"You *always* take my breath away, Sunta. Day after day."

"I know I've wanted you to say that, but I've been a little afraid of it, too."

"What's wrong, baby? Too soon?"

"No. Not too soon. We've been real close, almost from day one. But I'm still hurting from my divorce. He was abusive, Staff, and I'm still real unsure of myself."

"Sorry to push. But I won't take it back."

"Don't be sorry, big guy. You know I care for you a lot. If I can't say I love you just yet, please be patient."

"Okay, you got it. Here I was worried about the age thing."

"Age thing! Boy, are you dumb."

"What? Now I have to worry about the dumb thing."

Assunta punched him on the shoulder and stood up to kiss him full on the mouth, leaning over him as he sat there with his fingers snaking into her hair.

~~~

He dropped in on the Thursday night writer's group at the Athenaeum just as the meeting got started at seven o'clock. Ivan was reading from a biography he'd written about a nineteenth-century Newporter named Thomas Sergeant Perry. Constance smiled warmly when Boyle walked in. Trainor DeSales and Marilyn Rezendes looked surprised and nodded his way. When Ivan looked up, he made no sign of recognition and didn't pause until he had finished the chapter he was reading.

"That's all I have for tonight, folks," he said, placing the last page face down atop the others. "Any comments?"

The three regulars asked a number of questions and gave him a lot of encouragement. Boyle held back, feeling he wasn't qualified to comment. Ivan directed a sharp look his way but ignored him thereafter, starting a discussion about research that lasted for the balance of the session.

After the meeting, things became progressively more awkward. When he got him alone, Boyle's attempts at starting a conversation with Ivan were met with hasty monosyllables.

"Ivan," he said finally, "I have the feeling you'd rather not talk tonight, but something's come up I want you to know about."

"What would that be, I wonder?"

"Listen, you probably think I'm a phony, but I really am interested in writing crime fiction. I haven't got started yet, but I'm a part-time private investigator and I have some story ideas I want to pursue ... sooner or later."

"Sure. Good luck with that. What is it you want with me,

Boyle?"

Man oh man, he thought, Ivan sure is frosty tonight. Whatever was the matter, though, he couldn't postpone this. Might as well plow through and get things out in the open.

"I had a call from a client in Arizona today. He wants me to look for someone he last saw in 2003. A boy named Sam Dunnell."

Ivan winced. "What do you know about Sam?" he demanded.

"My client was living with Kathy Dunnell until she left Arizona with Sam. I know she was Kristi Darnell."

They were standing by Ivan's car, and Boyle watched him hesitate as if to compose himself. Then Ivan stepped in close and spoke in a furious whisper.

"You look, you sonuvabitch, and you listen. I don't know what you're trying to pull, but just back off. I've already taken more grief from you than I can handle. Thanks to you, Billy Moncton's wife calls me over and over to tell me what a mess I've made of her life. She's even threatened to sue me."

"Oh, Jesus, she shouldn't have ... I'm sorry, man."

"Yeah, I'll bet!"

"Look, I'm not a malicious guy. It was just a job. And you need to know that my client wants to adopt Sam. Can we talk about this?"

"Not likely, Boyle. My mother and I have custody of Sam because Kathy wanted it that way. And her grandparents know all about it."

Ivan was so angry he was quivering. Boyle backed away and put his hands up.

"I'm sorry, man, really sorry."

He walked off feeling like a heel. Damn, why did Theresa Moncton blow his cover? He never thought she'd do a thing like that.

In the morning, after a restless night, he thought hard about Guy Bosworth and Sam Dunnell. He knew Bosworth meant well, but he could not bring himself to complicate things for the Chitworths. A few hours later he made his final call to Arizona.

"I've drawn a blank in Newport and Alabama, Mr. Bosworth. I have no place left to look."

"You can't keep searching?" he asked. "You haven't been at it for long."

"I'm awfully sorry, sir. There's nothing more I can do for you."

CHAPTER 26

The news from California startled Claudia Chitworth. When she made her weekly call to San Francisco, she commiserated with Angela at length over the ugly rehash of the Shoo-fly scandal.

Closer to home, she noticed that Ivan had a high level of fascination with the new story. He had met that Cullion fellow, she remembered, when Angela married Sam Porter in 1999. While the Breastplate case stayed in the headlines, Ivan immersed himself in the newspapers each morning.

It didn't take long for him to draw the same conclusion she had – Angela and Brad must be told about Sam before some awful person found out who he was and broadcast it to the world. If there were ever a headline proclaiming 'Shoo-fly's second son,' Angela and Brad could *not* be blindsided. That would be inexcusable. Claudia and Ivan agreed that time was running out.

"Well, mother," he said one evening, "I suppose the first order of business is letting Sam know he has a brother."

Claudia cringed. It was hard to believe that Sam hadn't spoken to Ivan yet. She had held back, and now weeks had passed, putting her in a quandary. Sam asked the occasional question about Justin – far fewer than she had expected. And when Ivan said nothing, she was puzzled but reluctant to bring it into the open.

"Oh, Ivan, I feel like a meddling old woman," she said. "Sam knows. I told him a few weeks ago. I had an idea it was a way to force the issue of telling Brad and Angela. I was so sure Sam would ask you about Justin, I half expected you were punishing me by not mentioning it."

Ivan's jaw dropped. He stared at her and flipped the magazine he was reading to the coffee table between them.

"Exactly what did you tell Sam, mother?"

"That he has a half-brother living in San Francisco with his aunt and uncle."

"Aunt and uncle," he said derisively. "Another phony aunt and uncle like you and I. The poor kid has no blood relatives we know about except the Gores in Alabama."

"We still have to decide what's best for him, Ivan. No one else can, and Kathy Dunnell thought you were the logical choice for some reason."

"For some reason! I like that, mother. Apparently you're not of the same opinion."

"Ivan, Sam is like any other child. He needs the stability of a real family life. Because one of us is around all the time, he has it now. But just what kind of commitment will you have to tend him day and night when I'm gone? You know how old I am! Will you change your lifestyle just because your mother dies? Pardon me for doubting that."

Ivan stiffened and turned his face away. He took a deep breath and exhaled. She hoped he wouldn't take her up on the allusion she made. So many things were best left unsaid between people who loved each other.

Oh son, she thought, *please help me do what's right.*

When he turned back to her, Ivan spoke quietly.

"Telling Angela is one thing. I suspect what holds us back is not being able to gauge how hurt she'll be. And don't forget about Brad – Helena, too. They've all suffered. But you're introducing a new note here, Mother. I think you're saying Angela should be Sam's guardian. How do you think that makes me feel?"

"Ivan, I don't mean to hurt you. But a moment ago you said we were phony relatives, that Sam has only the Gores. That's not true. He has a brother he's never met. A brother he should be raised with. And I know Angela's very first thought will be to bring them together for just that reason. Could you raise two boys alone? Would you?"

Some questions just seem to answer themselves. Ivan looked at her a long moment with his fist under his chin. Then he got up from the armchair and walked off. Before he reached the staircase to the second floor, he turned and spoke.

"Well, mother, first things first. Call Angela by all means and tell her about Sam. Tell her about Kathy and the Gores and especially about me – Sam's guardian. And when you've done all that, let me know what she says."

He was washing his hands of the matter, she knew. It was on her head now. How unfair. An old woman shouldn't have worries like these, she said to herself.

~~~

Claudia thought things through and waited a day before calling Angela. Ivan said both Helena and Brad might suffer as well by this new revelation. And he was right – she hadn't considered that. In the end, it didn't make a great deal of difference, except that it increased the burden she felt. Would there ever be an end to the parade of misery started by that madman, Sam Porter?

It was late morning when she called San Francisco. As best she could, she related the whole story to Angela. While she looked out to the east through her bedroom windows, a mist was moving in from Easton's Bay and pooling in the low ground at the edge of her property. Like the mist, her words and sentences piled up steadily. She had been afraid that her narration would be full of gaps and foolish repetitions, but it was clear and complete. She must have thought it out more thoroughly than she realized.

"Aunt Claudia, could there ever be a dispute over Ivan's status as guardian?" Angela asked when she finished.

"I can't see that happening, Angela. Sam's great grandparents know what Kathy wanted. She had a lawyer write a letter stating her wishes on the matter. Both Ivan and the Gores have a copy. We never sought a legal ruling here – it just didn't seem necessary."

"What does ... Sam think about all this? Does he ask about Justin?"

"It hasn't been so long since I told him. He can't quite grasp what a half-brother is."

"I see. Would you mind if I call Ivan about this, dear? I think we have a lot to discuss."

"Yes, I do too. And Angela ... please think how this will affect Brad and your sister as well."

"We're getting used to crises here, Auntie. They seem to show up with frightening regularity."

~~~

Sam repeated the word to himself ... half-brother. Half brother and half what? Was he a good kid like Joshua at school or a stupid bully like Miguel?

Justin didn't go to school, Aunt Claudia said, he had a tutor. But who wants a tutor following you around all day? What if you don't like him? At least he had more than one teacher. Like Mr. Norton was nice even though Miss

Grzebien was kind of crabby. He supposed it was better to go to school like he did and have friends than stay home all day.

He had grown used to his life in Newport with Ivan and Aunt Claudia. She was more like a grandmother than an aunt, he thought, and Ivan was a lot like an older brother.

Was there a reason why Ivan didn't talk about Justin? Maybe he didn't want another brother around.

Getting to meet Justin would be nice, but not if he was like the boy in the new dream. That would be scary. This boy came out of the night and looked in through his bedroom window. Sam would help him in after a while, raising the sash and standing aside. He wore a spotless white suit, and Sam wondered how he kept it so clean.

The boy told him things in a whispery voice, things he promised not to tell but could never remember when he woke up. Sam tried to hold on to some of them, but all that was left in the morning were bad feelings about a man the boy knew. Could bad feelings hurt you when you promised not to tell?

Chapter 27

Damn it to hell. Boyle was in a funk about that scene with Ivan Chitworth. He might have been able to put it out of his mind eventually – if it was only his reputation on the line. After all, a lot of folks figure a P.I. is a lowlife on his best day. But the Chitworths had to be afraid he could generate a whole lot of nasty publicity anytime he wanted. He couldn't let that stand.

From the street, Dismas Cottage was imposing. Surrounded by a wrought iron fence of a sturdy, yet baroque pattern, the house rose three full stories on its raised mound and was surrounded by mature landscaping. There was a vaguely European look about it that he couldn't pin down as to country of origin. Must have at least fifteen rooms. Driving by, he tried to surmise what the annual tax bite was on a pile like that. You add taxes to the yearly maintenance on the house and grounds, pretty soon you're talking a number well over thirty-five grand – without counting a mortgage even. He drove past through the quiet, tree-lined neighborhood until he saw sky meet water down by Ochre Point.

On Webster Street he spied an open parking space to the left of Ochre Court, the main administration building at Salve Regina University. Boyle pulled in and walked out onto Cliff Walk, the seaside promenade above Easton's Bay. On a clear day – and it was a clear day – you could see the lighthouse off Sakonnet Point in Little Compton to the southeast. To the north was the curving sand strip of the

City Beach. In all, it was a miles-wide and miles-long vista full of surging ocean and blue skies. Beyond the beach was the tony Middletown neighborhood of Tuckerman Road along Easton's Point.

Well, the view sure was nice, but what was he doing down here? Why hadn't he stopped at Dismas Cottage and gotten it over with? He'd already driven by twice, but couldn't pull the trigger. What a wimp. He figured on giving himself one more chance when he went back. For now, though, he may as well enjoy the scenery like everybody else.

Because it was high season, dozens of strollers were passing by on the path along Cliff Walk's edge. He sat on a bench high up the sloping lawn behind Ochre Court, next to a flagpole flanked by ill-tended bushes. Below him, a father and young son had stopped on the path and were looking out into the bay. Dad was pointing something out, and the boy was nodding gravely.

Boyle thought about the bond such a pair would have throughout their lives so long as nothing came between them. A sacred thing, no doubt – a cornerstone for trust and human feeling. He had missed that in his life, but he liked to think most people had someone to count on, a treasured and lasting relationship dating back to childhood.

In only a few minutes, he had relaxed and grown thoughtful. It was time to drive back to Dismas Cottage and set things right.

He heard chimes toll inside when he pushed the doorbell. A pretty young Hispanic woman answered the door.

"I'm sorry," she told him. "Mr. Chitworth is not at

home."

"I see. Would you please give Claudia Chitworth my card and ask if she could see me for a moment. It's very important."

The young woman frowned at his card and searched his face for a second.

"Wait in here, please," she said, a barely perceptible smile lighting her eyes.

Before long, an elegant old lady in an ankle length lavender dress appeared in the arched doorway to his left and signaled him forward. When he reached the archway, she had retreated to the middle of the room and was sitting there expectantly, a full twenty-five feet away. And a very spectacular room it was, he thought.

As he walked towards her, she glanced at his card and spoke out.

"Mr. Boyle, I don't know you. Maria tells me you asked first for my son. Are you acquainted with him?"

"We've met, Mrs. Chitworth. At the writer's group."

"I don't understand. Are you a writer or a private investigator?"

Boyle could see Ivan hadn't spoken to her about him. He could steer clear of the whole Billy Moncton affair, which would simplify things.

"I'm no writer, Mrs. Chitworth. I went to Ivan's group on Thursday to talk about something else. He knows I have a client interested in Sam. But he didn't let me explain the situation. He was so angry I thought it best to leave."

"Why are you here with this now, Mr. Boyle?"

"Only to say that I haven't told anyone about Sam. And I won't. I let my client know that I couldn't locate him.

Please convey my apology to your son. Since this is obviously news to you, you have my regrets as well, ma'am."

Just as he finished speaking, Mrs. Chitworth looked to the doorway. He turned as well and heard footsteps clattering through the marble foyer. It was Ivan, who began to yell as soon as he saw him.

"You! Get the hell out of here! Now!"

Boyle was facing Ivan and opened his mouth to object, but he could tell it was no use. He turned and walked away as Ivan spoke to his mother in a quavering voice.

"You mustn't believe anything that man said. I can prove he's a liar. I don't know why he's doing this. What did he say, mother? We may have to go to the police about him."

Taking deep breaths, Boyle fled the house and piled into his car. As he grabbed the wheel, he shook his head sharply and muttered to himself. What a goddamn mess.

~~~

Until he figured it out, Boyle sat at home sulking like a whipped puppy. Ivan Chitworth must have thought he came to Dismas Cottage to out him to his mother. Jesus! They might even have him pegged for a blackmailer.

He hated the idea of backing off at a sticky pass like this, but what in God's name was he supposed to do? Before he went to see Mrs. Chitworth, he had been sure things couldn't possibly get any worse – yet they did. In spades, no less.

Lying in bed Saturday after another restless night, he greeted the morning with a baleful eye. He propped himself up on one elbow and considered the day ahead without enthusiasm. He'd have to get up, of course; there was no excuse for lying there much longer. Sun was barging through his bedroom window, and the day's heat and humidity were rising in tandem. After breakfast, he'd wash up, take a long walk, and spend some time cleaning house. That was as much as he could handle.

Was he thinking metaphorically about cleaning house, fixing the mess he made yesterday? No, he needed to tackle the task literally – by doing something about his dusty rooms and slovenly kitchen.

By early afternoon, he had made progress – three rooms clean and only the kitchen and bathroom to go. These last were the worst of the lot, he thought, but progress is progress. He was pulling a mop and bucket out of the kitchen closet when the phone rang.

"Stafford Boyle here."

A pause. "This is Ivan Chitworth."

Boyle held on to the phone and cringed mentally, waiting for whatever should come next.

"You may want to hang up on me, but don't. Maybe you can understand my reaction yesterday – at least I hope so. My mother told me you stopped by to apologize. She was pretty horrified at the way I acted. I guess it's my turn to say I'm sorry. I really am."

Boyle exhaled loudly; he didn't try to hide it.

"This is a big relief for me." he said. "Thanks for calling. And since Mrs. Moncton blew my cover like that, I need to tell you something. I refused to investigate any further after the preliminary work. There's nothing in writing that refers to sexual orientation or a relationship."

"She drew the conclusion herself?"

"I was obligated to tell her what I thought. I observed Billy at your house twice and I saw you go off to Boston together. But that doesn't constitute proof of anything, and I wasn't about to take the case further."

"That's good to know, I'm glad you told me. Anyway, I'll be out of town for a while, and my lawyer can deal with the Monctons. Both of them."

Whatever the relationship was between Billy and Ivan, it had apparently ended. There was no need to comment, and Boyle was silent. But Ivan hadn't finished.

"You know ... my mother and I have been talking something over. We need someone whose discretion we can rely on. After everything that's happened, I'm thinking you may be the guy."

Was he going to get an assignment out of this? He couldn't imagine a stranger result from a botched job, but he couldn't afford not to listen.

"I'd be pleased to help out if I can," he said.

~~~

They agreed to meet that afternoon at four. Boyle spent an hour cleaning the kitchen and bathroom, then worked on himself. He showered, shaved, and went to his bedroom to dress.

It was hot outside, but shorts were out of the question for a business visit to Dismas Cottage. He pulled on a pair of summer weight black slacks and a silky blue short-sleeve shirt that he wouldn't have to tuck in. Everything was neatly pressed, and he thought his tan looked good against the light blue fabric. He inserted a small notebook into his back pocket and clipped a pen to the "v" of his t-shirt where it couldn't be seen. Just in case.

Ivan had told him the driveway gate would be open and that he should walk around to the back where he and his mother would be relaxing. When he had done so, Boyle was standing on an immaculate expanse of green velvet lawn that appeared to eat up about five acres of the most expensive neighborhood in town. There was a dazzling white gravel walkway down the center with low, trim bushes on either side and a huge urn in the middle spilling ivy, flowers, and floral vines down to the path.

He saw none of the common amenities he expected, such as a pool or tennis court. Instead, fountains, statues, and two enclosed gazebos dotted the grounds and terrace. Halfway to the back on the left was a rose garden with winding paths. To the right were stands of maple and copper beech trees. Across the back of the property a white marble balustrade separated a kind of sunken garden from the rest of the grounds.

Where the hell could Ivan and his mother be? Boyle had rounded the giant urn and still saw no one. Beyond the balustrade, he could make out walkways left and right with flowers and miniature examples of topiary. But the most eye-popping feature was the unbroken phalanx of towering beeches at the back edge of the property, weeping beech trees with heavy-laden branches bent to the ground in long, weird arcs.

Boyle was ready to turn back and look for someone in the house when a figure in white shorts stepped out of the dense foliage. It was Ivan. He and Mrs. Chitworth were there, under the weeping beeches. And it was easy to see why they preferred it, once he joined them. It felt twenty degrees cooler under the sheltering green arms. Words like 'oasis' and 'grotto' popped into his mind.

In this secluded spot sat two white cast-iron benches in

filigree and a large white cast iron table, in the middle of which was a tea service warmed by little candles. Yes, Mrs. Chitworth was serving him hot tea in a china cup on the hottest day of the year. Hard as this was to believe, the temperature under the trees seemed to justify the practice.

Boyle sat on one bench with Mrs. Chitworth while Ivan alternately paced the ground and sat alone on the other bench. When they had exhausted the usual polite conversation, Claudia Chitworth spoke up.

"Ivan and I have been discussing our relatives in San Francisco, Mr. Boyle. May I assume you know who they are?"

"Yes, ma'am. Helena Swann and Angela Styles. I understand Mrs. Styles has a son about Sam's age."

"That would be Justin, yes. Sam and he have the same father, you know."

That certainly was a graceful way of introducing her concern, Boyle said to himself. The poor kids shared the father from hell.

"As you can see, Mr. Boyle, my mother is a charitable person. Sam Porter, as I see it, is part of our problem. It seems that Justin has exhibited some difficult behavior lately. This is something Helena alerted us to. She doesn't know very much, but Justin is seeing a mental health professional in San Francisco."

"I see. And Mrs. Styles never mentioned it?"

"That's right," Ivan said. "Which would be her business only, except that we're talking about transferring guardianship of Sam to Angela and her husband. It may be best for Sam to be raised with his half-brother. As much as we love him, an elderly lady and a single man aren't the ideal parents for Sam."

"Angela is my niece," Mrs. Chitworth said. "A beautiful girl and a marvelous person,"

"Yes, ma'am, I'm sure she must be."

Ivan was pacing under the dome-like cover of the beech trees. Occasional shafts of sunlight pierced the branches and cast him alternately in bright light and dim silhouette as he walked back and forth.

"So we're of two minds here," he said. "Justin and Sam should be together. But not at the expense of Sam's welfare."

"Can't you talk frankly with Mrs. Styles about all this?" Boyle asked.

"We don't see how. Angela tells us Justin is in perfect health. And we don't want to claim that we heard otherwise. Rather than confront her with Helena's assertion to the contrary, we would like you to consider investigating for us."

"Shouldn't you find someone in San Francisco?"

"Mr. Boyle, we wouldn't know where to start." Mrs. Chitworth was standing now, having placed her teacup and saucer on the cast iron table.

"Our fear of someone discovering Sam's parentage is intense," she said. "In San Francisco, this information would be explosive, to say the least. Finding someone we could feel confident about would be a long process."

"My mother's right, Boyle. We trust you. Will you go to San Francisco for us and look into this?"

He was thinking about Assunta and the disruption a trip like this would cause. Never mind that he wasn't looking for full-time employment.

"I'll have to think about it. Tell me exactly what my mission would be."

Ivan spoke. "Well ... to find out what Justin's problems are so we can decide whether to let Sam live there with him."

"Would I be able to speak with Helena Swann or Brad Styles?"

"Not Brad, no. But Helena ... well, yes, if you can't make progress otherwise. We'll introduce you if it comes to that."

"An investigation like this is problematic, folks. If Justin has a psychiatric condition, there's no way I could legally obtain the medical records to prove it. I should be able to find out who treats him, interview people who know him, things like that. But the picture I might develop from that wouldn't be complete. Then there's the time factor. I can't say how long it would take."

They were both nodding. "We understand," Ivan said. "We want your best efforts, but the whole thing has to be handled discreetly. Angela and Brad can't know that we're looking into this."

Boyle wasn't at all sure this was a case he should take. But he had to say something, and he didn't want to refuse them outright. Not yet.

"Let me work up a weekly fee, including expenses, and get back to you. Airfare would be separate."

"Marvelous," said Ivan. "So you'll do it?"

CHAPTER 28

Boyle felt weird buying a one-way ticket to the west coast, as if he were never coming back. Even though he couldn't tell how long his investigation would run, it seemed all too final not to have his return passage paid in advance. Still, he hoped a couple of weeks would suffice.

He decided to leave from Logan airport in Boston since there were no direct flights out of T. F. Green in nearby Warwick. Assunta told him she couldn't spare the three plus hours it would take her to drive him to Logan and come back to Newport. That was a big disappointment and a sign she was miffed at the whole idea. At the last second, however, she came over to say goodbye and take him to the bus station. Rather than park at the airport indefinitely, he was saving the Chitworths a few bucks by catching a coach from Newport to Boston.

Boyle's 11:00 a.m. flight on United was full. To simplify things in the new age of airport insanity, he packed two bags and did without a carry-on. Booking an aisle seat for comfort's sake helped a little, but six and one-half hours in the air was bound to make you sticky and cranky.

He tried to kill time by mulling over his plan of action and figuring out how he might gather information on Justin Styles. Mostly, he caught up on his sleep – until the flight attendant asked him to raise his seat all the way for their landing at San Francisco International.

Within an hour after that, he had picked up his rental car and was driving into town.

The Junipero Arms was a modest hotel in the downtown area with an old-fashioned feel to it. It was a relief to check in, take a shower, and unpack his things. Afterwards, he looked out the window and daydreamed about the California of twenty-five years ago, when he was last here.

Back then he was in the Navy, a second-class petty officer enrolled in the Russian language program at the Defense Language Institute in Monterey. School was okay, a terrific break from sea duty, but San Francisco was the big attraction for weekends. It was just his luck to have all of the Monterey Peninsula as his playground and a great city just two hours away – when he was way too poor to enjoy it.

Of course, that was then and this is now, he thought. Best to cut the daydream short and do a little work.

He needed to visit the main library, a new building with a kind of faux beaux-arts façade at 100 Larkin Street in the Civic Center. It was open until eight o'clock, which meant he'd be able to get in a couple hours of research before dinner. He settled in with microfiche records and read for two hours straight all the old stories and columns he could find pertaining to the Shoo-fly case. That would serve as general background and a primer for understanding what the Styles family had been through.

Until he could speak to someone like Helena Swann, there wasn't a heckuva lot more he could do. But Ivan was still reluctant to set up a meeting between him and Mrs. Swann. He was afraid she might, despite her best intentions, let it slip to Brad or Angela that he and his mother had hired a private detective.

In the meantime, he thought it useful to find out who

the most prominent child psychiatrists in San Francisco were. The Styles family was likely to engage the very best. And he knew the address of the Marina district mansion, so why not tail Angela Styles a few times, especially when she had her little boy with her? Maybe he could match the addresses she visited with those of the best kiddy shrinks.

Sounds like a plan, he said to himself.

Back at the hotel, he called a local hospital and asked for the physician's referral service. That yielded four therapists and two child psychiatrists. He got similar results looking through the yellow pages directory in his room. Next morning, Boyle made a second trip to the main library for an Internet search. He found several references to a Dr. LaFreniere, a child psychiatrist who had reached near celebrity status.

Until then, he hadn't paid much attention to the addresses he had written down. When he did, he found that Dr. LaFreniere's office wasn't far from the Tremont Building, which housed Sharples Communications. A very promising result, he thought. This guy had to be Justin's shrink.

On his third day in San Francisco, Boyle drove to the Marina district. After he found the Sharples' impressive stucco mansion, he spent time looking through the shops on Chestnut Street, strolling the area around Marina Park, and roaming the nearby Presidio. When he felt well acquainted with the downtown area, Pacific Heights, and the Marina district, he prepared to stake out the Sharples mansion.

Mornings would be a good time to start, he figured. He'd be fresh, alert and hopeful. He hated tails and stakeouts, never thought he was good at them, and was always miserable after a couple of hours of waiting around. So he'd give it just that much time – two to three hours each morning. If he didn't have results within a week, he'd think of something else.

On his first try, Monday, the stakeout was a success but the tail was a flop. He picked up Angela leaving home alone at ten-thirty. The gates to the mansion's driveway opened, she flew out into light traffic, and he lost her downtown.

On Thursday, she left home with Justin in the car. It was nine o'clock. He was absolutely determined to do better this time, but still lost her in Union Square. At least he knew where the hell he was this time, and it occurred to him that Doctor LaFreniere's address was close by. He parked in the first legal spot he found, stuffed the meter full of quarters and walked over to the building where the doctor had his practice.

Inside, he noted the floor and suite number for Raynor LaFreniere, M.D. on the office directory. He saw no reason not to go up there and chat with the receptionist, who turned out to be a middle-aged woman with a kind, maternal manner.

"Pardon me Miss, may I ask a few questions?"

"What can I do for you, sir?"

He hadn't thought ahead, he knew the lies would come easily.

"I work in the neighborhood and thought I'd stop by. The doctor treats children, doesn't he? My daughter is having problems at school."

"That's right. Doctor LaFreniere treats preadolescent children. Would you care to make an appointment for your daughter?"

"No, not just yet," he said, backing away from the counter. "I wanted to make sure Dr. LaFreniere was the right kind of specialist. I have to speak to my wife about this."

In his peripheral vision, Boyle had seen Angela Styles in the waiting room, flipping through a magazine. That gave him enough information to complete his first report to the Chitworths.

Moving on from there would be the real challenge. When he called Newport, Ivan and Claudia were pleased to know Justin was seeing San Francisco's foremost child psychiatrist. Understandably, they wanted to know much more. He pressed for an introduction to Helena Swann.

"Look," he said, "I might as well make arrangements to come home. Without some help and direction, I'll be wasting your money here."

"But you've hardly started, Mr. Boyle," said Claudia Chitworth. "And your progress is quite satisfactory."

"I know when I've hit a wall, ma'am. Only sheer luck will get me any further. After an interview with Mrs. Swann, though, I'd likely have a few notions how to proceed."

Ivan, who was on another extension, spoke up.

"All right Boyle, you'll have your interview. I'll call Helena myself. Where do you propose to meet her?"

"We don't have to meet, and she won't have to know my name. Better she doesn't, in fact. Just get me her cell phone number and a time for me to call when she can speak freely.

~~~

When it was time to call Helena Swann two days later, Boyle was at Marina Park, just a few blocks away from the

Styles mansion. Rather than hang around the Junipero Arms, he had driven over to the Marina district to stroll the beachfront. Flipping open his cell phone, he punched in her number. She answered on the second ring.

"Mrs. Swann?"

"Yes."

"I'm the investigator your cousin Ivan hired. How are you today, ma'am?"

"I'm well, thanks. Tell me, what's that I hear in the background?"

He looked around. "Well, there's a little traffic noise. And two kids in front of me running and screaming. Their dad is helping them get a kite launched. I'm at Marina Park."

"You are? Well, that's close by. The last time I was there, you know, was in 1999. I was with another investigator at the time."

"Ah," he said. "That would be Pedro Brunetti. Last week I brushed up on the old case at the library. Fascinating stuff."

"Yes, I suppose. Well what can I do for you, Mister Private Eye?"

He walked off the grass and onto the narrow strip of beach sand. "I'd just like to ask a few questions, Mrs. Swann."

"Please call me Helena. Some prefer Black Widow, but I rather like my given name."

Boyle didn't know whether to laugh or not, but he did. It seemed a better course than keeping silent. Why was she so flippant?

"Thank you for agreeing to speak with me," he said. "I

certainly appreciate it."

"My pleasure," she said. "You may ask anything you wish. If a question troubles me, I'll tell you."

"Fair enough. Why don't I start by asking your general impressions of Angela and Brad's family life – how they get along, how they interact with Justin."

"Angela and Brad have a magical relationship. Love and support in both directions, never a cross word in public. Truly enviable. Everyone who knows them will tell you this. Individually, they are both renowned for niceness. Does this sound a little too much, as if I'm being ironic or something? I don't mean it that way."

"No, go on please."

"Well, you know I was once engaged to Brad and that Angela is my stepsister. So I've known both of them intimately. I've always thought their relationship with Justin perfect in every way. But there are strains now. Brad was the model dad in my estimation, but there's a distance between him and Justin now – he seems to judge him more. And Angela frets about the boy constantly. It seems to me that I get along with Justin better than either of them right now. He seems more ... natural with me, more like a boy should be at that age."

"Does he confide in you?"

"Yes, but there's never been anything unusual or out of the way."

"Does he talk about his parents with you?"

"Ah, he used to. But not now."

"So far as you know, what makes them think he needs psychiatric help?"

"I only know a little. Justin has thrown some tantrums

lately. He didn't do that as a tyke. And his mother thinks he abused a kitten he had. She took it away from him."

"Has anyone spoken to you about his visits to the psychiatrist?"

"Angela told me only that Justin is seeing Ray LaFreniere to ... understand himself better. That's what she said when I asked about a diagnosis."

Thinking about the effort he put into finding out who Justin's shrink was, Boyle was miffed at the Chitworths. They shouldn't have kept him away from Helena Swann until now.

"I don't think Justin cares for these visits," she continued. "I've been told not to ask him about his ... treatment, but I've noticed he becomes agitated nearly every Wednesday, the day before he goes."

"How did your sister and brother-in-law react to the news about Sam Dunnell living in Newport with the Chitworths?"

"Right away, Angela thought about bringing him to San Francisco to be with his brother. Brad's reaction was less enthusiastic. Personally, I think he was horrified."

"May I ask your reaction?"

"Oh, I was horrified too, at first. But I can understand Angela wanting to have custody."

"Help me understand it then."

"Well ... despite everything that happened, I believe she still loves her first husband. If she couldn't save him, she can at least save his boys."

"I hesitate to ask this, but all the news articles about Sam Porter pointed to a ... relationship between you and him. That must have had quite an impact on your sister."

"Tabloid nonsense! It had a terrible effect on all of us, but we got through it. And when all was said and done, who was pregnant? She was, not I."

Boyle heard the anger in her voice and decided not to press. The breeze from the bay was stiffening now and he hunched his shoulders, turning away from the sudden cold.

"Can you think of anything we haven't discussed that I should know?" he asked.

"Not really. Perhaps you should know that I'm making plans to live on my own. I hope to move within a few weeks."

"May I ask your reason for leaving?"

Long pause.

"Let's just say it's time I struck out on my own."

"Well, I wish you the best of luck. Oh ... one last thing. The Cullion murder case made headlines everywhere. Did it cause you folks much trouble?"

"What on earth do you mean?" she snapped.

He thought her reaction strong. What the heck was that about?

"Well, the news stories rehashed the old Shoo-fly case," he said. "I wondered if that caused any problems at home. Did Justin ask about his father, for instance?"

"Oh, I see," she said. "Justin is home-schooled just so he won't hear these things from other children. He is also sheltered from the 'wrong' kind of news coverage. I don't know what Angela and Brad's timetable is for explaining all that to him. I'm quite sure they haven't yet."

When they said goodbye Boyle shut down his cell phone and stuffed it into his jacket pocket. He thought a moment, then strolled over to Baker Street by the Palace of Fine Arts to study the rotunda across the pond. Something was bothering him. He couldn't understand why Helena Swann didn't ask any questions about Sam. Not that he had a lot of answers, but why wasn't she curious about him? He thought she was straightforward about most everything else ... but was he really supposed to believe she hadn't been screwing Shoo-fly behind her sister's back?

CHAPTER 29

Helena Swann sat at home in her sister's mansion, lost in a sour reverie. Oh, how it rankled! Her former lover had not just one son, but two. And the woman who bore young Sam was merely a name from the tabloids, someone she didn't know. Two sons by two women, and nothing for her except this ... ongoing humiliation. She may have had his love, such as it was, but they bore his children. So much had been lost, so much denied her. That was why she couldn't countenance learning more about this new boy Sam, another piece of his father that belonged to someone else.

As he often did, Justin Styles pulled open the door to Helena's suite without knocking and came running up to her. She smiled and barely managed to kiss him before he skipped away, plunking himself down on an ottoman and looking back to her expectantly. Now that was just like him, she thought. First he demands your attention, and then backs away.

"Well, what is it Justin?" she asked. "I can tell you're up to something."

"I'm not up to anything, Aunt Helena. I want to know where you were, that's all. I didn't see you all morning."

"Did you miss me, dear?"

"I guess so. When I had my break, you were gone. What were you doing?"

"I was out on the terrace, Justin. Didn't Mr. Danzig tell you?"

"Probably. He says I don't always listen good."

"He may be right about that, you know. He's a very smart man."

"That's what mommy says. But if he's so smart, why does he have to hang around with a little kid all day?"

She laughed. "There are some questions your Aunt Helena won't try to answer for you, and that is one of them."

Justin smiled at her comeback. Then he furrowed his brow and leaned back on his elbows.

"What about my other question?" he asked.

"Other question?"

"About what you were doing on the terrace."

"Such persistence! Well, young man, I needed a little privacy this morning for a telephone call. From a gentleman."

"What did you talk about?"

"It was business – a kind of interview, actually."

"What did he want to know, Aunt Helena?"

"Lots of things. He even asked about you."

"Really? What did you say?"

"Oh, just that you're a good boy – most of the time – who loves his mommy and daddy, and even his old Aunt Helena."

She could see she had made him uncomfortable. He squirmed on the ottoman and ran an anxious finger around the braiding. His mouth puckered as he looked up at her through long lashes.

"What's the matter, Justin?"

"Why do they make me go to Doctor LaFreniere, Aunt Helena? They think I'm crazy, don't they?"

"Justin, I know your mother has talked to you about

this. Have you talked to your dad also?"

"He ... isn't like he used to be. Mommy is different too. I don't like to talk to Doctor LaFreniere any more."

Helena looked directly at Justin for a long time before speaking. Gradually, he stopped fidgeting and sat upright, looking back at her intently. Lately she felt closer than ever to her nephew. He was at loose ends in this house just as she was. Like her, he knew he didn't fit in. All manner of money was expended in making them happy, she thought. So much money and so little understanding.

"Justin, these are things your mom and dad would want you to talk over with them. You have to trust them and give them a chance to help you."

"I like to talk things over with you more. I get the feeling everything I say freaks ... makes them upset."

"They're just worried about you, Justin."

"I know. But why? You don't worry about me."

"Well, I do, but maybe in a different way."

"Then it's a better way. When they tell me what bothers them, I don't even understand what they're saying. Am I bad, Aunt Helena?"

"We all do bad things sometimes, Justin. That doesn't make us bad."

"I would do anything for you, Aunt Helena. Anything at all."

"Would you now?"

Helena gazed down at his sweet face and wondered how she had inspired this adulation. He was just a needy little boy, she thought. She knew without question that he was an object of devotion to his parents. But he wanted something more and was looking to her for it. When he came close again, she kissed his cheek and ran her fingers through the silky black hair. The exact same shade and texture as his father's, she thought.

"Justin ... maybe there is something we can talk about doing together."

~~~

Gunther Danzig came to the United States for postgraduate studies in 1976 and never left. His first jobs were as tutor for the children of American families of German heritage who wanted their kids to be fluent in that language. Thirty years later he was still tutoring, albeit for a broader spectrum of knowledge and a wider sampling of wealthy families. He home-schooled the children of the rich in San Francisco, and most of the time he liked it.

But Justin Styles was unique in his experience. He could be self-disciplined and industrious for long periods. At other times, he was dreamy and disorganized. "A mature child with astonishing insights," he had written just a year ago when he started working with the boy. Lately, however, he was just as likely to be stubborn and moody.

His mother had echoed that last phrase a few weeks ago, not long before she told Danzig she would be consulting a – how do you call it? – mental health professional. Perhaps that will do some good, he thought.

For his part, he had asked for more leeway to discipline Justin – he simply wouldn't listen sometimes. Well, nothing came of that. He wasn't even sure what sort of discipline he had in mind. He certainly hoped Mrs. Styles – such a fine woman – didn't think he wished to strike the child. That, of course, was the furthest thing from his mind. But people in this country became suspicious when a German spoke of discipline. Yes, he should have explained himself more fully.

Today, Justin was rather ill-prepared for his French lesson, but his attention was adequate. The history lesson went longer than planned, mostly because of the boy's interest in the American Revolution. Danzig had emphasized the importance of the Battle of Trenton and the boy had questioned him closely about the Hessian mercenaries.

"They were Germans, weren't they, Mr. Danzig, like you?"

"That is correct, Justin."

"And mercenary just means they fought for anyone who would pay, not because they believed in something."

"Correct also."

"What is my nationality, Mr. Danzig?"

"I understand that your mother is English. But your father ... I don't know."

Justin heard the hesitation, Danzig could tell. He had been instructed to avoid any reference to the boy's natural father. Mentally, he admonished himself for not proceeding as if it were Brad Styles's nationality in question.

Justin had an awfully smug look on his face. "Oh, you don't know what kind of name Porter is, Mr. Danzig?"

"There are many things I don't know, Justin. Let us go on with the lesson."

"Tell me one thing first. Are your parents both German?"

"Yes they are. Now ...."

"But if one of them was ... different, would that be a reason to be ashamed?"

"I shouldn't think so. But Justin, these are questions for your father and mother – they are not for me to answer."

Now that was precisely what disturbed him about the boy. He would secure these little advantages over you and use them to act in a condescending manner. As soon as he saw you squirm, he wished to prolong his enjoyment of it. It was a species of schadenfreude.

For the rest of the day, Justin was perfectly attentive and responsive, but he kept a knowing smile on his face that infuriated Gunther Danzig. He had a feeling Justin was capable of doing wicked things.

CHAPTER 30

The little article with the black border around it on the Chronicle's front page caught Boyle's attention. Apparently, it was a late-breaking item that would be treated more fully in future editions. But it made him want to pack up and go home when he read it. Hell, this family's life was too damn complicated and drama-filled for his taste.

Bradford Styles– Noted Business Leader and Philanthropist

"Mr. Bradford Styles, 45, prominent San Francisco publisher, died last night in his Marina district home, as the result of a fall. While details are sketchy, a source close to the family stated that the housekeeper, after hearing a loud noise, found Mr. Styles lying at the foot of the staircase to the second floor of the Spanish style mansion. Apparently, death was instantaneous.

No statement from the Styles family was available at the press deadline for this story. Police officials have not commented. Mr. Styles's wife, Angela Sharples Porter Styles, is said to be in seclusion.

Bradford Styles was a highly respected businessman, long serving as Executive Director in charge of Sharples Communications. He also served on the boards of several area charities. His father-in-law Sam Sharples, legendary San Francisco newspaperman, founded the San Francisco Record, the flagship company of Sharples

Communications. Mr. Styles, though a lifelong San Franciscan, was himself scion of a wealthy San Joaquin Valley family. He is survived by his wife Angela, president of Sharples Communications, his son Justin, his mother Nuala, and a sister-in-law, Helena Sharples Swann.

The family was recently in the news when Michael Cullion was charged with the murder of Jake Snider at a storefront mission called The Breastplate of Faith and Love. The story generated a renewal of interest in the 1999 slayings attributed to Samson "Shoo-fly" Porter. Cullion was a known accomplice of Mr. Porter, the first husband of Angela Styles.

Funeral arrangements for Mr. Styles are said to be incomplete at this time."

Boyle calculated the time difference between San Francisco and Newport and called the Chitworth residence. It would be 11:30 a.m. there. When the call went through, Ivan answered.

"Hello."

"Ivan, this is Staff Boyle. Has anyone else called you this morning?"

"I just got off the phone with Helena, Staff. We're kind of reeling here, you know?"

"I understand. Is there anything I can do for you?"

"Uh, well, yes. You could get us rooms where you're staying. Where is that?"

"The Junipero Arms. It's downtown."

"Don't know it."

"It's pretty ... old-school. Fine service. Not so much on bells and whistles."

"That's okay. I don't know what time we'll be there, but you could book rooms for my mother and me. Angela may want us at her place, but we'll stay where you are until we're sure. My room will be for two. I'm taking Sam out of school."

"Whatever you say."

"Thanks for calling. Now I can concentrate on airline reservations. Is there anything else you need from me?"

"I kind of assumed you'd want me to call off the investigation and come home."

"Not yet, no. Please stay where you are."

"All right. Listen, the newspaper account was brief. But there was a hint that a police investigation may follow."

"Hunh? That seems ridiculous!"

"You're probably right. Maybe I'm reading more into it than I should."

CHAPTER 31

Maynard Bennett didn't come home until eleven thirty the night Brad Styles died. From the time he was called out at seven twenty-five until he left at eleven-fifteen, his every action was thoughtful and measured. All the more so, as he was totally cognizant of the power and influence wielded by the occupants of the Styles household.

His wife was sleeping when he got in, so he changed into sweat clothes and hung his suit in the hall closet without going into their bedroom. Then he traversed the hall to the spare room they used as a combination office and den.

It had been his son's room. Nathan, the Bennetts' only child, had graduated from San Francisco State two years before and left for an accounting position in L.A. Maynard Bennett thought of him every time he walked into the room and sat at the desktop computer, as he was doing tonight.

He supposed he could wait until tomorrow to organize his notes and make his report, but he forced himself to get started now. Experience told him that work tomorrow would start with a bang. It always did when the cops had a role, however small, in a headline story about a big name. His boss Al and the Chief would be all over him looking for answers to fifty questions. A completed report might short-circuit that – and it would get a host of the city's brass off their backs.

He probably wouldn't be as fresh as he'd like in the morning after losing four hours sleep, but he'd save himself an awful lot of grief.

~~~

Bennett wouldn't have been called out at all if the patrol car officer had been able to secure the scene before the arrival of the Medical Examiner. Justin Styles kept darting around asking questions of the EMT's, going in and out of rooms – just acting up, really. And Miss Jarndyce was in no condition to take control. Mrs. Styles had taken a sedative, and Helena Swann had locked herself in her upstairs suite.

The patrol officer knew she was dealing with a famous family and asked headquarters how to proceed. Bennett took the callout from the duty sergeant and found Justin on the terrace when he arrived. He appeared to be hiding something in an earthenware pot out there. He corralled the boy gently and guided him inside, then took an initial statement from Miss Jarndyce and asked her to take Justin in hand.

Bennett interviewed Helena Swann as well. He knocked at the doors to her suite for some time before she responded. Repeatedly, he called her name and identified himself. Finally the doors opened. She was in her motorized chair.

"I was in bed, Detective," she claimed.

He noted she was dressed in a white silk blouse with a pleated front, fitted black slacks, and black open toe Joan Crawfords. Nothing that might be considered sleepwear.

"Sorry to disturb you, Mrs. Swann. Are you aware of what happened?" he asked.

Her eyelashes fluttered and her hands steepled in front of her mouth. "Oh no ... he's dead, isn't he?" she whispered.

"Yes, ma'am," he replied. "Can you tell me what you

saw?"

"I heard a shout, then someone rushing by my door. When I heard my sister sobbing, I came out towards the balcony to find out what happened. But I retreated to my room after seeing Brad on the stairs. It was just too much for me. I couldn't bear to watch."

Bennett thought she was awfully pulled together for someone who couldn't stomach the scene.

"Can you tell me how my nephew is?" she asked.

"He was acting out, to be frank. But Miss Jarndyce is attending to him."

"If necessary, we can call his doctor. I'm sure Ray LaFreniere would come over if we ask him."

Bennett knew the name – a kiddie shrink. When he thought it through, he decided to call his boss about what Justin had done. He needed to find out what the boy hid on the terrace. But if it was evidence of a crime, he would have to acquire it in a defensible manner.

"Al, I'm going to be up with this half the night," he said. "Could you start the paper for a warrant and call in some favors to get it issued?"

"Serving paper on Angela Styles won't be easy, pardner. Tell you what, though. If we make it real specific – just to search the soil in that one pot on the terrace – I can maybe get it executed tonight."

"Great idea, Al."

"If it was anybody else, we could get one for the whole house. Do you intend to serve it tonight?"

"Tonight won't work. Mrs. Styles is in no shape to talk."

When Miss Jarndyce put Justin to bed, Bennett grilled her again. Upset as she was, he had her relate the night's events slowly and thoroughly, coming back to the same points over and over. But she remained adamant on the question of Helena Swann.

"Not again, Detective, please," she said at last. "I feel that you're pressuring me. I've told you and told you Mrs. Swann never came out of her room. I would have seen her."

Before leaving the Styles mansion, Bennett called a technician in from Metro Division to shoot a video with him.

CHAPTER 32

Two days after Brad Styles died, Boyle picked up the Chitworths at San Francisco International. It was late by the time they wrangled the baggage out of the car and checked in at the hotel. He stayed with the bellhop and the luggage cart, delivering first to Mrs. Chitworth, who asked him to call her in the morning at seven.

When he dropped into Ivan's suite next door, Boyle could see Sam through the bedroom doorway. He was already asleep. Ivan asked the bellhop to put his large bag on the foldout stand and everything else in the far corner of the sitting room. He thrust a few bucks at the man, who thanked him and left.

Before leaving, Boyle spoke up. "If there's nothing more, I'll say goodnight."

Ivan wiped a hand over his tired face and forced a smile.

"Let me see," he said. "I'll need you to baby-sit tomorrow, if you'd do that for us. We don't think Sam is ready for a wake and funeral."

"Be glad to. The newspapers said it would be private. Does that mean just family?"

"It means you need to be invited. My mother talked to Angela briefly, and she got the impression it won't be a small affair. I'm willing to bet there'll be a crush from San Francisco society and the business world. Brad and Angela know vast numbers of people."

"So you and your mother will have a busy two days. She asked me to give her a wake-up call at seven tomorrow morning. Want me to call you too?"

"Uh, sure. Why don't you have breakfast with us? I need to get you acquainted with Sam. You'll be seeing a lot of each other for the next two days."

~~~

At 9:00 a.m., a car was waiting to bring Ivan and Claudia to the Styles mansion. Before leaving, they conferred with Boyle in Ivan's sitting room while Sam watched the cartoon channel in the bedroom. Once again, Boyle tried to point out the difficulty of investigating further.

"I need your help to keep this going, folks. Justin's shrink will never talk to me without permission from Mrs. Styles. There is *no way* to get more information unless I can talk to people."

"I despise that word 'shrink,' Mr. Boyle," said Mrs. Chitworth, her voice cresting high on 'shrink'.

She hadn't contributed to their discussion until that moment. He supposed he could have been more diplomatic, but what did these people want – the answers they claimed to be looking for ... or something else?

"Sorry, ma'am," Boyle said, deciding on a different tack. "Do either of you know his tutor?"

"No," said Ivan, "but Esther Jarndyce knows Mr. Danzig. And she has the week off, I understand. Right, mother?"

"Yes, she was so upset after the police interviews, Angela told her to take time off."

"She's the housekeeper, Boyle. Would it help to speak to her?"

"Yes, I think so. Can you be straightforward with her

about the kinds of questions I'll have to ask?"

"Maybe we can tell her you're looking into Justin's behavior, that we have some concerns. Mother, you know her awfully well. Could you call and ask her not to say anything to Angela about this?"

"I'll do it if that will help."

"If she knows Danzig," said Boyle, "will I be able to get to him through her?"

"I just can't say," said Mrs. Chitworth. "But you may talk to her about Mr. Danzig and ask what she thinks about his relationship with Justin."

They left it at that. Boyle was irritated at their lack of clarity and figured he might have to follow the case where it led. Forget about the Chitworths' fine sensibilities. Otherwise, nothing was going to happen.

At least he and Sam were getting along great. Ivan had introduced them earlier at breakfast and they were practically old buddies now. The boy seemed very bright and was curious about his babysitter.

"Do you live here, Mr. Boyle?" he asked when they were alone.

"Just call me Staff, Sam. You mean do I live in San Francisco?"

"No, do you live in this hotel?"

He laughed. "No Sam, I'm here because your aunt and uncle asked me to help them out while the three of you are in San Francisco."

"They're not really my aunt and uncle, but I call them that."

"I see. Your mother brought you to live with Ivan and Mrs. Chitworth, didn't she?"

"That's right. We came from Alabama, where my great grandparents live. My mother died two years ago."

"You must miss her, Sam."

"Yes. She was very pretty."

"I'll bet she was."

"Will we stay here in San Francisco a long time, Mr. Boyle?"

"I don't know, Sam," he said.

The boy stared intently, then looked away. He had done that several times this morning. Boyle judged him a little anxious. Did he have an inkling that his future was in question? Well, that would do it. He was only seven years old, after all, and had already lost his mother. Add that to being shuttled around cross-country, adjusting to different lives with different people, and what you had was less than a recipe for trust and security.

Hoping to make him feel at ease, Boyle took his hand and told him they would be together all day and he wanted him to stay real close. A shy smile spread across Sam's face.

A little sightseeing wouldn't hurt, Boyle figured. Now he hadn't the least idea what a seven-year-old would want to do in a big city, but he'd try to convey his own enthusiasm for the things he'd like to see again after so many years.

They scrambled onto a Powell/Hyde cable car at the Market Street turntable, getting seats on an outside-facing bench. Fisherman's Wharf lay at the end of the route. Boyle pointed out landmarks like Union Square along the way.

At the steepest section of Nob Hill, the gripman asked all able-bodied men to get off and push. It was part of his practiced routine for tourists. Sam was thrilled to be part of the bogus crew, jumping off and leaning hard into the rear of the car for a few seconds before being called back on board as they cleared the hilltop and headed downhill. Boyle was glad he took a camera along. His first shot caught the Fairmont Hotel for a backdrop while Sam pushed along with the cable car crew.

As they approached Fisherman's Wharf, the boy stood to get a better look at something a passenger was pointing to in the bay.

"What's that island, Staff?" he asked.

"That's Alcatraz, Sam. Ever hear of it?"

"I think so. Is it a prison?"

"It was. A famous one. It's been closed a long time. Would you like to go there?"

"Can we do that?"

~~~

The line for the Blue and Gold ferry to Alcatraz was monstrous long. But it didn't dampen Sam's sense of anticipation. If the boy was keyed up, that was all right – Boyle could enjoy the tourist thing through Sam's eyes even more than through his own.

Their whole day was captured in the snapshots Boyle took. Sam on the ferry. Sam on "Broadway." Sam behind bars. Sam in the shower room. Sam in the prison yard with the water tower as background. The kid crowded close to Boyle after every shot to check the results on the little digital screen.

"You got a scrapbook or a picture album, Sam?"

"There's a scrapbook Maria helps me with. No pictures, though."

"We'll look for an album then. When I get these shots processed, you'll want to organize them somehow."

"They're for me? You don't want them?"

"Well, sure, but they're all of you, Sam."

The kid was ecstatic. Boyle smiled at how easy he was to please.

Back at Fisherman's Wharf after the Alcatraz tour, they looked for a place to eat, finding a Johnny Rockets and piling into a booth for burgers, fries, shakes, and apple pie. The Latino waiter in the paper hat was happy to take the camera and get a shot of them together in the red leatherette booth, heads together and sucking their shakes through red-striped straws.

Boyle brought Sam back to the hotel at five o'clock. Ivan and Claudia wouldn't be able to see him later, he learned. They were exhausted from the crush at the wake.

"Will you pick Sam up in the morning, Boyle?" asked Ivan. "The funeral's tomorrow."

"My pleasure," he said.

CHAPTER 33

The funeral cars had taken the spaces reserved for them along the curb on California Street. Claudia Chitworth looked out from the car window toward the twin belfries of Grace Cathedral. Through the great open doors at the top of the steps, six men in black suits and ties could be seen accompanying Brad's casket in the narthex of the church, ready to advance into the nave. The cathedral's organ groaned like a muted calliope.

So young, she thought, and such a good man. This was a dreadful, dreadful day for her niece. Claudia remembered a happier time when Angela phoned to tell her that she and Brad would marry. How thrilled she had been for her – and how surprised to learn that it was Helena's old beau who would be Angela's second husband.

Six years had passed – years filled with crises, accomplishment, and much love – and now Angela must bury him. Claudia watched her niece get out of the lead car and ascend the cathedral steps with Justin and Brad's tiny mother, Nuala Styles. Before going inside, Angela turned to speak to the boy.

Her face had a kind of tragic glow. It was as if the black dress, the long blond hair and the deeply felt misery conspired to elevate Angela's image beyond its everyday loveliness. Claudia wept at the sight. The catch in her throat became a sob, and Ivan put his arm around her.

"Look how composed Justin is," he said. "What a brave little boy."

Yes, she thought – quiet, calm, and composed. But why would that be? A chill ran through her. Something was very wrong here, something she didn't care to think about. She said nothing to Ivan.

Their driver appeared then and opened the car door for Claudia – just as Angela and Justin stepped through the entrance of the cavernous old church.

PART III

BROTHERHOOD

CHAPTER 34

On the day of the funeral, Boyle feigned interest in showing Sam more of the city, but something weighed on his mind. Sam and he were linked in some way he didn't quite comprehend. He had made a futile effort last night to think it through but hadn't drawn any conclusions.

When he knocked on Ivan's door in the morning, Sam fairly vaulted out of the hotel room.

"Hi, Staff!" he chirped, eyes shining.

Boyle winked and smiled, but delayed his response while Ivan greeted him and said goodbye to Sam.

"Be good for Mr. Boyle, son."

"I will, Ivan, I promise."

"Hey, Tiger, ready for more?" Boyle asked, taking Sam's hand as Ivan closed the door.

"I can't wait. Where we going?"

First they went to Telegraph Hill and checked out the WPA murals inside Coit Tower. Sam was delighted at the details Boyle pointed out, like the thief plying his trade by the newsstand. At the top, in the observation room, he took a picture of Sam on tiptoe, peeking out through one of the arched windows to the city below.

For the boy's sake, he made an effort to recapture the previous day's sense of fun. They toured Ghirardelli Square and Aquatic Park. Later, they went to Pacific Heights and killed time in Lafayette Park. All through the morning, as Boyle took pictures of him, Sam wanted to return the favor. So he showed him how to point, focus and shoot. From then on, every shot of Sam next to a monument or building had to be repeated with Boyle as the subject. Sam would even instruct him solemnly to move right or left as he made a show of composing his scene, much as Boyle had done.

How could he not love it?

Back on Market Street at one o'clock, he figured they had just enough time to tour Mission Dolores before calling it a day. As they walked over to the church, he did his best to explain the significance of the old Spanish missions in California. The last snapshot he took was of Sam in the cemetery gardens. That was a false note, gloomy somehow – he looked forlorn among the flowers and tombstones, standing next to the garden wall. That aside, Boyle hoped he had enjoyed himself.

He pigeonholed Ivan when he brought the boy back to the Junipero Arms.

"May I see you and your mother tonight?" he asked. "It's important."

"Can't it wait until tomorrow, Boyle?"

"Please don't put me off. You've been with Justin and Mrs. Styles for two days, and I need your observations while they're still fresh."

Ivan looked annoyed. "Very well," he sighed. "Will eight o'clock do?"

"Yes, and thanks. See you then."

In his room, he gave his thoughts free range. They had been gathering all day. This was about Sam, and yet it was about him too. Maybe more so. Fact was, every time he looked at Sam, he saw himself.

Why had the boy gotten to him like that? Boyle wasn't a family-oriented guy, so what was all this effort to be the kid's best pal and chief protector? Maybe anybody who babysat for such an appealing child would feel the same. But no, the tightness in his throat told him something else was going on.

For Chrissake, pal, get a grip.

When evening came on, he left his room thinking that a walk around town would serve to get the kinks out and clear his mind. As the elevator car descended to the lobby, he became aware of his reflection in the mirrored panel surrounding the floor buttons. His lips were pursed and his shoulders slumped. Not a healthy picture. He was looking at a guy with a problem, a loser. It came to him that his focus was gone, that his feeling for Sam was getting in his way somehow. In the way of ... what?

Before reaching the hotel's front entrance, Boyle stopped short, causing the bell captain to look his way. He wasn't going out for a walk, he realized, he was going out for a drink. That might not be wise, but screw it – he'd have as many as he wanted. And if he met with Ivan and Claudia after a few too many, maybe they'd fire him and he could leave for home. Home, and Assunta.

He took the revolving door out of the hotel and turned left. The early evening air was cool and damp. Less than a block away, he found the kind of place he was looking for. Outside, it had a classic wood-paneled pub façade with a black and gold lettered sign that said *Virgil*. There were short green velvet drapes on a brass rod that covered just enough of the front windows to give the clientele some privacy.

Boyle pushed through the brass-plated front door to find it quiet inside and nearly empty of customers. When he sat down, the bartender came over and stood in front of him with an expectant smile.

He's not even going to ask what I want, Boyle thought. He admired that. An efficient professional discharging his duties always used the least possible amount of effort.

"Bourbon, straight up," he said, settling in on the upholstered barstool.

"No ice?"

"Separate glass."

Boyle turned on his stool and looked around the room. Low-level lighting, dark colors, paisley wallpaper above the fine wood paneling, and a lofty tin ceiling with recessed lighting. To his left, the doors to the building's lobby opened out, their beveled glass panes picking up light from the chandeliers in the concourse.

"Cash, sir?" asked the bartender, setting the drink and ice down with napkins.

Boyle fished out his wallet and put three twenties in front of him. "Unless you get busy and lose count, stop me after six."

"Certainly, sir. And I won't lose count."

The first drink slid down nicely in three short pulls. After the first mouthful, he flipped an ice cube into the amber liquid. By the time his second drink arrived, he was smiling to himself.

Simple logic underlay his whole predicament, he figured. He was feeling *through* Sam. Boyle was the lonely little boy with the fucked-up life. It was a kind of self-pity every time he looked at the child and wanted to help, to ease his burden. But he had put all that behind him long ago, hadn't he? The loneliness and pain had all been an accident of time and place.

Boyle's mother had died young, too. And when his father became a daily drunk, there were stretches of weeks and months when his young anger was the only emotion he felt. No love, no hope, no comfort. Just anger and the determination to roll everything back. He couldn't remember wanting to leave his father or run away, he just needed his life back.

Where could he go with this? What good did it do to know what he felt? Two things had happened since he came to San Francisco, he thought. The Chitworths proved themselves to be impossible clients, and Sam had showed himself to be a kid worth rooting for.

Ivan and Claudia talked about wanting the best for Sam, but God forbid Boyle should rock the boat while ferreting out information. In the end, he suspected the only solution they would find acceptable was a clean bill of health for Justin Styles. They wanted everything nice so they could dump Sam with a clear conscience.

Well, screw that. Sam was his client now, nobody else. From here on, where he went and who he talked to would be dictated by Sam's interests.

By quarter to eight, he was buzzed. Let's see what ol' Ivan and Claudia are up to, he thought.

"That was number six, sir," said the bartender.

"Yeah, I figured."

He picked up his change, left ten bucks on the bar, took a deep breath, and headed for the door to the street. He'd have to remember this place.

~~~

Whether it was anger Boyle was feeling or just

frustration, it had propelled him out of his chair, made his face go scarlet.

"This is incredible!" he shouted, looking first to Mrs. Chitworth, then to Ivan. "Why were you holding this back?"

"Take it easy, Boyle," said Ivan. "We're telling you now, aren't we?"

Mrs. Chitworth's eyebrows rose in tandem, and she looked him up and down.

"Can't you understand our reluctance to disclose a secret of this nature?" she asked. "I should think you would!"

"With all due respect, ma'am, I'm trying to do the job you hired me for. If the primary concern is Sam's welfare, how can you justify not telling me that Mrs. Styles and Mrs. Swann were involved in a murder case?"

Every feature in Claudia Chitworth's face seemed to sharpen.

"They weren't involved in murder!" she snapped. "They were being blackmailed!"

The three of them had gathered in Ivan's suite shortly after eight. Mrs. Chitworth had just recounted the day's events from her perspective. When she decried the media presence after the funeral service, she let it slip that Brad Styles had kept Helena and Angela's involvement in the Snider case out of the newspapers only with the greatest difficulty.

Boyle's reaction had been swift, but he might have gone too far. Was his anger even logical? After all, clients held back embarrassing information all the time. He supposed the liquor had compromised his ability to keep his temper under control. And maybe that was a blessing. These people needed a push, a poke, a prod. Something.

Ivan was standing also, his face ashen and cocked at an angle. "We appreciate your efforts and even your ... passion for Sam's welfare. But this won't do, Boyle."

"You're right," he said, sitting back down and glancing at Mrs. Chitworth.

"I was out of line and I apologize. To you especially, ma'am. I shouldn't have exploded like that. But I have to make something clear. I told you the newspapers are hinting about an investigation. Can't you see how the Breastplate murder and everything concerning it would have a bearing on that? Murder ... blackmail ... old allegations ... blocking press coverage. What must the police be thinking?"

"But how does this relate to Justin's behavior?" asked Mrs. Chitworth. "That's what you were hired to look into."

"I thought I was looking into the suitability of Sam's living in that household."

"Why, I don't believe it!" she said, lifting her chin and flinging her hands up. "You're questioning the appropriateness of my niece's ... *home*?"

All three fell silent. Boyle glanced toward the door to Ivan and Sam's bedroom, which was closed. He hoped the boy hadn't been listening. Ivan must have had a similar thought, because he walked to the door and opened it. A blare of television noise escaped.

"Everything all right, Sam?"

"Yes, Ivan."

"That's good. We'll be done here soon."

Ivan eased the door shut and took his seat again. The silence resumed. Boyle looked at his watch. Eight thirty-five. He thought it best to forge ahead and cover every topic he could think of.

"If you'll bear with me a few more minutes, we can get through my questions and I'll be able to get started early tomorrow ... unless you've had enough of me."

Mrs. Chitworth stared at him, disapproval in her eyes. "I'm going to my room, Ivan," she said. "You gentlemen will settle this, I'm sure. I am simply too upset to continue. Good *night*, Mr. Boyle."

He said nothing as she stood, spoke to Ivan, and left through the door to her adjoining suite. Ivan turned to him as the door closed.

"Are you drunk, Boyle, or just pathologically stupid!"

"Don't, man. Don't even start down that road. I may be a little buzzed, but we had to have this out. I can't think of anybody, anywhere I'd rather help than Sam. He's one hell of a nice kid, and he deserves the best. But how can I do anything for him while you and your mother keep holding back on me? '*Don't interview that one, Boyle. Don't fuss about a little old murder, Boyle. Don't make waves.*' It won't work."

"It's not that simple, and it doesn't help matters when you mis-characterize our instructions."

"Mis-characterize ...? Listen, Ivan, where are we going with this? I'm on your dime, man, and I intend to give value. Fire me if you want less than my best. Please."

Ivan exhaled and spoke through clenched teeth.

"When you took this job, you knew we were relying on your discretion. Assure me of that now, and you can go off in any direction you want. Talk to anybody you can reach, whatever."

"That's it. That's what I need."

"But know this, Boyle. You can't reach Angela Styles. We can't help you with that. And if she finds out we hired a private investigator, you will not have been discreet – you'll have destroyed a close family relationship. Do you know what I mean by discretion now?"

"All right. That makes it tough, but it's clear. I understand what you're saying."

"Good. You get to do things your way now, but don't disappoint us."

"I'll try not to."

"I repeat: *Don't disappoint us*. Now what do you need from me?"

"First, tell me about Mrs. Styles and Justin. You've seen a lot of them during the past two days. Give me your observations."

"I barely know what to say. Angela is grieving, as you'd expect. It's heartbreaking to watch. At the same time, she's tending to Justin very dutifully."

"And Justin?"

"Justin is very quiet. Self-contained, I'd say. He's very brave about this, watches his mother constantly."

"Does he cry, does he seem upset when his mother cries?"

"I ... no, I can't say he does. Maybe we have to remember that Brad wasn't his father."

"Pardon me, but I thought Brad Styles was the only father he ever knew."

Ivan got up and began to pace. "Yes, that's true," he said.

"And you don't think Justin's ... lack of emotion is

troubling?"

"I can't say. I didn't look at it that way. How can I judge him?"

"You're raising a little boy who's the same age, Ivan."

"They're nothing alike, I can say that."

"Then tell me how they're different."

"Let me take that back, they have two things in common. They *look* very much alike, except that Sam is blond and Justin has dark hair. And they're both very intelligent."

"I thought you'd say they're both shy."

"Well, I might have, but the quality of their shyness ... I don't quite know how to put it. It seems to me Justin is more aloof than shy, he keeps to himself because he likes his own company best. Sam is shy with strangers, yes, but he's gregarious with friends, and he warms up to most anyone who takes an interest in him. But this makes me uncomfortable, Boyle, analyzing seven-year-old boys."

"It seems to me your observation about Sam was perfectly accurate. And you said nothing bad about Justin."

"I suppose, but I made him sound like a robot. I just don't know him well enough to say much. And I'm sensitive to young children being stereotyped. That happened to me as a kid, and it wasn't pleasant."

Boyle wanted to acknowledge Ivan's admission, but he wasn't sure he even cared. Instead, he stayed on course.

"Well, it helps me to get a sense of his personality before I talk to the housekeeper and the tutor."

"By the way, Boyle, Danzig doesn't tutor Justin anymore. He resigned."

"What happened?"

"Sorry, I just know he's gone. You also need to know Angela insisted we stay with her as long as we're in San Francisco. We're checking out of here tomorrow."

"From my point of view, that's great. Sooner or later, I need to get into that house."

Ivan raised his head and stared at him wide-eyed.

"You do?" he asked.

CHAPTER 35

When he had learned as much as Ivan knew about Angela and Helena's involvement with the Breastplate case, Boyle began to think about motives. If foul play were involved in Brad Styles's death, there would be a motive somewhere. Could it lay close to home? Did it have anything to do with Jake Snider and the reason he tried to blackmail Angela Styles?

Although he didn't intend to mess with a police investigation, it could happen inadvertently. He hoped to avoid that by staying behind the cops. They had already interviewed Esther Jarndyce and probably Gunther Danzig as well. And with Ivan and Mrs. Chitworth staying in the Marina district mansion, Boyle should hear of any continuing interest by the police.

For the moment, he saw no problem in moving ahead. The only danger lay in some action of his being reported back to Angela Styles. That would violate his understanding with Ivan and screw up any chance he had to help Sam.

The bald truth was his investigation had just gone beyond determining the mental condition of Justin Styles. What he was also looking into was whether or not Brad Styles was a murder victim. If that seemed far-fetched, so be it. His objective now was to protect Sam Dunnell's interests. If danger was lurking in the Styles mansion, he intended to flush it out.

More and more, Ivan's definition of discretion was coming clear to him. His promise not to intrude on Angela

Styles meant he could not expect direct access to either Justin or his shrink. Which was why he insisted on gaining access to the mansion. Even though Ivan didn't like it, he'd have to help Boyle find a way to observe Justin first hand. It might be as simple as chaperoning both boys some day. But he'd need some pretext to make it credible, a role in Ivan and Claudia's life.

"We'll need a driver some days," Ivan said, "especially for my mother. How about chauffeur?"

"I can't see that. Chauffeurs wait outside. Why don't you tell everyone I'm a friend of yours who's staying in San Francisco? That's close to the truth – and it's what Sam believes. A cover like that, you can have me over without much explanation."

"Very well. I guess I'd buy it."

"Please make sure your mother buys it too."

Ivan laughed. "I'll do my best, but don't expect miracles. As you know, you're in her bad books."

Bad books, thought Boyle. Sometimes these people talked like characters in a Victorian novel.

~~~

Like Newport, much of San Francisco looked like a scene out of that same Victorian novel. Esther Jarndyce's apartment building in the Richmond district was a case in point. It was off Geary in the inner Richmond, and Esther had lived there for years. Modest, stuccoed, and well kept, it rose three stories, each of which had bay windows in front. Even though her apartment was tiny, she probably couldn't have afforded it without rent control.

She greeted Boyle with the formal politeness of people long in service to the rich.

"So pleased to meet you, Mr. Boyle. Won't you come in?

Mild voice, quiet manner, demure and decorous presence. Boyle was disposed to like her, whether or not she would be of use to him.

"Glad to meet you, Miss Jarndyce. I hope I'm not keeping you from anything."

"No, no. I was about to make coffee. Would you like some?"

"Yes, thanks."

Before long they settled into armchairs in the bay window alcove. Miss Jarndyce had arranged a plate of homemade cookies and a coffee service between them on a mahogany piecrust table.

Boyle sipped his coffee and turned to her. "I hope I can speak freely with you, Miss Jarndyce. I asked Mrs. Chitworth to tell you the sort of questions I would ask."

"Yes, we spoke."

"Then you know I'm here to protect Sam Dunnell. Whatever I ask, my goal is just that."

"Ask your questions, Mr. Boyle."

"How long has Justin been in treatment with Dr. LaFreniere?"

"Two months, I believe."

"Are you close to the boy?"

"There was a time when he was like my own."

"And now?"

"Children grow out of certain early attachments," she said. "I was a big factor in his first three years. Not so much since then."

She continued with a timorous gesture and a nervous laugh. "As soon as he realized I was the housekeeper – a glorified maid, really – he began to treat me accordingly."

"How would you characterize his behavior at home?"

"Justin can be utterly charming and affectionate. But he has a stubborn and willful side I'm sure you've heard about. One thing I might stress is that nothing escapes him. Justin is the most observant child I've ever known."

"Could you give me an example?"

"Well, he's a natural mimic. If he were to meet you today, he would pick up any mannerisms and speech patterns out of the ordinary. When he goes to a restaurant, he comes back home imitating the waiters and customers."

"Did Mr. or Mrs. Styles ever mention the reason Justin is seeing a psychiatrist?"

"No. Except that Justin told me himself, I wouldn't even have known Dr. LaFreniere was a psychiatrist."

"What did he say, exactly?"

She smiled. "As far as I can remember, he said he wasn't crazy, he just needed to understand himself."

Boyle smiled too. Just like a kid, he thought – most likely parroting something he heard.

"Miss Jarndyce, can you think of anything else I should know?"

"Well ... no, not really."

He thought she had been honest so far, but he could see she wasn't about to volunteer anything. "Does Justin have friends?" he asked.

"Well, he's home schooled, so ... "

"There are no other children in his life?"

"Not now, I think. Mrs. Styles had arranged for him to play with the children of friends, but that seems to have stopped."

"Do you know why?"

"No, I don't. I would never ask about a thing like that."

"What's your opinion of Justin's tutor?"

"Mr. Danzig is a lovely man. I like him very much"

"Do he and Justin get on well?"

"Generally, yes, I think. But I know Mr. Danzig is unhappy with Justin's schoolwork lately."

"Ivan Chitworth told me last night that Danzig resigned."

"Oh, that's too bad. I didn't know. I'll miss seeing him."

Boyle turned his head and looked out through the bay window a moment to the quiet street below. Miss Jarndyce was a charming old lady, he thought, but he was wasting his time. He already knew that Justin was a difficult kid in some respects. And so what?

He drank the last of his coffee and set the cup in its saucer. "Miss Jarndyce, I don't mean to upset you, but I want to ask some questions about what happened the night Brad Styles died."

"Oh?" She leaned back in her chair and crossed her arms.

"I hope you don't mind. Naturally, the Chitworths have told me what they know."

"Then why ...?

"Your testimony is first-hand. It might help me."

Esther Jarndyce tucked a stray lock of gray hair behind her ear. Her face told Boyle she hadn't expected this.

"Mr. Boyle, you don't know what I've been through. The police questioned me for hours, asking about the same things over and over. I was frightened. They made me feel I wasn't telling it right."

"I promise you that won't happen here. If you'll tell me what you remember, I'll just listen."

"Well . . ."

"No pressure, Miss Jarndyce. Whenever you're ready."

She sighed and stared straight ahead. "I was in the kitchen ... preparing tea to bring to Mrs. Swann. There was a voice somewhere, a shout ... then a noise, a loud thud. I wasn't alarmed, but I went to see what happened. I walked through the dining room ... towards the entrance. I thought someone might be coming home ... but no, everyone was in for the night.

"When I was a few steps into the foyer, I turned and saw Mr. Styles ... lying at the foot of the stairway to the second floor. His head had struck the marble tile ... blood was coming from his mouth. I felt dizzy, very dizzy. His body was mostly on the stairs ... twisted somehow. I took a few steps toward him ... I wanted to help. But I fell to my knees and thought I would pass out.

"I heard a door open upstairs ... well, just the squeak of a door – the hinge, you know. And I saw the toy on the stairs ... a little truck of Justin's. Later, they said Mr. Styles must have tripped over it.

"I think I shouted then, because Mrs. Styles came rushing downstairs. She went to him. I remember her calling his name, cradling him, moving him off the stairs so she could ... you know ... give him mouth-to-mouth resuscitation. I had recovered a little ... said I would call an ambulance. She turned to me and said: 'Yes, please call.' Her mouth and chin were covered in his blood ... that *awful* image, I see it still."

She was dabbing at her eyes with a handkerchief. Boyle

felt lousy knowing he had to question her further.

"I'm sorry to put you through that again, Miss Jarndyce. I can only imagine what it was like. But why do you think the police questioned you so extensively? It's obvious that Mr. Styles tripped and fell. What made them hound you about it?"

She looked at him. "I don't know. There was something bothering me, but I didn't tell them."

"What was that?"

"The toy truck."

"What about it?"

"Justin never leaves his things out."

"Oh, but Miss Jarndyce ...."

"Never," she said, clear-eyed and emphatic. "Not once in seven years."

She wasn't saying Justin did something, he realized. She was saying it didn't fit. And he believed her. But if she didn't tell the cops, what did *they* see that wasn't right? Why were they so persistent with her?

He was ready to excuse himself when he thought of a final question. "Miss Jarndyce, did you know Sam's and Justin's father?"

Her face tightened. "His biological father? I suppose you could say I knew him. Why do you ask?"

"No particular reason. It just occurred to me that I've always thought of him in a certain way, as a very evil man. But he couldn't have seemed that way to Mrs. Styles or to others in the household. To you, for instance."

She looked at him a moment, her eyes somehow fearful. "Sam Porter could be ... utterly charming," she said.

~~~

Gunther Danzig lived on Grove Street in Alamo Square. Boyle knew that was in the Western addition, not far from downtown. He called the tutor from Miss Jarndyce's apartment and arranged to meet him at one o'clock.

The dashboard clock said ten minutes to one as Boyle drove by the polychrome Victorian houses on the downside slope of Steiner Street. Alamo Square Park was to his left. Grove Street would be on the right, just past the "painted ladies," a standard feature in every guidebook to the city.

Danzig's place was a condo conversion on the second floor of what had been a two-family house. When the door opened, Boyle smelled something pungent that he couldn't quite place. Danzig smiled and gestured him in. He was in the middle of organizing stacks of old records.

"Sorry for the disorder, Mr. Boyle. I am taking advantage of time off to box these papers and send them to storage. It's amazing, is it not, how the paperwork gets ahead of one?"

"I can sympathize. I have file cabinets at home that need the same treatment."

"Well, I need to take ... the break now. We will sit in the living room – right through there. Will you have a beer?"

His offer had some heavy German ale written all over it, so Boyle declined, asking for ice water instead. While waiting, the smell came back to him. It was a cleaning product of some kind. Murphy's oil soap, he thought. A friend once referred to it as the German national scent.

When Danzig came back to the living room, the beer turned out to be Miller Lite. Boyle guessed this was one German who had been in the United States a very long time.

"Oh yes. Very long, indeed. Since 1976. Opportunities

here were so much better for me than in Germany. I go back from time to time, but this is home now, and I love my work."

He said 'luff' for love, and Boyle smiled.

"Yes, thirty years – and still I have the accent."

"But ... I didn't say . . ."

Danzig grinned. "Don't explain. I see the smile and I know. I have spoken English since I was young, but my teachers were German. They had the accent too!"

Boyle relaxed. This guy was okay. When he had drunk the ice water, Danzig looked at the empty glass.

"A beer now, perhaps?" he asked.

"Why yes," he laughed. "A beer would be great."

At first, Boyle suspected the interview would be unprofitable. Danzig idolized Angela Styles and thought that Brad Styles was a fine man. Moreover, he praised Justin's intelligence and academic potential.

"It sounds like a perfect position for you. Why did you leave?"

"My official reason had to do with Justin's progress. I thought someone else should take over. After an extraordinary first year, Justin was actually regressing, in my opinion."

"Unh-huh. Was there an *unofficial* reason?"

Danzig's clear blue eyes locked onto his. "Yes. I had grown to dislike the child. I found his attitude ... hateful. An awful word to describe a seven-year old boy, yes?"

Stafford Boyle felt the hair on his arms rise up.

"Well, yeah. I've heard Justin described as difficult and moody at times, but ... hateful is pretty strong. Did something happen?"

"There was no one thing. Over time Justin began to show contempt for me, and for others as well."

"Others?"

"Most authority figures, Mr. Styles included."

"I see. What about his mother?"

"No contempt, no, Justin loves his mother. But there have been strains, I believe, on account of his behavior."

"How does he relate to Mrs. Swann?"

"Oh, they are very close. Especially, I think, since Justin began seeing the psychiatrist."

"Was a diagnosis ever discussed with you?"

"No. I think if Mrs. Styles shared that, I might have ... accommodated her, adjusted to the situation."

"When exactly did you resign?"

"It was the day of Mr. Styles's death. I told Mrs. Styles in the morning. She was upset, I could tell, but she did not argue. Mr. Styles met with me in the afternoon to see if I wouldn't change my mind. I was to finish out the week, but after his accident ... I haven't been back."

"Have the police spoken to you?"

"Yes, a Sergeant Bennett. He seemed most interested in the condition of the balcony."

"What about the balcony?"

"You don't know? The support poles under the handrail ... balusters, I believe you call them ... were undercut along the balcony where it overlooks the foyer. Partially undercut, on the outside edge. I discovered it purely by chance. It was repaired just a few days ago. A very dangerous thing. Any undue pressure and someone might have fallen through."

"Were the cuts fresh? Could it have been done a long time ago?"

Danzig shrugged. "I can't say."

~~~

A strange little boy; a toy truck left on the stairs; a balcony with the balusters undercut. But the boy in question never, ever leaves his things about. And a sabotaged handrail seemed beyond the capacity of a seven-year-old – it takes experience to undercut a row of balusters so the damage isn't obvious. No matter who was involved, had there been a preliminary plan to kill Brad Styles, one that had to be abandoned? Was the toy on the staircase a second, successful attempt?

As he pondered, Boyle handed the car keys from his rental to the valet at the Junipero Arms and started for the front entrance. Just before going inside, he veered off to the right when he thought of the bar ... *Virgil.* Virgil was Dante's guide in hell, wasn't he? Well, he could use a guide – shit, even a signpost would do.

Eddie, the bartender, remembered him. He poured two fingers of Jim Beam into an Old Fashioned glass and served it with a tumbler of ice. Boyle settled in. There were just enough customers, just enough murmuring voices, and just enough quiet music to fill up the spaces in the conversation he was having with himself.

Would the cops have a case by now? They had everything he had – and more, probably. Besides talking to Jarndyce and Danzig, they would have spoken to Angela Styles, Helena Swann and ... even Justin, perhaps. And they would certainly have inspected the scene thoroughly. If Mrs. Styles had granted the police an interview with Justin, would that have led to the shrink? And if so, would she permit them to question him?

So many wonderful questions, all in all. And every one of them subject to the Chitworth taboo – Thou shalt not be indiscreet. Would it be less than discreet, he wondered, to talk to a benefactor of the Styles family – someone especially helpful to Angela Styles and Helena Swann? A benefactor who had been through two scandals with them and helped to cover up a certain blackmail attempt just before Brad died? At least that's what Ivan told him about Mickey Cullion.

Virgil had done its job, with the help of Jim Beam. Guided him right out of hell and into the dark heart of *Shoo-fly*, the definitive San Francisco scandal. Would he like it any better there? He left ten bucks on the bar, waved goodbye to Eddie, and took a long walk through downtown.

CHAPTER 36

When they were introduced that morning, Sam tried to remember everything Aunt Claudia told him about Justin. The only thing that came back to him, though, was – half-brother. Their mothers were different, their father the same. The father who died before either of them was born.

"Justin, would you like to take Sam up to your room?" Aunt Angela asked when the adults were settled in the living room. "You may play there if you wish."

"Sure, mommy," he said, revealing deep dimples with his smile.

First, Justin showed Sam around the house. They went through the kitchen, the library, and out to the terrace where they looked at the bay. Upstairs, he introduced him to his Aunt Helena, the lady in the wheelchair. When they entered her room, she acted pleased to meet him.

"Come close, Sam, and let me look at you. Have you boys any idea how much alike you are?" she asked, glancing at each of them in turn.

They shook their heads, then looked at each other doubtfully. She laughed at them.

"Sam," she said, "I want you to call me Aunt Helena. Will you do that?"

"Yes ma'am," he replied.

She ruffled his hair and held his face in her hand a second. She smelled good to him, almost like a garden. Then she went off to join the adults downstairs.

When Helena had gone some distance along the corridor, Sam turned to Justin. "How will she get down there?" he asked.

"There's an elevator for her. I'll show you later, but I'm not supposed to use it."

Justin's room was on the other end of the corridor, just off the balcony. It was a big room. His bed was big too, and he had a desk, a bookcase, and a library table of bird's eye maple with four painted chairs around it.

But it was Justin's closet that floored Sam. It was a whole room by itself. On one side were clothes, shoes, and bedclothes all neatly hung, stacked, and folded. There were shelves and containers, chests for underwear and socks, a floor rack for shoes and sneakers, and a long pole across the top divided into sections for suits, shirts, jeans and slacks, jackets and coats. Sam thought Justin had ten times as many clothes as he did.

The other side of the closet looked like an aisle in Toys 'R' Us. The floor-to-ceiling shelving held trucks and helicopters, model cars, board games, musical instruments, action figures, rocket ships and space platforms ... just everything you could imagine.

Sam giggled and stared. "I used to think I had a lot of stuff, Justin. And you can see everything here ... mine is all jammed in my toy chest."

Sam found himself admiring Justin more and more. He thought he must be very smart. They were in the same grade, but Justin had extra lessons. Maybe that was what the special tutor was all about.

"Do you take American history in Newport, Sam?"

"No. It's mostly reading stories, writing practice, and

arithmetic. I take French."

"Bonjour, Sam!"

"Bonjour, Justin. Comment allez-vous?"

"Très bien, merci. You're really supposed to say, 'Comment vas-tu?' because we're both kids."

"Oh."

"History is my favorite subject. Mr. Danzig knew a lot about American history, even though he's German. He said regular schools don't teach it until eighth grade."

Sam couldn't imagine he'd be studying history any time soon. Not that it mattered to him. He liked his school in Newport, and the things he was learning were plenty for him. He sure wouldn't want to spend time on extra stuff.

After they had picked out toys and played for a while, Justin sat back on the floor and watched Sam with the helicopter. For a moment, Sam wondered if he were doing something wrong.

"What?" he said, looking back at Justin.

"Nothing. Everybody says we look alike, but I'm not so sure."

"I don't think we do. Look how different our hair is."

"Once my Aunt Helena said I have the exact same hair as my father. But I think she was sorry she told me."

"Why?"

"Because I started asking questions, and her face turned red. She wouldn't say more."

When Sam tried to think of his parents, only his mother came to mind. His father was a blank. "Well, what did you ask her?"

"If he was a bad man."

Sam stopped playing with the helicopter and sat back

on his heels. Should he tell Justin the things he knew?

"I was named after him," he said finally.

"I thought so. Is your name Samson?"

"No, just Sam."

"His name was Samson Porter."

He didn't know that. There was a lot he didn't know and a lot he couldn't figure out.

"I heard my Aunt Claudia talking to Ivan one day. She said he was a terrible man. I think she hated him."

Justin nodded like he understood. "I saw a picture once when my mother was getting rid of stuff. I figured it was him by the way he had his arm around her. She said it was just an old friend. But I'm sure it was him."

"What did he look like?" asked Sam.

"He was tall and he looked real strong. He had dark hair like me."

"My mother was blond, like me. She looked a lot like your mom."

"What happened to her?"

"She died when I was five. She was real sick when she took me to Newport. She wanted me to grow up with Ivan and Aunt Claudia."

"Know something?"

"What?"

"Some people didn't like our real dad, but I bet he wasn't bad like they say. I saw a movie once where the guy everybody thought was bad turned out to be the hero because he wasn't afraid of anything."

Sam couldn't figure it one way or the other. Aunt Claudia never lied, but that didn't mean she was always right. That boy, though, the one in the dream he had? The boy was afraid of some man.

"There was a bad man in a dream I had, Justin," he said.

When there was no reply, Sam looked over to find his brother staring at him.

"Do you dream a lot, Sam?" Justin asked in a quiet voice.

"I guess so."

"I don't tell my dreams to anybody – not anymore. Not even to Doctor LaFreniere."

Both boys fell silent. Justin stepped over to the table and sat down. Sam waited, knowing somehow that Justin would speak first.

"But you're my brother, Sam. I guess I could tell you."

He was right, Sam thought. They were brothers and they could share their dreams.

CHAPTER 37

Shonda Wallace hated to answer her phone at work. With so many clients and so much going on in the Public Defender's office, she found it impossible to concentrate there. When asked for her number at work, she gave out her personal cell phone number instead, finding it convenient to divert her callers to voice mail and get back to them in quiet moments outside the office.

That's why the jangling sound of the landline extension startled her. It was early morning. She was at her desk, filling out her monthly mileage expense report. The caller identified himself as Stafford Boyle, and he wanted to talk about Michael Cullion. At first, she thought she was speaking to an old line San Franciscan – the accent was similar. But he was from New England.

"Now why would a P.I. from Newport, Rhode Island be interested in Michael Cullion?" she asked.

"My clients are from Newport. They're related to Angela Styles and Helena Swann."

Shonda remembered a certain name from her research into the old Shoo-fly case. She came across it again two days ago in a newspaper story about Brad Styles's funeral.

"Are you saying the *Chitworths* want something from my client?" she asked.

"Very good, Ms. Wallace," he laughed. "The reason for my investigation is confidential, of course, but I can tell you my clients have no interest in Mickey Cullion. They hired me on a personal matter. Still, I think it would help me out if I understood the Breastplate case from Cullion's perspective. Especially his relationship with the Sharples girls. That's what you call them around here, isn't it?"

"M-m-m, yeah, that was their maiden name. Frankly though, I don't see why Michael should speak to anyone associated with that family. He's being held pending trial, I'm sure you know that. Do you have something to offer us?"

"I can't say for sure. But I think you and I are in a similar bind. I hear that Cullion hasn't been as open with you as he should be. I also hear some pressure came your way to help keep Angela Styles and Helena Swann out of the spotlight."

"That may or may not describe my situation. But ... so what?"

"The Chitworths aren't very good clients either," he said. "Because of that, and for reasons I won't get into, I've decided to look into Brad Styles's death. Which gives you something that could put me between a rock and a hard place."

"The rock being your clients, and the hard place ... the SFPD, maybe?"

"We begin to understand each other."

"Well, you interest me, Mr. Boyle. But I don't see how it signifies. The 'powers that be' came down on me – like you said. But that in itself gives me some leverage to help Michael now."

"Maybe I could give you insurance on that."

"How so?"

"If you encourage him to speak freely to me about his relationships with Sam Porter, the Sharples girls, and Brad Styles, I believe I can tell you what Jake Snider had on

Helena Swann."

Shonda fell quiet. She had been hunched over the telephone, hand over ear, blocking out the office noise. Now she sat back in her chair and let all the chatter, door closings and office machine sounds wash over her.

"Hello. Ms. Wallace, you there?"

"I'll have to be there," she said.

"What?"

"I'll have to be there when you meet with Michael."

~ ~ ~

When the guard escorted Boyle into the room, Shonda Wallace and Cullion were already there, sitting on one side of a beat up table with a bible between them. As they looked up, Cullion's right index finger was still pointing to a verse in the open book. Boyle took a chair across from them. Cullion closed the bible and handed it to Shonda, who placed it in her briefcase.

Boyle spoke first: "Nice to see you Ms. Wallace. And you, Mickey."

"The name's Michael," he said, his smile fading.

"Sorry," he apologized. "The newspaper stories ...."

"Yeah, I know. 'Mickey' sounds better to those coyotes."

Shonda Wallace spoke up. "I have to tell you something up front, Mr. Boyle. Michael sees no good reason to talk to you about the Breastplate or the people involved in the case."

She was trying to tell him something, he thought. But what? He couldn't read her expression. Boyle took his time glancing from her to Cullion and back.

"Well, then ... what am I doing here?" he asked.

"I had already promised you an interview, so Michael

agreed to meet and hear you out. You'll just have to convince him you mean no harm to Angela Styles or her family before he'll discuss anything."

He couldn't imagine why Cullion should care about anyone in that family, but there it was. Shonda was letting him know that her client wasn't looking out for his own interests, and he'd have to play it accordingly. Well, when had anything been easy or straightforward in this case? The stickier things got, the more the truth looked like his only alternative.

"Look, I have to think Ms. Wallace has told you everything I told her – except maybe one thing. Let's start with that."

Shonda reacted quickly, tucking her chin in and starting up from the table.

"This interview is over! Michael ...."

Cullion's eyes had grown wide and the corners of his mouth turned up. He put his left hand up to her in a wait-a-minute gesture.

"Looks like the man got my attention," he said. "Let's hear him out."

Shonda Wallace had a helluva glare. Boyle felt its burn even as he tried to ignore it.

"I know Jake Snider made an accusation in his blackmail note about Helena Swann being accessory in the Wanda Buckley murder. And I know about Brad and Angela Styles's dealings with Pedro Brunetti. I know it because my client knows it – and neither of us is interested in making this stuff public. Ms. Wallace here can verify that."

Shonda sighed and crossed her arms. "What he's not telling you, Michael, is that his clients are related to Angela and Helena. They're the Chitworths from Rhode Island."

"All I'm trying to do is help them protect a young boy," he said, "and to do what's best for him. There's no danger of my spilling the secret. But I don't have access to Angela Styles or Helena Swann, so I have to tease out information the best way I can. That's what I'm doing here."

Cullion looked curious. "What do you think I can tell you?" he asked.

"Like Ms. Wallace said, I need a better understanding of the Breastplate case and everybody involved. I can't prove anything, but I'm afraid that Brad Styles was murdered. If I'm right, a whole houseful of people may still be at risk."

They probably thought his major concern was Justin Styles. At least, that was the misdirection he tried to lay down. Something in Cullion's sad brown eyes told Boyle he was ready to talk.

Shonda, on the other hand, had stepped back into neutrality – she merely watched her client and waited. She was smart enough to realize Boyle had already given her exactly what she needed. Knowing what was in the blackmail letter put plenty of leverage in her hands. She could cut the best possible deal now on Cullion's sentence without half trying.

"All right, Boyle, I'll talk about the Breastplate," he said. "But what you're looking for starts even further back ... when Sam Porter met Helena Swann."

~~~

An hour later, Boyle and Shonda Wallace found themselves in the visitor parking lot, squinting at each other under a glaring sun. She cocked her head to one side and nodded to him.

"For a minute there, I thought I was going to have to kill you."

"Nah," he said. "Too damn hard to get rid of the body."

"Right. That's what stopped me."

Boyle grinned at her, then shook his head slowly. He was trying to work his mind around the implications of Cullion's long narrative.

"Helluva of story, Ms. Wallace. You already knew it?"

"Not even half of it. Michael has been trying to put this stuff behind him for a long time. I think you struck a chord when you said your job was to protect that little boy."

"If you don't mind, I still have one question for you."

"What's that?"

"The bible. What were you two looking at when I came in?"

A low chuckle rumbled up from her chest.

"It was a verse from Isaiah," she said. "It goes, '*He hath sent me to bind up the broken-hearted, to proclaim liberty to the captives, and the opening of the prison to them that are bound.*' Maybe Michael can believe that now."

"Do you have a verse for me, Shonda Wallace?"

"You're sure you want one, Boyle? I don't kid about that stuff."

"I'm desperate. I'll listen."

"Then try this from Proverbs: '*Surely in vain the net is spread in the sight of the bird.*' "

Boyle could only stare and frown while she smirked at him, then turned and walked away to find her car.

CHAPTER 38

The wrought-iron gates were open as Boyle pulled into
the circular drive of Angela Styles's home. Pushing the
car door shut behind him, he blinked up at the rambling
Mediterranean style villa and thought of Norma Desmond's
spooky old mansion in *Sunset Boulevard*. Except that this
one wasn't spooky, just kind of overwhelming, and he was
sure there'd be no Joe Gillis floating face down and bug-
eyed in the pool out back.

No, the Styles family was subtler than that, he said to
himself. There would be nothing obviously wrong, no
creepy butler to answer the bell and no blast of lugubrious
organ music as the door opened to admit him. He'd have to
make do with the hint of menace that had come to invade
his sense of the case.

This dark mood of his was the result of Mickey Cullion's
narrative, he figured. The whole epic of Shoo-fly – and the
Breastplate – had a depressing inevitability to it, a kind of
forward motion that hadn't yet run its course. And here he
was, at the temple of its ghosts, where a second generation
was being raised. The story was his constant companion
now. More than a story, it was a puzzle to figure out, a
playscript with the answer to Brad Styles's fate.

Today marked a week since his meeting with Cullion. In
that time, he had been twice to the Marina district mansion
at Ivan's invitation. He was on a first name basis now with
Angela Styles and Helena Swann. In fact, he had grown
uncomfortable in his guise as Ivan's 'friend.' Increasingly,

he felt the gals had him pegged for his new pal's lover.

Adding to his discomfort was Assunta's cool reception when he called her last night. It pissed him off to be playing a phony game in San Francisco while the only person he cared about was slipping away from him in Newport.

Despite all that, today represented the chance he was waiting for. This evening he'd be in the house for two hours while Angela, Ivan, Claudia, and Helena attended a memorial service for Brad Styles at Yerba Buena Gardens. The ceremony was being hosted by one of Brad's pet causes, the San Francisco Neighborhood Theater Foundation. Just yesterday, Ivan had called to ask whether Boyle would baby-sit the boys.

"Will Esther Jarndyce be around?" he had asked.

"She's back, yes. I let her know you visit from time to time."

"Good. Does she understand you and I are 'buddies' now?"

"Hey, you're the one who made that bed, Boyle. Now you've got to lie in it."

"You need to reconsider the choice of words, pal."

Ivan went hysterical at that, choking with laughter. Boyle suggested he drop dead.

Grimacing at the memory, he locked his car, trod over the cobblestones to the front portico, and rang the bell. Esther answered the door, and they chatted a moment before he sought out the boys.

"They're in Justin's room, Mr. Boyle," she said, securing the door behind them.

"I know the way, Miss Jarndyce. I'll find them."

He took his time climbing the stairs from the foyer to

the second floor, noting the carpet runner, the stair treads, the ornate handrail and balusters. A man died here, he thought, at the peak of his career, the height of his powers. Was it a tragic accident in a posh setting, or an evil deed with a hidden motive?

Sam was excited to see him. Justin was curious and friendly. Before long, he told the boys they were on their own – he'd be in the library reading. Already plugged in to Xbox 360, they planned to stay in Justin's room. As he left, Boyle half-closed the door and heard the telltale squeak. Justin's head came up from his game, but Boyle could see he wasn't alarmed. He smiled and made a gesture to signify he'd be downstairs, and Justin turned back to Sam and the game they were playing.

Boyle fished out a small notebook from his back pocket and prepared to sketch the layout of the house. Besides Justin's room, the second floor housed Helena's suite, Angela and Brad's master bedroom and two guest bedrooms. Each of these had a private bath. Helena's suite was the largest of the second floor rooms, closely followed by the master bedroom. Justin's room was located across from the balcony – it was the only room with a quick and direct access to the stairs, the only one with a clear sight line from its door to the balcony, the stairs, and the foyer below.

Leaning over the handrail, he looked at the balusters. No way to tell something had been wrong. It might be useful to know exactly which ones were undercut. He made a note to find out who the repairman was and who hired him.

An alcove just beyond Helena's suite housed the elevator entrance and a stairway to the third floor. Two bedrooms up there were designated for servant stayovers.

Both of them shared a bath. The rest of the floor was devoted to storage space – where boxes, old furniture, and toys were piled up haphazardly. Boyle remembered that Miss Jarndyce generally stayed at the mansion two nights a week. The other third-floor bedroom was only occasionally used when extra help was required.

Downstairs, he knew that Esther would be in the kitchen watching television. Later, she would seek out him and the boys for a snack. Instead of heading directly for the library, Boyle stepped out to the foyer to sketch as much as he could see of the first floor layout.

With his back to the front door, the foyer stretched out in front of him to the sweeping staircase twenty-five feet ahead. The French doors to the terrace were to his left. On his right were the kitchen and dining room. The library entrance was to the left of the staircase, while an enormous double parlor lay behind the stairs, accessed by two arched doorways. From his previous visits, he recalled seeing two lavatories downstairs, one off the kitchen and one through the library.

There was a service entrance in the kitchen and two doors to the basement area: one leading from the kitchen, as well as one concealed in the paneling behind the staircase in the hallway area between the back of the stairs and the grand parlor.

It was hard to envision Brad Styles lying twisted at the bottom of the staircase with blood oozing from his mouth onto the floor tiles. To Boyle's mind, any spectacle of that sort was preposterous in these ordered and elegant spaces.

But once he got into imagining it, he could see Esther start out from the kitchen and advance through the foyer –

only to feel faint, fall to her knees and shout when she spotted the body. On the second floor, the hinge of a door shrieks. Soon after, a rush of panicked footsteps beats time along the upstairs corridor, and Angela flies down the stairs to embrace her dying husband.

Was Justin's door open or closed when she ran down that corridor? Did she see him before racing down the stairs? Has either she or Doctor LaFreniere talked to the boy about that night? Well, those were the questions he would have asked. Did the police ask ... and did they have answers?

~~~

Angela, Helena, and the Chitworths were subdued when they returned from the memorial service. It seemed to Boyle that he shouldn't linger.

"Well, folks, I'm going to leave now. Ivan, the boys behaved beautifully, just like you said they would."

"Thanks, Staff," he said. "Sure you won't stay for a drink?"

Angela spoke up. "Yes, do stay. I'm much obliged to you for minding Justin and Sam."

From the expressionless faces of Helena and Claudia, he could tell Angela's sentiments weren't unanimous. Was it possible Helena recognized his voice from their telephone interview when he first came to San Francisco? That thought had been nagging at him for days.

"It was my pleasure, really," he said. "But I have to get going. Ivan, I'll call you tomorrow."

Outside in the night air, he was relieved to be out of the house. He thought of his clients and their relatives going off to bed, each of them alone, all of them burdened with their secrets, their knowledge of each other, and the questions that remained unasked and unanswered.

CHAPTER 39

The phone rang as Bowers was pulling on his suit jacket, ready for lunch. He glowered at the thing, knowing he'd probably regret not letting it roll over to voice mail. Bennett stood waiting for him, hand on doorknob and poised to leave the Homicide Detail's office.

He picked up. "Homicide, Bowers here."

"Lieutenant Bowers?"

"Yeah, right. Who is this?"

"My name is Stafford Boyle, Lieutenant. I'd like to meet with you about the investigation into Brad Styles's death."

"Investigation? There is no investigation. What are you talking about, Mr. Boyle?"

"Sorry to put it like that. The newspapers ...."

"Yes, I know they're hinting, that's something they're good at. What is it you'd like to tell me, sir?"

"I'm an acquaintance of Angela Styles and Helena Swann. More specifically, a friend of Ivan Chitworth, their cousin from Rhode Island. I'd like to see you about something I learned when I visited them."

"Uh-huh. Why don't you just tell me what you know?"

"My friends would take it hard to find out I had gone behind their backs. I need to see you to feel comfortable about this."

"Well, I wouldn't betray a confidence unless it were illegal to do otherwise."

"Uh-huh. Is that supposed to reassure me?"

Bowers laughed. "Didn't think it would. Look, what do

you propose? We could meet here at 850 Bryant Street this afternoon."

"I'd feel better about meeting at my hotel. I'm at the Junipero Arms."

"I know the place. Just so you know, the management will recognize me as soon as I walk in. I've had occasion to go there in the past."

"That's okay. My room number is 420. Can you make it today?"

"Meet me in the lobby. Let's say one-thirty. Describe yourself for me, will you?"

When Bowers hung up, Maynard Bennett was standing in front of his desk, hands in pockets, his thick brown eyebrows arched up high.

"Some guy wants to talk about Brad Styles, May."

"When do we meet him?"

"He wants to see me alone. Tell you what, though. Be in the lobby of the Junipero Arms about quarter past one. This guy is six-one, one ninety, brown hair, mustache and goatee, forty-seven years old. You can leave after I come in to meet him, but we'll both be able to identify him later. And if you can manage it without being seen, use your cell phone to get a shot of him."

"If I can manage it? What the hell, Al!"

Ever since the Breastplate case, Bennett was getting mighty touchy, Bowers thought.

"Aw, c'mon May, let's go eat."

~~~

It hadn't been the right time for Boyle to say he was a P.I. Not on the phone, anyway. He'd leave that for later. When they met, he'd judge for himself what kind of person

Bowers was. If he made a connection with the guy, and if that led to confidence in each other, maybe they could share some information. That was the plan, anyway.

Hell, he swore he'd keep clear of the police, yet here he was – playing informer on his clients' relatives. But something was wrong in that house. He'd find it hard to forgive himself if anything happened to Sam and he hadn't done what he could to prevent it.

He left his room for the lobby at ten past one. Five minutes later, a big guy walked in who looked like a police detective. Cheap suit, soft hat, hangdog face. But the man didn't glance his way, and when he took the hat off his bald head, Boyle figured the baldness could explain the hat. Still, that was a cop face and a cop way of sitting and waiting.

While he was puzzling that out, a conservatively dressed black man pushed in through the front door and advanced to the lobby area where Boyle stood looking at a display of pamphlets touting local attractions and restaurants. Another cop face, another cop walk. The man smiled and signaled to someone he knew behind the reservations counter. Then he spotted Boyle, who had turned to face him directly.

They padded toward each other over the plush lobby carpeting and shook hands. Boyle spoke first.

"Nice meeting you, Lieutenant. Your partner over there didn't introduce himself."

Bowers chuckled. Boyle was glad he didn't try to deny it.

"Well, I should have known Detective Bennett couldn't make himself invisible. But I have to be careful, too. Things aren't always what they seem, you know?"

"Fair enough. You'll excuse me, though, if I don't want to talk in the lobby now. Shall we go up?"

Bowers stuck his arm out in the direction of the elevators.

"By all means," he said. "Lead the way."

Neither of them spoke until the elevator doors opened to the fourth floor.

"You a P.I., Boyle, or what?" Bowers asked as they stepped off.

"Touché, Lieutenant. I was hoping to tell you before you guessed it."

Boyle inserted his card key in the slot and pushed opened the door to his room when the green light flashed. Before he could even invite him to sit down, Bowers was ranging around the room with a kind of bloodhound determination, pulling aside curtains, poking around in the closet, checking drawers and lamps. When he was satisfied, he sat across from Boyle at the little table by the windows.

"Your driver's license, Boyle. And your P.I. ticket." He was making the 'gimme' motion with his right hand.

"Rhode Island?" he asked when Boyle handed them to him. "What's your story, man?"

Bowers's tone had become aggressive, almost threatening. Boyle felt himself go hot under the collar.

"What's *your* story, man! You gonna brace me? We can call this off right now, Lieutenant. I haven't done anything."

Bowers sighed, puffing out his lips and letting air escape out the sides.

"Okay, okay. Sorry. You said your friend was from Rhode Island too. What'd he do, bring you along? And what for?"

"Let's leave that aside for now. He's my client and what he hired me for is between him and me. It has nothing to do with Brad Styles."

"All right, so you called me as a concerned citizen. What have you got?"

"First I need something. You said there's no investigation about Styles. That's not quite true, is it?"

Bowers stared at him a moment, then blinked.

"Damn!" he snapped, leaning forward in the chair. "This is all you're getting from me until you tell me what it is you know. Officially, there's no investigation. But we have a couple unanswered questions."

That was the truth, Boyle could tell. So he wasn't the only one suspicious about the 'accident' at the Marina district mansion.

"You already know the only squeaky hinge in that house is on the door to Justin Styles's bedroom," said Boyle.

"Right. We even have it on videocam, for what it's worth. Which is nothing, by the way."

"I suppose. The only thing I have for you is something about Justin every member of the household knows, but failed to discuss when you questioned them."

"I'm listening, Boyle."

"In all his young life, Justin Styles has never, but never, been careless with his things. No toys scattered on the floor, no little trucks left on the stairs, nothing."

"Interesting. But useless."

"Sure it is, like all circumstantial evidence. Put everything together, sometimes you have a case."

"You saying you got more?"

"No. But I bet you do. As for me, I'm a friend of the

family now. I see them, talk to them, and I learn things. When I know more, maybe I can help you. Especially if I knew what you wanted me to watch for."

Bowers shook his head and looked out the window.

"Take the business about the balusters, Lieutenant," Boyle went on. "I know a little, but I'm sure you know more. Were those cuts fresh, for instance? Are you holding any evidence from the scene?"

"That's enough, Boyle. I'm not going there with you. Get to your bottom line, man."

"I'll do anything I can to help you as an insider, if only you'll give me a window into your case."

Bowers stood up, buttoned his suit jacket, and walked to the door. As he left the room, he turned to Boyle and spoke.

"I may get back to you," he said. "Just don't count on it."

CHAPTER 40

Ray LaFreniere had always liked Brad Styles and counted him as a friend. With such busy professional lives, however, they hadn't gotten together nearly as often as he wished, except for the occasional round of golf or odd tennis match.

If Ray had been married, he and Brad would undoubtedly have seen more of each other. They had the same taste in women, and you could bet their wives would have hit it off. Observing Angela at the wake, Ray couldn't help thinking how much he admired her. Always had, ever since he met her in the months before she married Brad.

Those were the days of the big scandal, and he liked to think he helped Brad through it. But Angela was Brad's ultimate saving grace. She gave the man something new and powerful to live for – a beautiful and gracious woman to love and protect.

Ray wished he could have that now. He wanted the love of a good woman – his friend's widow. Marriage was something that had slipped away from him more than once. First it was medical school and a gal who couldn't wait. As a young doctor in practice, he fell in love with a colleague who didn't believe in marriage. So they lived together until she changed her mind. By then, so had he.

After a certain age, a guy with a top-flight career is on autopilot. The career itself becomes his reason for staying engaged with the world, his platform for power and self-respect. A family might have slowed him down when he was coming into his own: first as a well-paid, later as a renowned psychiatrist. Without the encumbrance of a wife and children, he was able to travel light and go far.

And then things change. Values shift, maturity happens. You come to regret the lack of human warmth in your daily life. Perhaps you observe a young dad with his kids at the zoo, and you feel envy. He was forty-four now, and a perception had arrived that money and renown were third-rate substitutes for love and family.

Justin Styles had brought Angela to his office and into his mental life. Unfortunately, the boy hadn't made much progress. More and more, he resisted treatment. In turn, that brought Ray into rather frequent consultation with his mother – a compensation that had become a focus in his mind.

When Brad died, Ray had feelings of loss and guilt to deal with. The loss was only natural, the guilt was tied to the opportunity he imagined. Ray intended to keep in touch with Angela, and he hoped their acquaintance would develop into something deeper. He hesitated to admit it, but he was already in love with Angela Styles.

Today, however, was about Justin. It was a mild and fog-shrouded Sunday morning. He was alone in his office, sitting at his desk with a cup of strong, steaming coffee and his case notes. The boy had all but stopped communicating with him. His mother attributed this to Brad's death and dismissed its significance. But Justin's reluctance to talk pre-dated his father's ... accident. And Ray LaFreniere was worried. He couldn't shake the suspicion that Justin had something to do with it.

Until now, he had dismissed out of hand the silly notion

that Brad met with foul play. That was newspaper gossip, mere insinuation, wasn't it? He was going to depend on a totally objective reading of his case notes – something he had been postponing for weeks – to settle his mind on that score.

He should have done so at the outset. And he knew just what he had to review. All of it would have been noted way back when Justin began treatment. Two things were relevant – a recurring dream the boy had, and an incident Brad recounted during a telephone conversation on the day of Justin's first visit.

With his closest attention, Ray looked over his notes on the dream.

"When asked about recurring dreams, the patient smiled and recalled one with a few variations that always awakened him in an agitated state. In the dream he feels a threat to his own safety and that of the woman with him. A tall man with dark hair sometimes beats him, sometimes the woman, sometimes both. The man is a threat to their home as well. Using a kitchen match, he sets fire to things in the house. Once he set fire to the bed the patient and the woman are resting on. The patient recalls the man's laughter and his terrible temper.

In the dream, the patient is sad, angry, and frustrated. Sad because he can't understand why anyone would do such things. Angry because he wants revenge, yet frustrated because he feels powerless.

When asked who the man is, the patient doesn't know, but thinks he is related. When asked whether the relative is close, like a father, or not as close, like an uncle, he can't say. When asked for particulars of dress and grooming, the patient at first doesn't know, then mentions a smell the man has, a strong smell. His description of this points to something unpleasant, yet stimulating – a mixture of body odor and another substance he can't identify.

The dream contains a reversal. The patient flies at the man in a rage; the man disappears into a dark room. The patient and the woman are liberated.

After just moments of this freedom, they find a key that will unlock the door to the room where the man fled. They feel compelled to enter. The door opens to a darkened, chilly space. When a light comes on, they see the man dismembered on the bed. His arms and legs are severed from his trunk. His head is also severed, but his bloodshot eyes open and the head begins to talk. The woman screams and the patient runs and falls, runs and falls – in agonizing slow motion.

The dream ends at this point. When he wakes up, the patient's heart is racing, his fear is intense. The fear subsides when he opens his eyes and looks around his room. He reports returning to sleep after the dream without particular difficulty. The patient claims to have related his dream to no one before this.

Besides the dream content, two items are noteworthy:

1. Patient relates dream impassively, smiles and retains eye contact in a way that suggests he is observing the effect on the listener.

2. Patient has a descriptive power that makes the details of the dismemberment extremely vivid, especially the gore and blood-soaked bedclothes."

What bothered Ray LaFreniere at the time was Justin's detachment from the dream. There was neither enthusiasm in the telling, nor was there a residuum of fear. One of those would have been typical. With Justin, there was precision in the narrative but a kind of ... irony in his tone.

What bothered him now was the dream itself. What sort of little boy was Justin, after all? Was his dream merely Oedipal, or did he use it as a prompt for action of some kind? And he wondered if there was a piece of the dream left out. Is it possible the boy related the dream accurately, except for ... the act of dismemberment itself? Who had murdered the man? If it wasn't Justin, it had to be his mother.

Or did it? He never said the woman was his mother. She might have stood for someone else. Why hadn't he seen that before?

When Ray looked for the telephone conversation with Brad, he had only his longhand notes. They had never been transcribed. After reading them over several times, he found he could recall nearly the entire conversation.

Brad had been embarrassed about the whole episode and tried to tell it in a general way with few specifics. After a couple of false starts, Ray asked him to narrate all of it from start to finish, just as it happened.

"Think of me as a clinician, Brad," he had insisted. "That's what I am, after all. Forget I'm your friend."

"Easy for you to say, Ray."

"Yes, but the sooner you get it over with, the sooner I can evaluate it. And I'll still respect you in the morning."

He wanted him to take it as a joke, and it worked. Brad burst out laughing.

"All right, asshole," he said. "From the beginning ...."

He paused a moment before continuing, then inhaled audibly.

"Justin and I have always taken showers together. Less frequently in the last year, but it's something we've never been shy about ... until now.

"We play the game 'you-wash-my-back, I'll-wash-yours,' and I've always thought it the most innocent thing in the world. But last week, Justin took it to a different level and I got scared. Scared and angry.

"I soaped him up as usual and turned around for him to do the same. There was a little hesitation on his part this time, which barely registered. He started soaping my lower back kind of slowly, then suddenly one hand is going into the crack of my ass.

"It was a jolt, you know? I spun around to see what the hell he was up to, and he's standing there looking straight at me with a big grin on his face and a stiff erection. His thing is big for a kid his age, almost as big as an adult's.

"First, I'm just startled. Then he gropes me, puts his hand right out and takes my balls. Nothing like this ever happened before, not even close.

"I slapped his hand away and started yelling. I told him never to touch me or anybody else that way. I kind of pushed him out of the stall and told him he'd be taking showers on his own from now on. His face went all tight and angry, but he didn't say anything. Didn't apologize, didn't cry, nothing.

"Later, when I had calmed down, I went to his room and talked to him for a long time. And he did apologize. But I can't get over the feeling he wasn't sorry at all. He was playing a computer game when I came in to see him, and he went right back to it when I turned to go.

"In the end, Ray, it was Justin's attitude that bothered me most. The whole sex thing was uncomfortable for me, but I understand the aspects of curiosity and experimentation. No, it was that damn grin on his face and the lack of remorse that rankled."

It took a few weeks of visits before Ray began to see what Brad meant. What bothered *everybody* about Justin was ... nothing ever bothered Justin very much. He was impervious to correction or criticism. The only opinion that mattered to him was his own.

Ray looked up from his notes. It was one o'clock, and he stood at his office window, mesmerized by the non-stop foot traffic in the plaza below. He had grown hungry and was ready to leave for home. But an idea began to nag at him, and he went back to the patient files, where he pulled out Justin's records again. Knowing beforehand what he would find, he nevertheless flipped through his notes and looked at the transcript of the dream once more.

The man's genitalia weren't mentioned. In the boy's dream, were they severed as well? Was that another important detail Justin left out?

CHAPTER 41

If Alfonso Bowers had his way, he'd be getting mighty aggressive with Helena Swann. Lawyer or no lawyer, clout or no clout, he'd lead her right down the path toward a charge of conspiracy – conspiracy with a little boy, for Chrissake – in the murder of Brad Styles. He not only suspected her, he actually had some proof, such as it was, before having his investigation shut down by the usual apostles of political cowardice, Hilary Saunders and her D.A., Winston Garrett. 'Her' D.A. because that's what he was, her fuckin' pussy lap dog.

Right now, Dan Cinzano was grilling Bowers on every last detail of the case. And that was fine, he would need to be sharp for the meeting fifteen minutes from now.

Bennett would be there, too. He could handle all the details of evidence collection and chain of custody. That would be important – pencil pushers like Saunders and Garrett loved to back away from difficult cases under the guise of evidence mishandling by the boys in blue.

After the pre-meeting session with Dan Cinzano, Bowers felt more relaxed. His boss was with him all the way. Five minutes before the meeting, he walked into the men's room, took a leak, washed his hands and patted cold water over his face with a paper towel.

Bennett popped the door open then and strolled to a urinal. Over his shoulder, he called out, "Hey Al, all set for my end of the presentation."

"Great, May. Thanks, buddy."

Bowers took a last look in the mirror and gave himself an exaggerated wink for encouragement.

~~~

A half-hour later, a video was playing out on the television monitor in Dan Cinzano's office. Bennett and a technician had shot it a few hours after Brad Styles died on the marble floor of the foyer in the Marina district mansion. It was like some boring short you'd see at an art house film festival – the opening and closing of every door in the Styles home, accompanied by an audio track with comments on each location.

This was the last of the evidence Bowers presented to Hilary Saunders and Winston Garrett. It proved conclusively that the only squeaking door in the house on that evening was the one to Justin's room.

The other evidence presented were the depositions from Esther Jarndyce, Gunther Danzig and the carpenter Osvaldo Gutierrez, the saw blade from the potted palm on the terrace, and transcripts of the interviews with Helena Swann and Angela Styles.

Ms. Saunders held back until the end. When she finally spoke, Bowers gritted his teeth at the sarcastic tone.

"Gentleman, what a fine little exhibition. For a moment there, I thought Lieutenant Bowers was going to pull out a collapsible pointer and dazzle us with a stack of colored transparencies. But what the hell, fellas? You've got *nothing*, less than nothing. A squeaking door, a statement from an alcoholic carpenter. You can't be serious about this."

Cinzano's face went red. "You forget we're not trying to prove anything, Commissioner. We're merely establishing the grounds for investigating further. We intend to interview Helena Swann and Angela Styles again. We know we won't get permission to interview the boy's psychiatrist, but we'll ask for it nevertheless. We're concerned about the boy and we're not satisfied we have a complete picture of what happened that night. The business with the balusters indicates ...."

"The balusters! The balusters are bullshit, Dan. Bogus beyond belief." Saunders turned away from him, shaking her head dismissively.

Winston Garrett piped up. "I have to agree with Hilary, Chief," he said.

"We know you *have to*, Garrett," Cinzano snapped. "That's your entire function in life, isn't it? Why not compliment her on the alliteration while you're at it. Awesome, wasn't it?"

The D.A.'s face crumpled, and he said nothing more. Cinzano had blown him out of the discussion. Hilary Saunders wouldn't be finished yet, but her demeanor had eased. Bowers figured the sarcasm would subside now.

"Dan, look," she said, "I don't mean to diminish the efforts of your team or their intentions, really I don't."

He sneered. "Then why give such a perfect imitation of someone who does?"

Saunders turned toward Bowers and Bennett. "Gentlemen, I apologize. But Dan," she continued, " the public and the press will not accept our harassment of these women. There is so little to warrant it. The Medical Examiner's report, after all ...."

"We all know what the M.E.'s report says, Hilary. Nobody's disputing how Brad Styles died. It's the circumstances surrounding his death we want to establish."

"To what purpose, though? Dan, please, I don't mean to patronize you, but you'll get killed in the media if you pursue this."

Bowers jumped in. "Not if you and the D.A. here don't encourage them. Not if you recuse yourself."

Saunders bristled and stared at him.

"Pardon?" She spit out the word like an accusation.

Dan Cinzano was nodding. "Al is right, Hilary. We want you to back off. Don't talk to the press about this."

Saunders stood up and crossed her arms, looking sharply from Cinzano to Bowers. "I will do precisely what I think is necessary for the good of this community. How dare you ...?"

Cinzano held up his hand to stop her.

"If you don't cooperate with us, Hilary, the press may hear rumblings that your lifelong friendship with the Sharples sisters and other members of the elite in San Francisco has clouded your judgment – led you into an ethical dilemma. For instance, who the hell told you the carpenter is an alcoholic? Helena Swann, maybe? Now there's a story to run with. I can't say how a rumor like that would get started, but nasty assumptions always seem to leak out."

Hilary Saunders's cheeks began to glow. She tried to hide her anger by sitting down and looking into her bag for something, but Bowers saw her hands tremble. The Chief had locked her in.

Bowers took the opportunity to signal to Bennett. "If you folks don't mind," he said, "Sergeant Bennett and I are done. We need to leave now."

Winston Garrett took the hint as well. "Yes Hilary, I ... uh ... have to make a call to my office. Excuse me."

Cinzano and Saunders were talking again as Bennett closed the door on them, but the heat had gone out of the debate. Bowers thought he had never seen the Chief look so serene, nor Ms. Saunders so deferential.

Back in their spaces, he looked at Bennett and grinned, his eyebrows straining upward.

"Never try to screw Dan Cinzano out of a donation to the Police Athletic League, May. It makes him crazy."

Maynard Bennett flopped into his chair and brayed like a donkey. Bowers could see the old silver fillings in his back teeth.

CHAPTER 42

Boyle heard the name Osvaldo Gutierrez from Esther Jarndyce. The Styles family had employed the carpenter on a number of occasions over the years. At one time, the fellow was much in demand for his restoration skills, but was often unemployed now.

"He drinks a bit," Esther had said.

Boyle smiled. "Like Bojangles."

"Excuse me?"

"An old song, Esther. Pay no attention."

Boyle couldn't bring himself to ask Esther where Gutierrez lived. He certainly had no good reason to look up the family's carpenter. Besides, his rule in talking to anyone in the Styles household was to stay under the radar. If he were careless, any importunate question or aggressive bid for information might be reported back to Angela Styles.

Still wanting to find out more, he phoned Gunther Danzig, who had told Brad Styles about those undercut balusters in the first place. Without hesitation, Danzig recalled hearing Gutierrez say he was from Oakland.

A computer search at the main library yielded an address of 115 Broadway for the Carpenters' Union Local in Oakland. When Boyle called, a man named Jack Palmer answered. He had a rough-hewn manner and a gravelly voice, and claimed to know every union carpenter in the Bay Area.

"You must know Osvaldo Gutierrez, then."

"'Course I know Wally."

"He was recommended to me. Can you give me his phone number?"

"Whatcha got?"

"Hunh?"

"What do you want Wally for?"

"Restoration work. I got a staircase needs repair."

"Well, you're lookin' for the right guy."

Palmer didn't have a telephone number for Gutierrez, but he gave him a William Street address that was close to the Union Local HQ and the 19th Street BART station. Boyle figured he might as well make the trip to Oakland and check it out.

When he found William Street, he thought it must be a wrong address. All he could see were commercial buildings: auto repair shops, welders, a dental clinic. But 17½ William was a converted garage with two apartments, and the name O. Gutierrez was on the mailbox for upstairs – 17½ B.

Boyle looked in the mailbox, found nothing, then climbed the set of outside stairs to the second floor, where he knocked and tried to look into the window to the side of the door. A middle-aged man in green work clothes appeared at the foot of the stairs, crossed his arms, and stared up at him.

"You need help there?" he called.

"Hi! I'm looking for Wally Gutierrez."

"You know him?"

"No, I've got a job for him."

The man nodded. "Wally left last week. He don't live here no more."

Boyle vaulted down the stairs, two at time, using the

handrails to propel himself.

"Can you tell me where he went?" he asked when they were face to face.

"I never asked."

The man's name was Phil. He owned the apartments and the repair shop next door.

"Is there anybody else I can talk to?" Boyle asked. "People he knew, maybe. Or customers?"

He shook his head. "Nah. Wally didn't have visitors, y'know? Well ... except for that one gal the day he left."

"Oh yeah? Who was that?"

"Didn't know her. Man, she was something, though. Elegant blond lady. Not what you expect to see around here."

CHAPTER 43

The week after Brad died, Angela Styles had an appointment with Ray LaFreniere to discuss Justin's progress. When she called to cancel, his heart sank. Ever since the funeral, she was on his mind constantly, and he looked forward to seeing her.

"I don't think I'm up to it this morning, Ray," she said.

"Angela, you need a little relaxation," he protested. "Instead of coming downtown, meet me for lunch somewhere. Think of it as 'doctor's orders.'"

"Lunch? I don't know, Ray. I wouldn't want to see people I know."

"Instead of any place local, we could go to Westlake Joe's in Daly City. How's that?"

"I haven't been there in years," she said. "Maybe that would work."

"Angela, I think you need this."

"Well, I suppose my cousin won't mind watching the boys," she said. "What if I meet you around noon?"

"Perfect for me."

And it was, for him. Angela was distracted most of the time during lunch, and kept coming back to topics like Justin's treatment and prognosis. On the other hand, she raved about the veal piccata he suggested, and she didn't draw her hand away when he took it to comfort her. It was perfectly natural that she became emotional at times. After all, she was a recent widow.

So they had a quiet meal in a nearby town. Even if they

had been seen, who could object? There was nothing amiss, except for his feelings. Still, it marked a milestone for Ray. Soon, perhaps, he could begin to visit her at home. There was no question of 'dating' for a while, although he would certainly use whatever leverage he had to see her as often as possible. Ethics aside, he intended to stay close to Angela Styles.

CHAPTER 44

A l Bowers was glad he decided to hold back Bennett's report on Dr. Raynor LaFreniere. There was only the one surveillance to discuss, but he and Cinzano figured Hilary Saunders would go right back to Angela Styles if they brought it up.

And he hadn't told anyone that Stafford Boyle contacted him. The P.I. presented a couple of problems. First off, could he trust him? He called the Newport police and found Boyle to be legit, but they barely knew him. Assuming his offer of help was genuine, was he skillful enough to be of use, or would he botch things up?

It hadn't been easy, after all, to convince his boss they should keep the investigation open. Now that Cinzano was on board, it was important not to fuck up. He could almost see the newspaper headline if he made use of Boyle and Hilary Saunders found out about it:

San Francisco Police Plant Private Dick
in Styles Mansion
Police Commission President Appalled

But Boyle had already brought him a piece of information that could prove useful down the line. And now, as the investigation reached a critical point, he could sure use a pair of eyes inside the Styles household. All day he thought it over, consulting with Bennett before he went home for the night.

The next morning he called Boyle's cell phone. The P. I.

sounded surprised.

"I had given up on you, Bowers. What's up?"

"There's something to talk about. I want to see you today."

"Let's not bother if it's gonna be a one-way street, Lieutenant."

"Meet with me and judge for yourself."

"Just remember that I expect information too."

"I haven't forgotten."

They were trying to out-hardass each other. Bowers smiled. He liked Boyle better for trying, but he was pretty sure that wasn't his style at all. They agreed to meet at the Continental Diner on Market Street for lunch.

~~~

Boyle was killing time on Powell Street before heading back towards Market. He had strolled into the heart of the shopping and hotel district around Union Square. As always, people rushed through the square and along the surrounding streets. He didn't think much of the new design of the plaza – it looked open and featureless. But there was more access now, not just at the corners like it used to be.

Walking back, he stayed on Powell, stopping to watch the tourists crowding around the cable car turntable when he reached Market Street. Heading right on Market, he crossed to the other side near the Civic Center BART station and kept going until he reached the Continental Diner.

From the outside, he spotted Bowers at a window booth. They looked at each other as he passed by to the entrance, neither of them making any sign of recognition. Kind of a hard guy, he thought. Once inside, he walked directly over to Bowers and slid into the seat opposite.

"You know this place, Boyle?'

He shook his head.

"Mickey Cullion was the grillman here."

"Oh. The Breastplate case."

"That's right. See that old man over there in the corner booth?"

"Uh-huh."

"That's the owner. Name's Theo. Nice old guy. He'll be a character witness at Mickey's trial. If Mickey ever goes to trial, that is."

Boyle was uncomfortable now. Bowers was sitting there grinning at him. Was he trying to tell him something? Did he know he met with Cullion?

"I called Newport, Boyle. Checked up on you."

"Yeah? I could have given you references."

"What good would they be? Four people maybe, all of them saying you're a prince. Shit!"

Boyle laughed, but said nothing.

"I got the police chief there. He was good enough to call a few people. You've stayed under the radar in Newport, and I'll give you a point for that."

"Great. So now I've got a point. How do I cash it in?"

The waitress came over holding a pad and pencil. They ordered Continental Burgers – ten-ounce burgers with cheddar cheese, Bermuda onion slice, lettuce, tomato, four bacon strips, and their special "Theo" sauce.

"How d'you want them?"

Boyle: "Medium."

Bowers: "Well."

"Both want fries?

Boyle: "Fries'll be fine."
Bowers: "Onion rings."
"Drinks?"
Boyle: "Diet Coke."
Bowers: "Regular Coke."

When the waitress left to put their order in, Bowers leaned back in his seat and drummed his fingers on the worn Formica tabletop.

"Cards on the table, Boyle. I want to use you and I'll tell you where we're at, but first I want to know everything – what you were hired for, and what you've found out so far."

"You're a cautious man, Bowers, and I'll give you a point for that," he deadpanned. "Thing is, I've already told you stuff. So when does it start coming the other way? When do I hear about your case?"

Bowers nodded and smiled. "One thing I got is that you interviewed Mickey Cullion. Wanna tell me about it?"

Boyle felt himself tense up. "Nothing much to tell. I wanted background on the Styles family. I got it."

"And Shonda Wallace got enough from you to bargain a murder charge down to practically nothing. On a case that was a sure win for us until you showed up."

He knew his face had gone red. He could feel the heat from his collar to his hairline. How did Bowers find out?

"Ah, the man has a conscience, I see. But don't let it bother you, Boyle. We knew Mickey was protecting the Sharples gals, and we didn't want to see him do much time. We just didn't know what-all was in Snider's letter. As a matter of fact, we still don't. But now that the D.A. knows, he says Mickey will waive trial and the sentence he gets will be reduced by time served."

"Lieutenant, gimme a break. That's a whole other case. If you want to know what Jake Snider had on Helena Swann, get Cullion or the D.A. to tell you."

Bowers had him to rights, but he had some integrity left. Having already bypassed his clients' instructions, he wasn't about to compound the error by revealing what Ivan told him concerning the Breastplate.

Bowers was staring at him hard, but his expression was almost ... amused.

"Everybody likes a stand-up guy, Boyle. Maybe you'll do, after all. And maybe I'll get Shonda Wallace to tell me. She and I go way back."

The waitress showed up with their order on a tray, setting the Cokes down first, then the mile-high burgers with the side orders in paper trays. Looking at those onion rings, Boyle wished he hadn't gone with the fries.

"Best onion rings you'll never taste, Boyle. Not the frozen kind. Just fresh-cut, tossed in the Fry-o-lator, golden crispy rings with succulent centers."

Bowers popped one in his mouth and chewed with his eyes half-closed, affecting a dreamy concentration.

"You're a prick, Bowers, you know that?"

"Yeah. It's like a point of honor. Here, have one of these bad boys."

CHAPTER 45

At lunch, Boyle related to Bowers how his case started in Newport, his attempts to help the Chitworths and Sam, and his growing concern about Brad Styles's death. After lunch, they strolled back up Market Street, turning left on Larkin towards the Civic Center where the lieutenant was parked. Bowers talked about Maynard Bennett's initial callout to the Styles mansion – and his own involvement afterwards.

"There would have been no need of a homicide detective in the first place if things hadn't been a little crazy at the scene. When Bennett got into it, too many things didn't make sense. The next day, I showed up at the house with him. Angela Styles didn't object to making a statement, and it dovetailed with everything Miss Jarndyce said, except she didn't hear the squeaking door."

Boyle nodded. "Not hard to understand under the circumstances."

"That's what we figured. And then I showed her the search warrant. She was livid, but there was nothing she could do, and we found the saw blade on the terrace where Bennett saw Justin hide something. It was one of those skinny things goes in a coping saw. She asked Justin about it. He said he didn't hide anything, knew nothing about a saw blade."

"So the kid lied."

"Troubling detail, maybe, but what did it mean? There was no relevance to Brad Styles or his death."

Boyle agreed. "Not then, anyway."

"Our involvement would have ended right there, but we needed to talk to the tutor, who had just resigned. He told us about the undercut balusters. That led to the carpenter, who swore the cuts were fresh. Which he told Angela Styles about – because she had made a point of asking him."

"More of the same, right? Something is wrong as hell, but how is it a police matter?"

"You got it. When the Chief informed us the investigation was over, we couldn't make much of an argument. But we let him know Helena Swann's seclusion at the scene made no sense and that Justin Styles was a disturbed little boy."

Boyle didn't get it. "If you closed the case, how come ...?"

Bowers was nodding. "When you told me the toy truck on the stairs was another thing that didn't add up, I was determined to dig a little further. I knew Angela Styles would never let us question LaFreniere, but maybe I could verify that Justin saw him on a regular basis. That would at least confirm our feeling the kid was a head case. If a little more evidence turned up down the line ... we'd be that much closer to prying the case open."

They had come into Civic Center Plaza. Bowers pointed at his car with the remote to unlock the driver's side door. Boyle thought they had finished.

"How can I help, Lieutenant?"

"Be patient, Boyle. I got more. Bennett had seen a calendar in the kitchen that was marked 'Dr. L. – 11:30' every Thursday, and he remembered that Helena Swann said Justin's doctor was Ray LaFreniere. We figured to watch LaFreniere's building a few weeks for Angela to show up with Justin. But the next week on Thursday the good doctor exits the building at quarter past eleven. Bennett had done his research, knew what the guy looked like. He tails our boy, and guess what? LaFreniere meets Angela Styles in a restaurant in Daly City. Is this a romance or what?"

Bowers opened the car door and sat inside, looking up at Boyle.

"So here's where you come in. My boss has put us back in the game. I want to know if LaFreniere comes to the house. And if so, how often. Can you find out?"

"I'll do what I can."

"Good."

"And you guys?" he asked. "What's your next step?"

"We're going to interview Helena Swann and Angela Styles all over again. And Justin too. Everything will probably be done with lawyers this time – lawyers, the D.A., city supervisors, social workers, whatever."

"Good luck with that."

"Right," he said, looking at his watch. "Anything else? I gotta go."

Boyle smiled. "Well, yeah. One thing I forgot and one I was holding back."

"Figures."

"Gutierrez is in the wind. I traced him to the Oakland address, but he doesn't live there anymore. And get this – Angela Styles came to see him just before he disappeared."

For the first time, Boyle saw surprise register in Bowers's face.

"Jesus," he said.

"What I forgot to mention is the Chitworths arranged a

telephone interview for me with Helena Swann when I first came to San Francisco. She doesn't know it was me, I didn't meet her in person for weeks. This was well before Brad Styles died. She told me then she was moving out soon."

"What reason did she give?"

"It was time to strike out on her own is what she said. But I wonder."

"You wonder what?"

"If she had been asked to move out."

"Wha ...?"

"From what I can make out, the Breastplate case caused a rift, and Brad Styles may have told Angela that he wanted Helena Swann out of their life. What if she became determined not to leave?"

CHAPTER 46

Mrs. Styles was gracious about subjecting herself to a second interview, and Bowers appreciated it. She said nothing about a lawyer attending, the condition he had expected. Of course, if one showed up when he got there ... he'd have to make the best of it. He wouldn't feel blindsided, he would adjust. Same game, different playmates.

It was ten-thirty when he pushed the doorbell and heard the chimes sound inside the Styles mansion. Esther Jarndyce answered the door and led him from the marble surface of the foyer, past the carpeted corridor behind the staircase and into the oak-floored living room, where she asked him to make himself comfortable.

She pointed out the seating arrangement by the fireplace, and he sat in one of the jacquard-upholstered armchairs facing a delicate looking sofa he thought might be in the Regency style. Every time he came to this house, he felt like he did when his wife took him into a fine furniture store.

He hadn't much time to look around at the tapestries and antiques in this paean to gracious living before Angela Styles came floating into the room through one of the arched doorways, her hand extended in greeting and her smile a tender benediction. She had a knack for making a guy feel he was the reason she got up in the morning.

Her oval green eyes locked into his as she sat across from him on the sofa.

"Good morning, Lieutenant Bowers. It's a pleasure to

see you again."

"The pleasure's mine, ma'am. I just wish it weren't under these circumstances. How are you getting along?"

"Well, it's a difficult time for all of us here. Will you take coffee with me, Lieutenant? My housekeeper will be in with a service in just a moment."

"Yes, I will. Thanks, Mrs. Styles."

Bowers took his notebook and pen from the breast pocket of his jacket and placed them on the little round table between them as a signal they needn't engage in more small talk if she didn't wish to. Mrs. Styles watched and smiled.

"You won't be looking for a statement that I'll need to sign, will you?" she asked.

"No, ma'am. I'll be taking notes on some questions I have to ask, is all. And I'm sorry the newspapers keep dropping hints about an investigation. Things got a bit ... frantic the night Mr. Styles died. I'd just like to clear up a few issues and get out of your way."

Her smile had grown wan. "Well then, let's get started."

The housekeeper came in with a coffee service and set it on a serving table just to his left. Mrs. Styles made a quiet gesture to her signifying that she could withdraw. When they were alone, she poured the coffee into two cups and handed one to Bowers. He would have liked milk and sugar, but took the cup and said nothing. After a token sip, he set it down and picked up his pen and notebook.

"On the night your husband died, Mrs. Styles, did you see your sister at any time following the accident?"

"No. She told me she came out to the corridor and saw what had happened, but I didn't notice. Does that surprise you?"

"No ma'am, not at all. Did you see her later that night?"

"No, I didn't. She told me she secluded herself. I have no reason to doubt it."

Bowers felt she wanted him to dispute that. He detected a note of exasperation in her voice that wasn't directed at him.

"When you first came out of your room and ran to the stairs, was Justin's door open or closed?"

She shook her head. "I couldn't tell you."

"Did you see him at any time after the accident that night?"

"Much later, yes, I remember seeing him. I had grown hysterical when the rescue squad came and Esther gave me one of my pills ... a sedative. Then I forgot and took another when I went to my bedroom. Before I fell asleep, Justin came into my room to comfort me. I was nearly delirious, I'm afraid. I don't remember much after that."

"Why do you think Justin denied leaving the toy on the stairs and hiding the saw blade?"

She sighed as if annoyed. "I believe the enormity of the situation caused him to be afraid, and he fibbed. Have you another explanation?"

"No, ma'am. I understand what you're saying."

He had assumed his most deferential manner, hoping to placate her, to keep her with him at first. Soon enough, he knew, she'd chafe at his questions.

"Would you say it was typical for Justin to leave a toy on the stairs like that?"

"Actually, not at all typical. He's very careful with his things."

"So there might be reason to believe it wasn't him, don't you think?"

He had taken her off guard, he could see it in her face.

"Well ... yes. But if not Justin, then who?" she asked, looking puzzled.

Bowers smiled and shrugged his shoulders as though he didn't have the least idea.

"Justin's doctor is Raynor LaFreniere, correct?"

"Yes. Justin sees Dr. LaFreniere."

"Does the boy have behavioral problems, Mrs. Styles?"

"I won't be getting into that with you, Lieutenant Bowers."

"Ma'am, Justin's behavior the night of the accident was ... atypical. We were concerned for the boy."

"Thank you," she said in a curt voice. She was shutting down his line of questioning, but he needed to go further.

"Dr. LaFreniere is a friend of yours, isn't he?" he asked.

"More a friend to Brad. They golfed together."

"Would you be willing to let us question him about Justin's actions that night? He may have discussed it with him by now."

She stared at him. "What an odd thing to ask me. Lieutenant, I think Justin has the right to a strictly confidential relationship with his doctor."

"Of course he does."

"Do you suspect my son of some crime I'm not aware of, Lieutenant Bowers?"

"I can't say that, ma'am, no. But we believe the saw blade we discovered was used to undercut the balusters along the second floor balcony. Since Justin was observed hiding it, we wonder if he knows when the balusters were cut."

"That probably happened a long time ago."

"Your carpenter told us otherwise. In fact, he said you asked him about it and he informed you the cuts were fresh."

"I can't say I recall that. It seemed such a trivial thing at the time. I didn't take it seriously."

"But it was a dangerous thing, and somebody did it very recently. Someone might have been badly hurt."

"You're right ... but why does it concern you?"

He ignored her question. "Mrs. Styles, in the week after your husband's death, did you make a trip to Oakland to see Osvaldo Gutierrez?"

"Yes. Why do you ask?"

"We wanted to check his statement. When we tried to contact him, he had quit that apartment. Were you aware he was leaving town?"

"Not until I saw him that day. As interested as you are in him, you probably know he drinks too much. I understood he was upset about the police questioning him. I wanted to pay him and make sure he was all right."

She was on edge now. Bowers figured to ease off a bit, then move on to his final questions.

"I see. Mrs. Styles, please understand that I don't want to be intrusive. I just want to clarify the things I didn't understand. A few more questions and I'll be done."

"I know you have to do your job, Lieutenant. Go on."

"I have some personal questions I hope you won't find offensive. First, let me ask how you and your husband and Mrs. Swann had been getting along. Were you experiencing any problems in your relationships?"

There were points of color in her cheeks now. She drew herself up a little before speaking.

"No problems whatsoever."

"And Justin, ma'am ... how had he been getting along with his dad and his aunt?"

"Perfectly well, as always."

He saw her nostrils flare as she spoke. It was time to end the interview. He tucked the notebook and pen into his jacket and rose from the chair.

"Mrs. Styles," he said, "Detective Bennett has a nice, easy way with children. I'd like him to interview Justin. Can we set a day for that, please?"

The lovely green eyes flashed. "Lieutenant Bowers, whatever is the point? I'll have to think about that ... and the conditions under which I might permit it."

"Right, ma'am. Please let me know."

He handed his card to her. She favored him with a smile, bur turned and left the room without taking it. The housekeeper was waiting in the foyer to show him out.

~~~

Angela was glad she granted the interview. Despite the anger and fright building inside her, she at least had some insight now into what the police were thinking. No matter how they downplayed it, they believed Brad was murdered – and they were looking at her, Helena, and Justin.

How humiliating it was, these ongoing contacts with disreputable people and the police – as well as the scandals and the newspaper headlines that resulted. They had been through so much already, and *still* it hadn't ended.

No matter the danger, she was prepared to protect her little boy. He would have a good life, a normal life, she would see to it. And Sam too – she loved him from the first moment she met him. She would raise the brothers together. Aunt Claudia was behind her in this, and she would win Ivan over. Even Helena wanted both boys with them.

Helena ... whom she should confront about Brad. Oh, the things that girl had gotten into over the years. She would keep on loving her stepsister, she supposed, in spite of the suspicions that tortured her, and as long as she didn't challenge her over them. It just wouldn't pay to stare too long into the deep well of Helena's motivations.

Take the night Brad told her and Helena to destroy the copies of Jake Snider's blackmail letter. What she had seen then burned through her mind daily now. She wasn't at all objective about it, she recognized that. If she could only get her head around it, decide what it meant one way or the other, she could perhaps move on. But it would be either/or when she came to a conclusion. She'd either stand by Helena once again – or let her twist slowly in the wind.

Brad had surprised her that morning when he said he would convince Helena to divulge her contacts with Mickey Cullion to the police. Angela thought he would never speak to her sister again after the awful scene they'd had the previous evening. But he changed his mind and was willing, anxious even, to try again.

It was etched in her consciousness now, that picture of her beloved husband walking out of Helena's suite afterwards. Angela had just come out of their room down the hall when he opened the door and took his first, unsteady step into the corridor. He was red-faced and glassy-eyed, a look she knew well, a look that spoke to her of sex and intimacy.

For the first time ever, she felt a rush of jealousy about her husband. After all, she mustn't forget that he and her sister were once lovers. And Helena *still* had wiles enough to attract men in a certain way. There had been signs before this of assignations with tradesmen and workers in the house. The only other explanation was that Brad had asked Helena to leave and precipitated a fierce row. Which was it?

He hadn't yet seen Angela standing there, so she called to him.

"Brad, what is it?" she asked. "What happened in there?"

But he hesitated, and her heart sank.

"Nothing, Angela. Nothing happened. I'm feeling dizzy all of a sudden. It must be the tension over that meeting. But Helena's agreed to cooperate, honey. Everything should be okay tomorrow."

Angela hadn't known what to believe then. And still she didn't.

CHAPTER 47

Mrs. Swann let him know right off that she'd have her lawyer at their meeting. No surprise there. What Bowers didn't expect when he walked into the library at the Styles mansion was Hilary Saunders. Her back was to him. She was examining a leather-bound volume from the large collection stored in the floor-to-ceiling bookcases that lined three of the library's walls.

The fourth wall backed onto the terrace, which he could see through the oversized windows. In the middle was a fireplace, serving as backdrop for Mrs. Swann and her lawyer, who sat facing him in matching armchairs. Her motorized chair was nearby. Esther Jarndyce, who had preceded him into the room, announced him and left.

His hostess held her hand out, encouraging him to approach. What a stunning woman, he thought. Ivory complexion, nearly black hair, full red mouth, tiny waist, substantial hips. Always attractive, today she seemed especially ... vivacious. Her smile intensified as she welcomed him.

"Good morning, Lieutenant Bowers. You know Hilary, I understand, so let me introduce you to my lawyer, Miles Skeffington."

Bowers advanced for a handshake and was put out when Skeffington just sat there. The lawyer received him with the offer of a pudgy pink hand, like some exiled ruler of a defunct principality.

"How do, Lieutenant," he crooned.

Instead of replying, Bowers turned and went to the sofa facing the armchairs, where he sat grim-faced.

Hilary Saunders was looking directly at him now, and gave a little wave. "Good to see you again," she lied. "And I don't want you to worry, Bowers. I'm not here as president of the Police Commission, but as Helena's best friend."

He tried to stay loose and hoped to disguise his anger by willing a smile across his face and pretending to be amused. When asked if he'd care for something to drink, he declined.

"Well, folks," he said, "I guess this is my meeting, so why don't I go ahead with my questions?"

After a pause, Helena Swann spoke. "Whatever you say, Lieutenant."

Hilary Saunders took up a position behind Helena's chair, standing with her arms crossed, as if she were that lady's protectress. Skeffington looked on with half-closed eyes, hands steepled under his chin. This was going to be short, Bowers figured. The interview would go nowhere, so why bother playing hardball? That would just oblige them and result in a complaint about harassment. Purely as a matter of form, he took out his notebook and looked inside.

"Mrs. Swann, you told Detective Bennett you came to the top of the stairs the night Mr. Styles died, then retreated to your suite when you saw Mrs. Styles trying to revive him. Is that correct?"

"Yes. It was very upsetting."

"I'm sure it was," he said. "Did anyone see you who could corroborate that?"

"Apparently not."

"I see. When Detective Bennett came to your door, you

told him you had been in bed. Can you confirm that?"

"I was lying down when he knocked, yes."

"Didn't you think to call 911, Mrs. Swann, after what you had seen?"

"I knew Esther would take care of it."

"Does that mean you also saw Miss Jarndyce when you came out to the stairs? You never mentioned that."

"Well ... no, I didn't see her, but I knew she was around."

Bowers grinned and looked at her a moment, but decided not to follow up. If this ever got to a jury, he'd bet anything that answer would undergo a change.

"Detective Bennett noted that you were fully dressed when you answered your door. Were you sleeping in your clothes when he knocked, Mrs. Swann?"

He had thrown out the question as much for Saunders and Skeffington as for Helena. Skeffington played it cool, but he could see Saunders bristle.

Helena smiled. "I didn't say I was sleeping, Lieutenant. That would have been callous, indeed. I lay down because I was distraught. When Detective Bennett knocked, I took time to pull myself together before answering."

It was the kind of answer he had expected. But now, he thought, let's give her something to think about.

"We understand that you were planning to move out of your sister's house before the ... accident occurred. Is that true, ma'am?"

Skeffington interrupted, but Bowers kept his eyes on Helena Swann. She was astonished, he could tell.

"Now Lieutenant, I can't imagine that Mrs. Swann wants to or needs to tell you about her personal affairs.

Since it has no relevance to the night in question, Helena, I wouldn't answer him."

It was all rather futile, but Bowers was glad he persisted. Boyle wouldn't be compromised because Helena had no idea he was the P.I. she had talked to earlier. Yes, he thought, let her chew that one over. She'd have to wonder if her sister or a close friend like Saunders had been talking too much.

~~~

Miles and Hilary assured her there was no legal significance to anything Bowers asked about.

"Believe me, Helena," he said, "that was just a fishing expedition."

"And a pathetic one at that," Hilary chimed in.

But she already knew that. She also knew that Al Bowers wasn't stupid. How in the world could it become known to the police that she had been facing a move before Brad died? She'd have to think hard about whom she had told – and what their motivation might be for repeating it.

Moving had been Brad's idea, of course. He brought it up weeks ago when he came to her suite for a visit. They needed to resolve their quarrel of the day before when she balked at telling the police about her phone call to Mickey Cullion. Brad came up with the simple, but clever suggestion to destroy the blackmail letter.

"There'll be nothing left of the accusations Snider made if the letter is gone," he said. "Angela destroyed the original. You need to get rid of the copy."

"But Brad, he said a friend of his had another copy in an e-mail file."

"What friends did Jake Snider have, Helena? Mickey

doesn't have a computer, and Snider lived in a halfway house. That was just a bluff. Anyhow, it's a chance we'll have to take."

Suddenly, it had been like old times. She felt closer to him than she had in years, almost as close as when they were engaged eight years ago. They even ... relaxed together on her sofa. But then he spoke to her of living on her own. It was an assault on her sense of security, a rebuke to her pride.

Brad had smiled sweetly, acting as though he knew what was best. "We'll arrange for everything, Helena. I don't want you to worry or feel abandoned."

So they wanted a life without her – the great encumbrance, the scandal magnet, the despised stepsister. Clear the bitch out of our lives! Admit it, she thought, that's what you're after. Oh, she had made noises in the past about leaving, but he knew she wouldn't. Why pretend it was her idea, or something she would welcome?

Well, she'd see about this. She knew Brad and Angela's vulnerabilities after all – she had been observing them for many years. There would be a way to short circuit this nonsense, and she'd find it.

Helena had sense enough to keep her composure and pretend it was something to think about. She took pains to make him feel totally comfortable, to accommodate him in every possible way. As in former days, she knew only too well how to satisfy Brad.

But when he left her suite, her slow burn had become a kind of silent rage.

On top of everything else, she thought, Brad was pushing her out of Justin's and Sam's lives, the children she might have had in a better world. Why should Angela be the only one to raise them and enjoy them?

Maybe the emotions lingering from that night were badly directed, she thought. She wasn't always as even-tempered as she should be. But you couldn't change the past, you could only move on. Which is exactly what she was trying to do.

CHAPTER 48

Ray LaFreniere was talking to Angela about the preadolescent program at Del Amo Hospital in Torrance, a private psychiatric facility. It was the first time he had broached the subject. She had let him into her life ever so slightly, and he meant to address her concerns about Justin as a way of consolidating his position with her. She wouldn't have drawn the conclusion he had – that Justin had a hand in Brad's accident – but it must have occurred to her that the police were suspicious.

"I'm sure it's a wonderful place and a wonderful program, but why are we talking about inpatient care, Ray? You can't be saying Justin needs that now."

"Think of it as an insurance policy, Angela. I know you've been concerned about the police and why they keep looking into what happened that night. I'm just telling you not to worry, that I'm in a position to put Justin beyond the reach of the legal system if it should come to that. Not that I expect it to."

Her mouth was a little distorted as she attempted not to cry. She reached into her bag and pulled out a handkerchief, applying it first to one eye, then the other.

"Well, here I go again," she said, trying to keep her composure. "It seems I spend half my time lately trying to hold myself together. But I appreciate your help, and I'll keep it in mind."

"Do me a favor and call your friend Hilary Saunders," he said. "She should be in a position to help us with this.

And then put it out of your mind. I brought it up out of an excess of caution – just to keep the base covered."

"I understand, Ray."

"Let me introduce one last topic, Angela. You've spoken a great deal about Sam lately, and I know how much you want to raise him and Justin together."

"And ... you agree with me, Ray?"

"In your case, yes I do. You love both of them and you're a wonderful parent. It certainly would be best for them."

He was going too far. How could he tell in advance if this were the best thing for either Angela or those boys? He barely knew Sam, after all. What he was really doing was telling her what she wanted to hear.

When the time came, LaFreniere was confident he could persuade her to place Justin at Del Amo. She didn't see it yet, but it would even help her gain custody of Sam. Once Justin was out of the reach of the legal system, everyone's level of anxiety would ease. He'd be able to assure them all, the Chitworths included, that Justin would respond to treatment and come back reasonably well-adjusted. Ivan could then be convinced to transfer custody of Sam, he was sure of it.

The Chitworths were an open book to him. Claudia thought the sun rose and set on Angela and was already convinced she should take custody. It was evident that Ivan wanted the very best for Sam, but the man was compromised. Life hadn't prepared him for fatherhood, and he wanted more personal freedom than he currently had; on the other hand, he took his guardianship seriously and would not hand Sam over if Justin's problems were severe.

And they were severe. But with his help, Angela could manage them. And a longish stay for Justin in an inpatient setting with a clear and positive prognosis would convince Ivan that the boy was on his way to a normal life. Ray LaFreniere knew he had the ability and the power to arrange it. One word from Angela is all it would take.

CHAPTER 49

Boyle thought he knew where Claudia Chitworth stood. Very likely, she had decided Sam would best be served with Angela Styles as his guardian. Still, it would be Ivan's opinion that counted most. Was he leaning in the same direction as his mother?

If Ivan were inclined to slough off the responsibility of raising Sam, how could Boyle stop him? No ... he would be fired the minute Ivan decided to cut bait.

But he hadn't been fired yet. He was still in the game, and he still had hopes of finding out exactly what happened the night Brad Styles died. The key to that, of course, was Justin Styles.

Justin, he discovered, was a very clever child, every bit as clever and charismatic as Esther Jarndyce and Gunther Danzig said he was. And his better qualities had made Sam into a kind of disciple. It disturbed him to watch the more impressionable boy fall under his spell, but there was nothing he could do about it. Justin was a leader and poor Sam a follower.

Was something really wrong with Justin Styles? Boyle had read enough on psychiatric disorders to have an idea, and he planned to do something about it. Before the Chitworths made their final decision, he would not only present them with his findings, but also make it a point to prod them into a confrontation with Angela.

To help Bowers, Boyle tried to keep an eye out for LaFreniere, but his access to the mansion was diminishing.

There were no longer any requests to babysit, and Ivan didn't always return his messages. He had to wonder if the Chitworths were getting ready to dump him. To keep a hand in, he had taken to following the doctor.

Raynor LaFreniere was fabulously consistent. Every workday at seven o'clock, he left his apartment for his practice. On the days he didn't see patients, Wednesday and Sunday, he nearly always went out to breakfast at nine. Except for the occasional golf or tennis match, he seemed to have no social life. If there was a woman in his life, Boyle hadn't seen her yet. Just once, he left town. Boyle followed until the doctor headed south on I-5. It looked like a long haul, so Boyle abandoned the tail.

This Wednesday was different. LaFreniere left home at ten o'clock, drove to the Marina district and pulled into the circular drive at the Styles mansion. Having followed him, Boyle found a parking space nearby where he could watch. Then he flipped open his cell phone and called Al Bowers.

~~~

Justin and his mother were on the terrace, cooled by a light misty breeze from the bay. They had eaten breakfast there earlier. Doctor LaFreniere showed up after the dishes were cleared away. And now the three of them sat around the big, glass-top table. They were supposed to be having a nice talk. That's what his mother said. But it wasn't nice, they were talking about a hospital, and Justin was angry.

He couldn't show it, they would know how to use that against him. He bit his lower lip to keep from saying what he felt. Before long, though, he had to speak up. They couldn't get away with this.

His voice had a shrill edge. "You said you'd never send

me away, Mommy. You promised, you know you did."

That hurt her, he could tell. And she couldn't deny it.

But it was LaFreniere who spoke up.

"Justin, it was my decision that you need this program. And you're not being 'sent away.' As soon as you're better, you'll come home."

Better? He was already better than either of them.

"But I'm not sick," he said. "And I don't care what you say. Mommy told me this would never happen. Tell him, Mommy!"

His mother held her hand out to him, and he saw the hot tears spring from her eyes. She was admitting he was right. But he didn't move toward her like she wanted. LaFreniere sat by her and passed his arm around her waist.

That's not right, he thought. She shouldn't let him get so close.

"I knew he was against me, Mommy, but you're supposed to be on my side."

She raised her head and seemed to pull herself together. Her eyes were red-rimmed, yet her voice was clear.

"Justin, no one is against you," she said. "I'm your mother and Doctor LaFreniere is a friend who wants the best for you. You don't see that now, but you will."

"But you promised! Why should I believe you now? You think I don't know what's going on, but I do."

They both looked startled then, defensive. Well, if they weren't going to say what this was all about, he would. He stood up from his chair and confronted them, squaring his shoulders and balling his fists.

"I didn't put the truck on the stairs, you know it wasn't me. I don't know where the saw blade came from either. I found it in my room, and I got scared because I remembered Daddy asking me about those spindles being cut like that. I didn't know *anything*, but he kept saying, 'Somebody could have been hurt,' like he thought it was me."

"Don't Justin," his mother said. "Don't deny everything. I know how upset you are. Keep in mind that you won't be at the hospital very long, I promise. Isn't that right, Ray?"

He saw LaFreniere hesitate before speaking.

"That's right, Justin, it won't be too long."

His mother knelt in front of him on the terrace tiles and held him close. It wasn't her fault, he knew that. But she was weak, not strong like his real father, and not like him. LaFreniere was the one he had to deal with.

"I'm sorry, Mommy," he said, loosening his fists and flinging his arms around her neck.

He let himself cry. Until now, he had been holding back. But why bother? What was it the doctor said once? Something about his not showing 'appropriate emotion.' If he cried and if he cooperated, could he get them back on his side?

Doctor LaFreniere smiled and spoke softly. "Justin," he said, "maybe we could talk this over. Just the two of us. I can help you understand if you'll let me."

His mother nodded. "Would you do that, honey? I think it's a good idea."

He wiped his eyes with the back of his hand, then took out his handkerchief and blew his nose. They were both anxious to please him now, he could tell.

"All right, Mommy," he said. "I will if you want me to."

The doctor was looking at him now like they were pals.

"Tell you what, Justin. We could go downtown, take a walk, and go to my office. No one's there today. Would you like that?"

"I suppose so," he lied.

~~~

For lunch, they strolled down to Market Street and ordered burgers at Wendy's. Justin let Doctor LaFreniere hold his hand on the way, even though it made him feel funny. It was like Mr. Danzig had told him many times – discipline meant doing necessary things whether they were to your taste or not.

What was important now was figuring out how to explain what happened the night his father died. That was everything. If going to the hospital couldn't be avoided, he'd best not fight it. But all the talk in the house lately about police detectives and lawyers worried him.

It was almost one o'clock when they walked into LaFreniere's office building and signed in with the security guard. The doctor showed his ID, and the guard gave Justin a visitor's pass, bending down and clipping the temporary ID to his collar as if it were some big deal. But this sort of thing was old news, he had been downtown with his parents many times.

Once inside the doctor's suite, Justin settled in the playroom while Doctor LaFreniere went to his office. After a while he came back and watched from the doorway. When he finally spoke, he was smiling and holding out his hand.

"Okay, Justin, let's go to my office and have that talk now."

Justin abandoned the puzzle he was pretending to work at and took Doctor LaFreniere's hand. They walked out of the playroom and into his office, where they sat in the armchairs by the window. There was a digital recorder on the little table between them.

"Justin, as you can see, we're recording our session today. And I'm sure you know what I'm going to ask you."

"It's about the night Daddy died, isn't it?"

"I think that's part of it, son. You haven't had much to say to me for weeks. So why don't you tell me what's been on your mind all that time?"

Justin looked up and tried to figure out why Doctor LaFreniere wanted to put him in that hospital. Did he want to help like he said, or did he just want him out of the way?

"I cut those spindles, Doctor LaFreniere," he said quietly. "Aunt Helena caught me. She thought I was setting a trap for my father. She said the police would see the cuts I made, and they'd know I planned to hurt him. I know it was a bad thing to do, but I wasn't trying to hurt him or anybody else – I was just copying what I saw in a movie."

"Think about that, Justin. Your aunt must have had a reason to think you wanted to hurt your father."

"She knew I didn't like it when he scolded me. We talked about that. But I wasn't planning anything bad. Honest."

"That saw blade, Justin – where did you get it?"

"I saw Mr. Gutierrez using it one day. I stole it from his tool box when he wasn't looking."

"I see. So your aunt caught you using the saw blade on the balusters. What happened then?"

"She told me Daddy was making her leave the house, and she was going to get back at him by playing a trick. She asked me to help her. On the night Daddy fell, I put my toy truck on the stairs like she wanted, right where the staircase turns. Coming downstairs, he wouldn't see it."

Justin was weeping openly now, gulping in air and choking the words out. "I didn't want my daddy to die, Doctor LaFreniere, honest. Aunt Helena knows I didn't."

"Take it easy, son. It'll be all right. Tell me what happened after that."

"I saw Daddy pass by my door on his way downstairs. Then I heard Aunt Helena call his name. That must have been when he tripped, because he shouted. I got scared and ran to close my door. I didn't even look."

His eyes were still wet, but the tears were spent now. Justin was looking down into his lap and sniffling. Doctor LaFreniere had thrust some tissues into his hand, and he wiped his face with them.

The doctor sat motionless in front of him. He was judging him now, Justin knew. Rather than stare back at him, he looked out the office window. A light rain was falling. He didn't feel angry anymore, and he wasn't afraid in the least.

CHAPTER 50

Ray LaFreniere believed the boy. He wasn't at all sure about his protestations of innocence, but the outline of what happened – combined with what he knew about Helena Swann's past – had the ring of truth. This lady had enlisted a seven-year-old boy in a plan to murder her brother-in-law and former lover. It was astonishing, quite beyond belief.

Helena's personality, her past and her motivations made this new horror seem plausible, but how could she think the boy would keep her secret? And when he thought of Justin's biological father and Helena's ties to the old Shoo-fly scandal, Ray LaFreniere had to shake his head in wonderment. There were pathologies here that went beyond any ready understanding.

He hoped Angela would do the right thing and inform the police, stepsister or no. She might balk – he realized how strongly she felt about family matters. His duty was clear, however. He had to convince her, and he believed he had the means to do it.

But when he finished relating Justin's confession to her, Angela's reaction bewildered him. They sat in her library, cocooned in the antique leather club chairs with their tall backs curved over at the top like monks' hoods. He expected tears and confusion, disbelief and anger. Instead, her face was a pale mask.

At first, he thought she was resigning herself to a new and difficult burden, but her demeanor said otherwise.

When she spoke, she was alert, organized, and quite sure of herself.

"There's no need to call in the police, Ray. They'll come to us. Detective Bennett phoned and left a message about it just this morning, after you and Justin went downtown."

Confused, he stared at her a moment.

"Angela, I don't understand," he said.

"The police want an interview with Justin," she said, a note of triumph in her voice. "I was ready to call in favors from every politician and city official I know. If the interview with Justin took place at all, it was going to be monitored by a team of lawyers and health care providers. But that won't be necessary now."

He squinted at her, head cocked. "What are you saying, Angela?"

"I mean to let Sergeant Bennett have his interview with Justin alone. No lawyers, Ray. After encouraging Justin to tell the truth, I'll just walk away."

His face cleared, understanding her now.

"You realize, of course, that Helena will have a price to pay for this."

Angela looked away from him and stared at the artful, complex design of the tapestry over the mantel. As she spoke, her voice, strong at first, faded to a whisper.

"Yes, she will. For the very first time in her life, she'll pay for what she's done. It's long overdue, after all."

He wanted to reach out to her in some way, to comfort her by word or by touch. But there were depths here he could not fathom, and he held back.

CHAPTER 51

As Boyle watched the entrance to LaFreniere's office building on Wednesday, an idea began to insinuate itself. All this tailing and waiting was so much make-work. He needed to take direct action of some kind. The passive role he had assumed was unendurable. It's all there, he said to himself, everything I need to know is in that building. Why don't I just go in there and take it?

At the Salvation Army thrift store on Sutter Street, he found a blue Dickies work shirt and pair of pants that fit. Old clothes, he thought, would be best. And the shirt he picked had a name patch already sewn on the pocket. Which gave him his identity for the caper – Erik.

He had no idea what an elevator repairman would take to a job, but he figured a toolbox with the usual stuff plus some gauges and lubricants would look authentic enough. It wasn't as if he was going to do any actual work. He just had to get past the security guard.

He planned it for late Sunday morning. He would break into Raynor Lafreniere's office and find Justin's patient records. It was the only way he could possibly keep faith with his vow to do his best for Sam. He had already veered into unethical behavior by disregarding Ivan and Claudia'a wishes, and now he was breaking the law. Well, it wouldn't exactly be the first time, would it?

The payoff would be a clear and cogent recommendation for the Chitworths. Given Justin's problems, was it safe to relinquish custody of Sam to Angela

Styles – or wasn't it? His own psychiatrist's diagnosis would settle the matter.

Boyle chose Sunday for the break-in because the rent-a-cop industry reached its highest level of incompetence on the weekend. He'd be most likely to encounter a poorly trained guard on a Sunday, giving him a fighting chance to bluff his way through to the upper floors of the building.

At eleven o'clock, he drove into the underground lot at Union Square. Quickly, he found an isolated parking space and changed into his work clothes. He opened the glove compartment and pulled out the multi-part form he had filled in to fake a work order.

Taking a deep breath, he pivoted out of the car and walked around to the trunk, where he retrieved the toolbox. After locking up, he stood looking towards the exit for a moment and tried to predict what might go wrong. He was counting on not having to show ID – that was one potential problem. As for anything else, who could know?

Ten minutes later, he was pushing through the front door of LaFreniere's office building and walking up to the smiling, elderly security guard at the desk in the middle of the lobby.

"Hi, my name's Erik," he said. "Regis Elevator. I've got a work order to check out the elevator doors on floors ten and fifteen. Says here they've been sticking."

Boyle handed the form to the guard, who took it and read it solemnly. He was perhaps seventy years old, mild-mannered, yet alert.

"Nobody told me about a repairman," he said, frowning.

"We were supposed to get to it yesterday, but one of the

guys was out sick. My boss told me to check it out today so you wouldn't have any problems come Monday morning."

"Yeah, that would make sense. But I don't know ...."

"Look, if you don't want me to do it, I'll write down 'refused entry' and you can initial it for me. Okay?"

Boyle knew the guard would balk at his suggestion.

"Nah, that won't be necessary. I could call my boss in, but he wouldn't like that. Tell you what, just sign the register here."

He pushed the open register in front of Boyle, who signed it as Erik Andersen from Regis Elevator. There was an additional space, which he left blank.

"Oh, and lemme see your license," the guard said.

"My driver's license? What do you need that for?" he asked.

"I gotta write the license number down here."

"Here, I'll do that for you," Boyle said, going for his wallet with his left hand while his right tugged the register back across the desk. In one motion, he had his wallet open and was writing down some numbers on the space next to the borrowed name.

"Out-of-state, hunh?" the guard asked. "Write down the state name, too."

The old man must have noticed he didn't have a California license, but it was unlikely he could read his real name upside down from where he sat.

Boyle chuckled and put his wallet away. "Yup. Moved here two months ago from Rhode Island. Still haven't got down to the DMV. You know how that goes."

"Well, Erik," he said, looking down at the register, "my name's Fred. You're the only one in the building now besides me. How long you gonna be?"

"An hour, tops."

"Okay. I lock 'er down and leave at one," he said, looking at his watch. "You got an hour and a half."

"Sure thing, Fred. I'll be out before one."

"Oh, by the way," he said, turning back to the desk, "I'm only going to be working on the north elevator. Where's the key?"

Fred opened the top desk drawer and pulled out a key with a blue tag. "Here you go," he said, tossing it to Boyle, who caught it and walked on.

Stopping first on ten, Boyle disabled the elevator with the key. Just outside in the corridor, he left a can of WD-40, a few gauges, and a screwdriver. Next he hustled up the service stairwell, coming out on fifteen, and laid out another set of tools outside the elevator doors there, the toolbox included. Then he turned to face Dr. LaFreniere's suite, which was directly opposite the south elevator – the one still in operation.

He let out a grateful sigh when he saw the lock to the double doors of the office suite was a simple affair, well suited to his basic burglar skills. From his back pocket, he fished out a set of locksmith picks. Despite a tremor in his hands and the flop sweat dripping into his eyes, he gained entry in less than a minute.

Leaving the office doors open, he stepped deep inside the waiting room and turned around to look back at the south elevator. As he had hoped, he would be able to see the floor number display above the elevator from where he stood. When the elevator car advanced a floor, he'd see the appropriate number light up.

The way he planned it, the setup on ten was a decoy. If Fred came snooping, he was likely to go there first, where the north elevator was stopped. Not finding him, he'd see the tools, look around the corridor, check the men's room. All of which would give Boyle a good minute or two. Then, as Fred took the south elevator up to fifteen, he'd still have time to lock up and get out. Even if the old guy decided to look for him on fifteen first, he should be able to track the elevator car as it rose above ten.

Now if Fred landed first on ten, then took the stairs to fifteen ... well, Boyle would be screwed. But what was the chance a seventy-year-old would do that?

All of this was contingent on his being in the waiting room, directly off the corridor, where he could watch the display over the south elevator doors. Which meant he had to find the patient files, wherever they were, and get back out to the waiting room as quickly as possible.

The first thing he did was eliminate from consideration any inner rooms unlikely to contain patient files. The playroom, staff break room, and lavatory were out. That left the receptionist/records area and LaFreniere's office to check out thoroughly.

One whole wall of the reception area was lined with built-in file cabinets, all locked. Finding the receptionist's desk locked as well, he surmised it a likely place to search. All of the drawers released when he jimmied open the lock to the top drawer. Rifling quickly through the contents, he found no keys.

Boyle knelt by the desk a moment and tried to think like the receptionist in charge of this stuff. Then he pulled open the top drawer again and yanked out the tray in front with the little compartments for rubber bands and paper clips. He grinned at the two sets of small keys lying there, snatched them from their hiding place, and walked up to the wall of file cabinets. There were numbers in nail polish painted on the keys that matched to the files. Within moments, he had access to all the paperwork in the office.

But it wasn't what he was looking for. Most of it had to do with insurance claims and settlements, supplies, correspondence – everything imaginable but patient records of the sort he needed. As he was about to unlock the very last of the twelve file cabinets, he heard the ding-ding that signified an elevator in motion.

Looking briefly at the disarray he caused in the reception area, Boyle decided to leave it as is. He scooted into the patient waiting room, looked outside to see the number three lit up on the elevator display, and walked out of the suite, closing but not locking the doors behind him.

Could he get down to ten before Fred? He'd better try.

Steadying himself with the handrails, he went careening down the service stairs two at a time. As he neared the tenth floor, he looked at his watch. Eleven fifty-five.

The staircase door had just eased itself shut when the south elevator doors opened on ten. Fred peered around to his right and grinned at Boyle, who sat on the floor smiling up at him. He made a pretense of wiping his hands off with a bandana handkerchief.

"There you are," the old man said. "How's it goin'?"

"Good, Fred. What's up?"

"I was just gonna call out for lunch. You want anything, Erik?"

"Thanks for asking, but I'm going to work right through and get out as soon as I can. Just about done now on this floor."

"Okay, pal. See ya." Fred gave a little salute and withdrew.

With the old man out of his way, Boyle gathered his tools and took the north elevator up to fifteen, using the key to stop it with the doors open. The decoy on ten was useless now, after his chat with Fred. At any rate, lunch should take care of him for at least a half hour. With any luck, he'd be finished by then.

Back in LaFreniere's suite, Boyle opened the remaining file cabinet in the reception/records area. The first ivory-colored file jacket he picked out was a patient record spanning several months.

"Yessuh!" he whispered, feeling the exultation in his stomach.

When he looked for Justin's records, however, he came up empty-handed. He checked for misfiles, but no, it just wasn't there.

He was gritting his teeth and pulling other file jackets out to determine what was wrong when it dawned on him. These were closed records. Yes, the last entry in each jacket confirmed it; he was into the doctor's inactive file. Quickly, he stuffed everything back and locked up, returning the keys to the receptionist's desk and pushing the pop-out lock closed.

It was twelve-fifteen. He went to the doctor's private office next. Scanning the room, his eyes took in the window with the majestic city view, the neatly organized rosewood desk and matching furniture, and the paneled walls with the chair rail running around three sides of the room. No files, what the hell! The only hope seemed to be the little corner closet he spotted, but no, there he found only clothes hangers, an umbrella and a pair of beat-up running shoes. The doctor's desk was unlocked, but devoid of files also.

As he was about to give up and leave, he noticed a break in the chair rail behind LaFreniere's desk. Then he began to distinguish a groove running up the dark paneling that might have been taken for part of the grain pattern. Walking over to the wall, he could see it was a hidden panel – not disguised for secrecy so much as for uniformity in the décor.

There was no lock, it was just a push-to-open panel that yielded to a thumb's easy pressure. There was a putty-colored hanging file inside. He pulled up the metal face, slid it back in its groove, and pulled out the alphabetized file drawer.

When Boyle found them, he saw that Justin's records were too extensive for him to read thoroughly before one o'clock. He hurried to the waiting room with the file and pulled out a digital camera from his trouser pocket. Keeping an eye on the elevator, he positioned himself in back of the center table where some magazines were displayed. He made space for the file and began taking pictures.

Ding-ding, ding-ding. As he was finishing, he saw the numbers light up over the elevator and snapped his final picture when the car was on four. Flying back to LaFreniere's office with the file, he stashed it in place, closed the file drawer and the panel, then went back to the waiting room to see the number eleven blink on.

He made a quick, careful survey of the room. Everything seemed in order. He walked into the corridor and locked the office. Looking at his watch, he saw it was only twelve-forty. Did he really have to hurry so? It could only be Fred, after all. What would he want this time?

Well, it really didn't matter. He had stuffed everything into his toolbox by the time the elevator doors opened. But it wasn't Fred who emerged, it was Raynor LaFreniere.

He had met the man, for Chrissake, and no matter how brief it had been, he couldn't afford to be recognized by him here! The doctor was still in profile and hadn't turned to look when Boyle backed into the north elevator with his toolbox, pulled the elevator key and pushed the button for the ground floor.

"Hold it!" LaFreniere shouted. "Hold it."

Looking out through the closing doors, Boyle saw LaFreniere bend over to retrieve something from the floor with his left hand while he thrust his right arm between the doors to keep them open. The doctor had one of Boyle's lock picks and was trying to hand it into the elevator. Boyle kept his face angled to the inside control panel while he snatched the lock pick away and shoved LaFreniere backward into the corridor. The elevator doors clattered shut on a string of obscenities.

His heart was pounding in his chest all the way down to the lobby. Assuming LaFreniere would be on his heels, he couldn't waste time with Fred, whose startled face he glimpsed while sprinting past him.

"Erik! Erik!" the old man shouted, pushing his chair back and running after him.

"Gotta go, Fred. Can't stop!" he yelled over his shoulder.

"The key, boy! The elevator key!"

On the run, he fished the key with the blue tag out of his

pocket and threw it backwards without looking. Much later, he would wonder if Fred caught it on the fly.

~~~

Boyle was still in work clothes when he found a photo shop open on Van Ness Avenue. The clerk was happy to take his camera card and produce hard copies on letter-size paper. At the hotel, he read the file twice and mulled over its revelations in a sort of quiet despair before rousing himself to call the Styles mansion.

"Ivan, I want to give you my final report. Can you drop by this evening with Mrs. Chitworth? There's a suite here on the second floor the manager has agreed to let me use."

"Today? I'm sorry, Boyle, we can't. How about tomorrow?"

Exactly what he expected – putting him off was a habit now with the Chitworths. Well, he had anticipated it. Before dialing, he decided he could really use this evening to prepare.

"All right, but please make it early. How about ten o'clock?"

"You make it sound urgent."

"It is, believe me."

CHAPTER 52

On Monday morning, Justin was playing alone in his room. Ivan and Claudia had an appointment downtown, and Sam was downstairs somewhere with Esther. He knew Detective Bennett was coming to see him, and that could mean only one thing – another bunch of questions about what happened the night his father died.

His mother walked in, smiling.

"It's time, Justin," she said.

"I won't talk to him, Mommy."

She didn't reply, but her look was stern now.

"I mean it, Mommy," he said. "I don't want to see him."

"Justin, you will do this for me. It won't take long. All you need to do is answer his questions truthfully. If you don't understand something or don't know the answer, tell him so."

Why was she making him go through this again? When he talked to Doctor LaFreniere, he figured that was the end. Ever since, he had to avoid his Aunt Helena. More than anybody, she had been good to him, which made his betrayal hard to justify, even to himself. But what else was he supposed to do? He was beginning to look forward to the hospital they had talked about – anything to get away.

It occurred to Justin that no one was on his side any more. Even Aunt Helena's motives for being nice to him were selfish and easy to see through – she expected everybody to make up for her lousy life in a wheelchair. Besides, she wanted a little boy of her own, he knew, especially one who reminded her of Justin's real daddy.

That's why his mother didn't trust Aunt Helena now, he figured. She was her sister, but she was sick of sharing things with her. Adults didn't impress him like they used to – they were just as selfish as they said kids were.

Justin intended to make the questions stop. If he failed, it wouldn't be for lack of trying. And he knew one thing for sure. Whether you get your own way depends on how smart you are. Today, he needed to be smart.

~~~

Maynard Bennett and Beth Twomey pulled into the circular drive at the Styles mansion just after ten. The courtyard was flooded with morning sunshine. In the very center, lazy arcs of water burbled from the apex of the fountain and collected in the basin below. There was a calming effect to that sound, Bennett knew, but today he scarcely felt it.

Glancing at the cars in front of his, he saw they belonged to Mrs. Styles and Helena Swann. Unless someone was late, they weren't going to be monitored by a team of lawyers. That should make him feel better, shouldn't it?

Until last Wednesday, he assumed he was off the Styles investigation for good. After the initial round of questioning, the case became politicized, and he was shoved right out of the picture. So he was surprised and pleased when Al Bowers asked him to conduct the interview with Justin Styles.

"This is probably our last chance to clarify what went down that night," Bowers had said. "I didn't get anywhere with Mrs. Styles or Helena Swann. So it's up to you, May. If you can get a clear account of the boy's actions that night, maybe we can put this to bed."

The only request Bennett made was that a second detective accompany him. He hoped to interview Justin without any family members standing by, and he knew the presence of a female law officer would help make that happen.

When Bennett rang the front door bell, Esther Jarndyce answered. She greeted him and smiled at Beth as he took off his hat and introduced them.

"This is Detective Twomey, Miss Jarndyce."

"Won't you come in? Mrs. Styles and Justin should be down in a moment. I'll show you to the library."

As they walked through the foyer, Bennett recalled the night of Brad Styles's death. Esther's insistence that Helena Swann never came out of her room was the initial spark that fired the investigation. And here he was trying to pin down the other mystery of that night – the actions of a little boy whose biological father had been a notorious killer.

Why that last thought popped into his mind, he couldn't quite say, except that he always got a heavy dose of déjà vu in this place. Indeed, this was the third investigation that brought him into the life of Angela Styles. First was the old Shoo-fly case, then the Breastplate, and now ... what would this one become known as?

Beth and he stood up when Justin and Mrs. Styles came into the library. She made a lovely gesture with her hand and shoulder that seemed to say, 'Don't stand on ceremony, we're all the same here.' Although he didn't believe it for a second, Bennett was thoroughly charmed at her ability to carry it off.

Justin's body language said something else entirely, he noticed. In the first place, the boy wasn't holding his mother's hand as they came into the room. Then he walked off and stared out the windows overlooking the terrace while Mrs. Styles sat and spoke to them.

"I think my son is a little nervous about talking to you, Detective Bennett. Justin, please come over here and sit by Mommy."

She extended her arm toward the boy as she spoke. He turned and walked to her, sitting to her right on the sofa facing Bennett and Twomey, who sat across in matching armchairs. Justin's eyes were downcast, and a muscle along his jaw line rippled.

"How would you like to proceed, Detective?" she asked.

"Well, ma'am, is it possible you and I could change seats? Justin and I need to get acquainted. I'd like to tell him a little about myself."

Mrs. Styles looked startled, but she smiled and got up when he did. Justin's eyes immediately rose to meet his as he stepped over and sat next to him.

"I have a son, Justin," Bennett began. "He's grown up now, but when he was your age, he was really interested in police work. How about you?"

The boy hesitated just a moment. "I remember you from the night my dad died."

"That's right, we spoke out there on the terrace."

"Have you ever been in a gunfight, Detective?"

Angela Styles interrupted.

"Justin, what a question." She was smiling, but embarrassed.

"That's all right, Mrs. Styles. Boys always want to know

that. Fact is, Justin, that kind of thing is pretty rare. I have twenty-three years on the force, and I've only used my weapon on the firing range."

"Are you a good shot?"

Bennett smiled. "Yes, I am. Expert marksman."

Beth Twomey smoothed her skirt under her thighs and turned toward Angela Styles.

"You have such a lovely home, Mrs. Styles," she said. "You must be very proud."

"Thank you. Yes, we love it here. Why don't I show you the downstairs rooms while the boys here get better acquainted?"

"Would you? All right with you, Maynard?"

It was perfect. For the five minutes they were gone, Bennett was able to settle in with Justin and get a sense of him. There was no question of establishing intimacy with the boy – even at his tender age, he was cautious and reserved. Still, Bennett was satisfied that he had loosened up enough to cooperate.

When the gals strolled back into the library, Mrs. Styles looked over to Bennett and Justin. Before she said even a word, he knew she was at ease with the situation. Beth Twomey would have seen to that.

"Justin, honey, you know Detective Bennett has some questions to ask. If it's all right with you, I'm going to leave you with him and Mrs. Twomey. I'll be in the kitchen with Miss Jarndyce if you need me."

The boy considered for a moment. "Okay Mommy," he said.

Angela Styles smiled sweetly and left the room. Beth and he communicated their mutual relief with a silent glance.

"Justin," he began, "I'm only going to ask about two things – the saw blade and the night your dad had his accident. You'll see me taking notes while you speak, and I'll probably ask more questions when I don't understand something. Okay so far, son?"

Justin nodded. "What's she here for?" he asked, pointing to Beth.

Bennett explained as Beth looked on smiling. "Whenever possible, it's smart for a policeman to have a witness. Detective Twomey will be my witness."

"That's right, Justin," she said. "I'll be here with you the whole time, but I won't be asking any questions."

Justin was sizing her up, and Bennett sat back to let them get better acquainted. Beth was in her mid-thirties, tall, and girlishly attractive rather than pretty. Wholesome was the inadequate word that came to mind when Bennett thought of her. A conscientious investigator, she was also the mother of three boys.

"My son Jason is just your age," she said. "His favorite thing in the world right now is Xbox 360. I'll bet you know something about that."

Justin smiled at her and nodded.

Things were going very well, Bennett figured – couldn't be better, in fact – yet he had to remember it cut both ways. The boy was relaxing for them, sure, but weren't they doing the same for him?

He listened closely as Justin related his theft of the saw blade from Gutierrez, his extreme care in cutting through the balusters from the outside edge inward, his attempts at concealment by using soap to fill in the cuts, the discovery by Danzig, and finally, Brad Styles's suspicion that Justin had been the perpetrator. Bennett asked for the name of the movie Justin claimed to be copycatting – he'd want to screen it to make sure of that. To complete his understanding, he had one further question.

"You didn't tell the truth about this, Justin. Not to your father when he asked, and not even after his accident, when we asked your mother to talk to you. Can you tell me why?"

"I was afraid I'd get in trouble. I knew it was wrong, but I lied."

"Have you discussed it since then with anyone? Your mother or aunt or doctor – anyone at all?"

"No."

Could that be true? He bought the story so far, but how could they be the very first ones Justin confided in?

"All right Justin, we're half way there. Why don't you take your time and tell us what happened the night your father fell down the stairs. Tell us what you were doing, what you saw, and anything else you want us to know."

Justin had grown a little agitated, but the story he told was the one they already knew: Brad Styles passing by his bedroom, the shout from the stairs, the boy shutting his door in fear when he realized something awful had occurred.

"When did you come out of your room, Justin?"

"I heard a siren, then voices downstairs. I opened my door then, when the rescue squad came. My mother was screaming and crying, but pretty soon she went to bed. That's when I went downstairs. Nobody wanted to answer my questions. I was scared when Esther asked me about the toy truck. She believed me when I told her I didn't leave it out. I don't know why exactly, but I thought about the saw blade then, and went to hide it."

"When did you see your Aunt Helena?"

"I didn't. She never came out that I saw."

"And your mother? Did you see her again?"

"Yes. Esther brought me to my room and waited till I got in bed. But I didn't sleep long. I got up and went to see my mother."

"Wasn't she sleeping?"

Justin looked up at him. The boy's mouth was distorted and his chin trembled. Then he put his head down and remained quiet.

Bennett shifted closer to him on the couch. He draped his right arm over the boy's shoulders.

"Justin, if this is difficult, we can take a break."

"Mommy was crying when I went in her room," he blurted. "It was dark, but she saw the door open and asked me to come close. She switched on the lamp next to her bed. She said she was awful sleepy, but she kept waking up. And … and she kept talking about what happened."

Bennett looked down at this robust little boy who suddenly seemed so vulnerable. Beth's face showed concern as well. He wondered if he should stop now. But would they ever learn, if he did, what really went down in this house the night of the accident? Although it seemed unfair to press the boy now, he was ready – oh so ready – to pour it out.

Bennett rolled his eyes at Beth Twomey and decided to wade in. He tried to keep any trace of anxiety from affecting the tone of his voice.

"If you can remember what your mother said, son, why don't you tell me?"

Big tears ran down Justin's cheeks. "I told her I didn't want to see you," he cried. "I told her this morning not to let you ask me questions. But she said I had to tell you the truth."

"Go ahead, son. You can tell me."

"Mommy said it was *her* when we talked that night," he said, squeezing Bennett's hand. "She was mad at Daddy and Aunt Helena. He met with my aunt before they all went to the police that time. They met alone, in her room. Mommy was in the corridor outside. She said ... Daddy and Aunt Helena were doing a bad thing. She said Daddy used to love my aunt, and maybe he still did. That's why Mommy put my toy on the stairs, Detective Bennett. It wasn't me. She knows it wasn't me!"

Bennett felt the hot tears soak through his shirt as Justin's face burrowed into his side. Beth Twomey left her chair to sit with them and help comfort the boy.

After a few minutes, Justin grew quiet and withdrawn. Bennett had collected his thoughts by then, and spoke tenderly.

"Justin, I'm going to ask Miss Jarndyce to come in and take you upstairs. Then I'm going to speak to your mother. Is that okay with you?"

"She's going to know I told you. She's going to hate me."

"No, Justin, that's quite impossible," Beth said with conviction. "No mother can ever hate her own son."

CHAPTER 53

Boyle met the Chitworths in the hotel lobby. It was a little past ten o'clock. He hoped his anxiety didn't show. He had made a particular effort at professionalism this morning. After minutely inspecting the clothes he would wear, he dressed, combed his hair neatly, and trimmed his mustache and goatee. All the while making himself run through the main points he would make – over and over until it was rote.

When he ushered Ivan and Claudia into the second-floor suite, he wasted little time in small talk and preliminary explanation. Asking them to sit on the couch by the room's large window, he began his presentation in a passionate tone.

"These are the facts and no one can dispute them," he said, looking from one to the other. "Justin Styles shows all the symptoms of antisocial personality disorder. It used to be called sociopathic personality disorder."

Mrs. Chitworth took in air audibly and assumed her most imperious manner.

"How can you *possibly* know that!" she demanded.

"I've done the research, ma'am. And please don't forget that I wouldn't be here if you hadn't thought something was wrong."

"But you're calling Justin a sociopath," she cried. "That's ludicrous, Mr. Boyle!"

"Mrs. Chitworth, most of these cases have behavior problems prior to age fifteen. They have a dislike or show anger toward authority, get into legal trouble, are often cruel with animals. Some set fires. We can't sit back and wait for Justin to set fires."

Ivan spoke: "Boyle, don't ...."

"But you've got to listen to me," he insisted. "The major symptom of the antisocial personality is a pattern of disregard for the rights of others, a failure to conform to rules. You can imagine the result. We're talking about con men here, people who use trickery for personal profit. They're impulsive, given to angry outbursts – physical assaults, even – they don't consider the consequences of their behavior."

Mrs. Chitworth was adamant. "I can't believe my ears! You're suggesting Justin is dangerous?"

"He has a condition that could make him dangerous. You know the history of his recent problems. Tell me why the police are still coming around for interviews. Doesn't it have something to do with Justin?"

"I think that's absurd, Mr. Boyle."

He looked toward Ivan, determined to reach at least one of them. "You know, some experts argue these people have a reduced ability to feel empathy for others. Human suffering and emotion mean nothing to them. Think of Sam in close contact with ... someone who can commit violence without remorse."

Ivan looked tense and worried, but remained silent. His mother spoke up again.

"I think you're trying to scare us, and I demand to know the basis for your incredible assumptions!"

"They're not assumptions, ma'am. I only wish they were. Justin tells lies without remorse, abused a kitten he had, touched his dad inappropriately in a sexual way, was physically aggressive with playmates, has expressed hostility to authority any number of times. There is no formal diagnosis because of his age ... but it's clear that he has serious behavioral problems."

Ivan slumped in his chair. "Boyle," he said, "where did you learn all this?"

"No. You don't want to know. But ask his mother. Ask his psychiatrist. Confront them if you care for Sam as much as you say."

"That's quite enough, Boyle. Who the hell are you to judge us?"

He had gone too far. They were silent and angry, and he knew he had lost them. He could see that Ivan didn't have the strength it would take to confront his cousin Angela about her beloved son. Mrs. Chitworth must have seen it too. She regained her composure and was even willing to concede that Justin's troubles called for continued therapy. They went on discussing both boys for some time, but it was just a game now.

As they prepared to leave, Ivan thanked him for his efforts, although he refused to say what he would do.

"I don't know, Boyle. I'll speak to Angela about Sam and Justin soon. We'll sort it out then."

The job was over. In effect, he was fired. He took no solace in knowing he had proved his case. And he had – beyond the shadow of a doubt. This was a terrible result compared to the risk he had taken. He almost wished he hadn't destroyed his evidence before going to bed last night. Then again, what could he have done with it, except get into trouble?

When the Chitworths were gone, a scene in a prison visitors' room popped into his head. He found himself going over his interview with Mickey Cullion and Shonda Wallace. What was it she said to him about his case? *Surely in vain the net is spread … in the sight of the bird.*

CHAPTER 54

A *nd a little child shall lead them.* Sure, thought Bowers, but where to? Up the primrose path, maybe? Or straight to hell? As far as Justin Styles was concerned, he suspected the latter when Maynard Bennett and Beth Twomey laid their bombshell on him.

Three hours later, Raynor LaFreniere and Hilary Saunders dropped by to see him. At her request, Bowers found them a vacant conference room, although he wondered why she hadn't simply called him to her office.

When they had exchanged pleasantries and settled in, LaFreniere pulled a two-page transcript and a digital voice recorder out of his briefcase, laying both on the table in front of him. He played back the recording of Justin's *first* confession, the one pointing to Helena Swann as the mastermind behind the death of Brad Styles. Bowers followed along with the transcript, which the doctor had dated and signed.

As the recording ended, he looked from Saunders to LaFreniere.

"Tell me, Doctor, did you believe Justin when he made these ... admissions?" he asked.

"Well, yes. I couldn't be sure about the details, but I believed him."

"And between ... let's see ... last Wednesday when you recorded this and today – who did you tell?"

Hilary Saunders spoke up. "Doctor LaFreniere doesn't have to answer to you about that, Lieutenant."

"Then what is he doing here today, Ms. Saunders? If it's a matter of doctor-patient privilege, why is either one of you here divulging what happened in a therapy session? Someone must have given you permission, right? And would that person be Justin's mother? And would she have an ulterior motive for that? It wouldn't be to counteract a certain other confession, would it?"

Hilary Saunders lashed out.

"That's a heavy-handed brand of sarcasm, Lieutenant Bowers. I find it offensive and disrespectful to me personally."

He was too angry to be careful.

"Here's the point," he said. "You've come here for one reason only, to have me drop the investigation right now, to keep us away from Mrs. Styles and Justin. You wouldn't be giving me this information if Justin hadn't made a second confession, one that cuts even deeper than this. You're handing me a monkey wrench to fuck up my case, and you figure I won't ask these people for an accounting. It stinks!"

"It's quite evident you've lost your perspective, Bowers," she snarled. "I should have gone directly to Dan Cinzano."

"Oh no, Ms. Saunders. You didn't go to my boss because he would have read you the riot act before he sent you to me. You expected deference and cooperation from me today. Sorry to disappoint you. But I'll go see him, just as you knew I would in the end. We both know how this damn game works."

He tossed the transcript on the table with a dismissive gesture.

Raynor LaFreniere looked shell-shocked. "May I ask

where this leaves us?" he asked.

Ms. Saunders had eased back into her chair with a smile.

"I think Lieutenant Bowers was about to tell us how this works."

He nodded. "You want the investigation zapped at the source to prevent getting more people involved. Every further step you take up the ladder will increase the chance of a leak – and a lot of sensational publicity. Ms. Saunders here can squash me like a bug, Doctor LaFreniere. But she knows that a big ol' squashed bug makes a mess."

"He's telling you that he gets to dictate some terms here, Ray."

LaFreniere looked bewildered. It was Bowers's turn to smile.

"Correct. I want a full report on Justin Styles for our files. Diagnosis, symptoms, prognosis – the works. In addition, I want a proposed course of treatment from his *new* doctor. I think you're too close to ... the family ... to continue with Justin as a patient. Are we agreed?"

LaFreniere's face went scarlet and his voice slid up an octave.

"Now wait a minute, Lieutenant! What will Mrs. Styles think?"

Then, making an effort to bring his voice under control, he continued.

"She ... she'll have to consent to all this, and I don't think I can advise her to do that."

"Your choice, doctor," he said.

"It's okay, Ray," Ms. Saunders said gently. "We'll both speak to her."

LaFreniere hadn't figured out what hit him yet. Bowers knew Saunders would bring him into line. He gave them a mock-friendly wave as they got up and moved toward the conference room door. They didn't wave back.

He hadn't the least right to demand those things from LaFreniere. That was Winston Garrett's province. But he figured Ms. Saunders didn't trust her lapdog any more and wanted to avoid getting the D.A's office involved. He was happy to take advantage. At least now the record would clearly show the police had recognized a troubled child and made sure he received appropriate treatment.

Smiling grimly, he shook his head. Twice now, his non-investigation of Brad Styles's death was shut down – this time by the cleverness of a seven-year old. Justin had to know what he was doing by pointing first one way, then another. He had muddied things so badly, the case was incoherent.

His biological father had been clever too, Bowers thought. Clever and deadly. Thirteen years from now Justin would be twenty. What in hell would he be like at twenty? Thank God, Bowers would be retired then.

CHAPTER 55

Not many P.I.s would stake out a former client's place of residence for two days after his services were terminated, but Boyle thought he might piece together a few fragments of the puzzle that way. If he could track the comings and goings of the household members for a day or so, he might see a pattern emerge that would hint at why he failed so miserably. Or maybe he was just morbidly obsessive, a glutton for punishment.

On Tuesday, Raynor LaFreniere and Hilary Saunders showed up early at the Styles mansion, in separate cars. Three hours later, at eleven o'clock, Saunders left alone. Not long after that, LaFreniere's car purred out of the gates. Justin and Mrs. Styles were with him.

Boyle followed as far as I-5, where he abandoned the tail. They were headed south. He recalled the doctor starting on such a trip before. He could either follow or take a break and go back to the stakeout later, betting on their return.

Easy enough choice, he thought, for a guy not getting paid. He took the break and came back at three o'clock after checking the parking lot at LaFreniere's apartment building to make sure the doctor's Lincoln Town Car hadn't returned.

It was close to midnight when the Lincoln finally pulled into the cobblestone driveway at the Marina district mansion. LaFreniere stayed only long enough to drop Angela Styles off. Justin was not with them. While he drove back to his hotel, Boyle considered the theory Bowers had about LaFreniere and Mrs. Styles. If this was a romance, he thought, somebody better tell those two to turn up the heat.

In the morning, Boyle reminded himself it was Wednesday, the last day for this horseshit. He got up early and killed some time at Marina Park with a coffee and scone, getting back and into position near the Styles mansion by eight.

Then the skies opened. At quarter past ten, Ivan drove off in heavy rain with Mrs. Chitworth and Helena. They were in Helena's car, and Boyle followed them to the airport. It seemed pointless to get involved in parking hassles and security lines, so he drove back to the city, had lunch, and resumed the stakeout. Somebody would have to bring the car back, after all. He figured that person would be Ivan, and he was right. Ivan returned with Helena before two o'clock.

That was enough for Boyle. A few comings and goings had given him more than he expected. Claudia Chitworth was on her way home to Newport and Justin ... well, Justin was out of harm's reach somewhere, a psychiatric facility most likely.

Mrs. Chitworth had probably left for home with a sense of having accomplished her mission. Until Monday, Boyle hadn't known she was the reason he failed. In effect, Ivan was his only legitimate client – albeit a weak one who needed a smarter P.I. than the one he hired. Everything conveyed to Claudia Chitworth – the evidence he uncovered, the conversations he reported, even his real identity – was relayed back to either Helena or Angela to help them subvert his case. He was sure of it. Mrs.

Chitworth's behavior on Monday was half out of anger – he finally had the goods on Justin – and half out of fear – the terror she felt that Ivan might refuse to relinquish custody when he understood the nature of Justin's problem.

Of course, there was a benign side to her machinations. She was an old woman who believed her son could not be an effective parent on his own. But who was to say Ivan wouldn't have risen to the challenge? There was irony here. She had likely fostered Ivan's dependence on her in order to have a companion in her old age. And now she would deny him parenthood. He doubted people did these terrible things to each other deliberately, but where should the victims apply for relief?

Boyle wondered if Ivan's eyes had been opened to his mother's intentions. He was staying on in San Francisco, after all. Why? Perhaps he was making a belated move toward independence – at the very least, he hoped that Ivan meant to provide a smooth transition for Sam. If so, Boyle's persistence in the case may have paid a small dividend.

As for the rest of his unanswered questions ... would the cops be willing to talk?

~~~

After the rain Wednesday and early Thursday, the air had a freshened quality that joined with the newly minted blue sky in one of those late summer interludes that point toward autumn. This perfection called for a long walk – even better, a trip out of town. But he'd think about that tomorrow.

In a few minutes, he'd be meeting with Al Bowers. Until now, he and the lieutenant hadn't helped each other much, but they had forged a bond out of mutual respect. Bowers knew he was a straight shooter who could be trusted. For his part, Boyle saw in the black man a kindred soul, someone who wanted to do the right thing in the right way for the right reasons.

"Sure we can talk," Bowers had said when he phoned him earlier. "Come on over. I'll grab a conference room somewhere in the building and maybe have Bennett sit in."

Boyle had a different idea. "I want to see you, Bowers, but not in official surroundings. Christ, you might be inclined to book me if I unload down there."

He laughed. "You tell me where, then."

"There's a quiet bar I like near my hotel called Virgil. How about meeting me for drinks after work?"

"Five-thirty okay?"

"Great. Bennett's welcome too. See you then."

Boyle was glad to see Eddie tending bar when he pushed through the front door. Dropping in at Virgil had become a routine for him. He figured routine and ritual were important to everybody, whether they admitted it or not – half the comfort of daily life was knowing what came next.

"Good evening, sir."

He nodded.

"Bourbon straight up?"

"Thanks, yes. A friend will be joining me, so I'll take it to a table."

"It's slow tonight, Mr. Boyle. Let me serve you there."

While he sat in the velvety dark, waiting for Bowers and Bennett, he watched the streetscape outside illuminated by the afternoon sun. During a long stretch of his life, Boyle thought of quiet city bars as safe harbors. Even on the sunniest days, with a bartender his only company, he had enjoyed sitting in the half-dark with a drink, peeking out at life through a bright window. It wasn't much different than spending your daylight hours at a movie theater. He felt like one of those anonymous fans Gloria Swanson refers to in the staircase scene at the end of *Sunset Boulevard*: " ... those wonderful people out there in the dark."

Bowers walked in at five forty-five without Bennett. Eddie came over and took his order while they were still discussing the weather.

"Very fine out there today, Boyle."

"Yeah. Hope it lasts for a spell."

"You said you were canned. Aren't you leaving for home?"

"Hotel room's paid for through the weekend. I think I'll take in the sights. Might even do a side trip to wine country."

"Everybody does."

Bowers thanked Eddie, who had just returned with his Irish whiskey and rocks. He smiled and raised his glass to Boyle.

"Here's to lost causes."

"Right, lost causes," he repeated. "Where's Bennett?"

"My man May doesn't frequent bars, Boyle. Always heads home when the day is done. Loves his wife and his home life."

"Sounds like a good man."

"The best. I'm no carouser myself, but I need a little relief now and then before the trek home. Nice quiet place here, by the way."

"It is. Tell me, Lieutenant, is there a case left? Will

somebody answer for what happened to Brad Styles?"

Boyle hadn't noticed before, but Bowers had hazel eyes. In the dark, they verged on a striking green. The lieutenant looked at him with a mocking grin.

"Not in this lifetime. The case is a shambles. I killed it Monday afternoon when LaFreniere showed up with Justin's first confession."

"Wha ...?"

"While you were getting canned by the Chitworths, Bennett was getting Justin's *second* confession, the one where he said Mommy did it. Then LaFreniere hauls his ass to headquarters with a transcript of Justin's *first* confession, where he told the good doctor Auntie Helena did it."

"Christ. That wasn't in the file."

Bowers put his drink down and stared.

"What the fuck you saying, Boyle?"

"I broke into LaFreniere's office Sunday and copied his file on Justin."

"Say what!"

"I was determined to prove to Ivan he shouldn't transfer custody of Sam Dunnell to Angela."

"Oh yeah, the second son." He was shaking his head. "Jesus, Boyle, I can't believe you went that far."

"Sam's a great kid, Lieutenant. He deserves everything I could do for him. I wouldn't be so worried about him except that he's come to idolize his brother."

Bowers tossed down the rest of his drink and wiped his mouth.

"That would be a worry, all right," he agreed.

In considerable detail, Boyle explained what was in

Justin's file. The lieutenant took out his notebook and pen and jotted everything down, stopping often to ask questions.

"This is going to help, Boyle. I have a feeling LaFreniere might try to sugarcoat his diagnosis or postpone the referral to another shrink. Now I'll be ready for him."

"Why do you think the boy needs a different doc, Bowers? I found squat to show LaFreniere was getting involved with Mrs. Styles."

"Turns out it's pretty one-sided, but there's no doubt he has the hots for her. It was Bennett found him out. He noticed him first at Brad Styles's wake. The guy sat alone and never once took his eyes off Angela Styles. Then there was the lunch in Daly City the next week. Every time she spilled a tear, Bennett saw LaFreniere's hand go for hers or his arm go around her waist. And you should have heard the guy when I said he had to find another doctor for Justin. It was embarrassing."

"I do know he's got almost no life beyond work."

"Right. Great professional reputation, but socially a loser. Good taste in women, though."

"Yeah, what you see first with Mrs. Styles is Angela the knockout. Then you get to know her a little, and she's a lot more – the type you put on a pedestal."

Bowers sighed and shook his head.

"She got to you too, hunh? You know, Boyle, I've watched these women through two highly publicized scandals – and now this. In the public mind, Helena is the evil twin, Angela's bad-girl sister. But that's never been so clear to me."

Boyle's jaw dropped. "Really? What's your take?"

"Well, there's a kind of competitive struggle between those gals that nobody seems to notice. When Angela married Shoo-fly, she was stealing him away from Helena. To spite Angela, Helena took him on the side as her lover. After Shoo-fly was shot down, Angela got Brad Styles away from Helena and married him. And now she's taking the boys and attempting to turn her sister out of her home."

"She hasn't kicked her out yet."

"You're right. And maybe she never will. Despite the things they've done to each other, there's also an incredibly strong bond between them. Starting with their father, they have always loved the same men. It's what they have in common as well as what tears them apart."

"Looks to me like you've become one of the men in their lives, pal."

Bowers grimaced. "Bite my balls, man! *Jesus*, I hope you're not right."

They were quiet a moment, Boyle gloating a little over his ability to make the lieutenant cringe like that. But there was something more important to dig into. He still wanted to assign blame.

"Bowers, who killed Brad Styles? You've got to have the best insight. Or was it just an accident?"

He shrugged. "I can't say, Boyle. Until Monday, I was absolutely positive Helena Swann talked Justin into helping her do it. If I had seen LaFreniere's transcript before Justin pulled that stunt with Bennett, I would have been pressing her hard. But now? Well, I'm not so sure."

Boyle looked over Bowers's head to the still-bright window. "I'm thinking it was Justin alone," he said. "No doubt he was picking up clues, though – from both Helena and his mother. Maybe he saw himself as their rescuer."

"Poor Brad Styles," Bowers said. "He was the best thing that ever happened to those people. But somebody was slated to pay for their sins. Isn't that what the scapegoat does? Like I always say – no good deed goes unpunished. Maybe Brad was too good to live."

"Lovely thought. Damn, you're a cynical bastard."

Bowers grinned wide. "Occupational hazard."

Eddie was signaling from behind the bar, holding up two fingers and looking at them with a question mark. They both nodded yes.

"Where is Justin now?" Boyle asked.

"Del Amo Hospital. It's a private psych facility in Torrance."

"Uh-huh. Tell me, what route would you take to get there."

"I'd go south on Interstate 5."

Boyle nodded. Just then Eddie walked up with a smile and served their drinks from a little cork-lined tray. Bowers reached for his and tossed it off.

"Thanks for the liquor and conversation, Boyle. Give me a chance to stand you before you head back East." He had gotten up and was adjusting his trousers.

"One more question, Lieutenant. You said Shonda Wallace was a friend of yours. After I interviewed Mickey Cullion, she quoted a bible verse to tell me my investigation was compromised. Turns out she was right. Old lady Chitworth was reporting everything I did back to Helena and Angela. How in hell did Shonda figure that out?"

"Shonda Wallace is a bright gal, but I suspect she was just telling you what you should've known – when you're close to a beehive you gotta take care."

"Damn ol' queen bee screwed me up."

"She might not have been the only one."

"Huh?"

"Yeah, I might have helped. To shake Helena Swann up, I asked about her plans to move out of her sister's house. If she thought about who she told ...."

"She would have remembered a certain P.I.! But you interviewed her pretty late in the game. I think she already knew who I was. Must have been a jolt to old lady Chitworth, though, finding out I was talking to the cops."

"You're lucky you didn't find a toy truck on your stairs."

Boyle grimaced and felt the gooseflesh rise on his arms.

"Jesus, Bowers, have a heart!"

CHAPTER 56

He had postponed it for too long, this adventure. Back home in Newport, the name had called up an image from the Middle Ages when he saw it blazoned across the newspaper headlines. That, and a certain pit-of-the-stomach feeling. But until today, Boyle had stayed away from The Breastplate of Faith and Love. Now, on this glorious day, his last in San Francisco, he walked in bright sunshine from his hotel to the Mission District and stood before the little storefront church.

The two-story building looked like a gaudy jewel box between the two decrepit Victorian hulks on either side. It was royal blue with white trim, and gold-tone letters spelled out its unlikely moniker on the two big windows flanking the mission door. Inside, the hall had been divided into a chapel on one side and an activity room on the other by means of a jury-rigged partition of two-by-fours covered by cheap paneling.

Boyle struck up a conversation with the preacher who ran the mission now. He was a black man in his sixties with a warm and encouraging manner. After Cullion's arrest, he came out of retirement to keep the mission open, renting out the apartment the same way Cullion had, and living in the spare room himself. Like Cullion, he scraped by, sending Mrs. Hendrickson enough money each month to keep up the mortgage payments.

"Michael will be released in just a couple of months," the preacher told him.

379

"Will he settle here, Reverend?"

"For a time, yes. He's promised to help me when he gets out of prison. But San Francisco has some terrible associations for the boy. I can't see that he'll stay long."

"I know what you mean," Boyle said. "Who could blame him?"

"Indeed."

It was Sunday afternoon, and services were over. The hall, however, was still bustling with activity. A dozen or so men and women, most of them toting bibles, stood chatting toward the rear of the activity room.

"You'll pardon me, Mr. Boyle," the preacher said. "I have to lead the bible study group now. Will you join us?"

"Thank you, Reverend, not today. Would you mind if I sat in the chapel for a while?"

"Certainly not. Stay as long as you like. You may find an elderly gent cleaning up in there. His name is Theo. He helps me out whenever he can.

He remembered the name. The old Greek was bent over near the altar table, wielding a broom and dustpan. When finished, he turned and spotted Boyle, who smiled at him. Theo nodded and walked over to a wastepaper basket, where he dumped the contents of his dustpan. Then he disappeared through the partition.

The room was very plain. A simple wooden cross and a large, embossed bible sat on the altar table, which was covered with a white tablecloth. A few ornate, though worn chairs stood along the far wall. The whole area was rather dimly backlit by the storefront window behind him. Two dozen carved oak pews faced the altar table, lending a formal note to the scene. They looked like surplus goods from an old Roman Catholic church.

Taking a seat in one of the backmost pews, he rested his hands in his lap and tried to meditate. When thoughts of the people who inhabited the case began to drift into his mind, he didn't fight it, entertaining instead a series of images.

He saw Justin in an all-white hospital room, sullen and staring. And there was Sam, playing quietly in the Marina district mansion while Angela and Helena looked on. Ivan Chitworth walked a street somewhere in the Castro – while his mother sat at home in Newport, gazing out from the great room windows to her beloved weeping beech trees.

Bowers had formulated what Boyle now believed – that both sisters harbored a terrible love for each other and for the men in their lives. And some day, maybe soon, Justin would rejoin them to continue the old pattern. Would Justin ever change? And would Sam survive?

Boyle wanted to find meaning in what happened, a little salvage from the shipwreck. But there was nothing of value, no keepsake for the mantel. He would leave for home tomorrow without any increase in wisdom or any feeling of accomplishment. In this family's history, he was part of a closed and dubious episode. If the Styleses and the Chitworths were weaving a tapestry, he was a dropped thread.

Perhaps there was one dimension of the story he could delineate. He considered himself a student of history, and he knew that no matter how big the town or country, the world of the controlling elite was very small. A covenant is recognized among them, no less powerful for being unwritten. It has ever been thus, he thought: in Persia as in Paris, in Lydia as in London, in Sumer as in San Francisco.

He admired Angela's position in this town's ruling echelon because she stayed out of the daily power stream – until her own universe was threatened. Then, of course, she would do anything to intervene, like a sovereign from antiquity raising a sceptered hand to summon the protection of her warriors.

This burden of thought and feeling wouldn't linger, Boyle knew, if the life waiting for him in Newport were as he had left it – if he could go back to a good woman and a promising future. But no, Assunta had moved on, he was sure. The last time he talked to her, she was distant. When he phoned last night, her number was no longer in use, and his heart sank into his shoes.

"Say, the preacher tells me your name is Boyle," said the thickly accented voice in back of him.

It was Theo, standing just behind the pew. They introduced themselves. Boyle scooted over and gestured for Theo to join him.

"Michael told me about you, Mr. Boyle. He said you helped him."

"Well, he gave me a leg up too, Mr. Staphos. We exchanged a little information is all. How is he doing?"

"Pretty good some days. Not so good other times. But he knows it won't be long now."

"He should be proud of the way he kept this place going. You know, the name is impressive – The Breastplate of Faith and Love."

Theo nodded with enthusiasm. "Michael loves the name. You know what it is, don't you? What it means?"

"Well ... no. No, I don't."

"It's the armor of the true Christian, Mr. Boyle. Faith

and Love. But like I tell Michael, there's more."

"What's the rest, then?"

"The rest of it is the Helmet of Hope, hope for salvation."

Boyle tried to let it sink in.

"I tell Michael all the time, 'Put on the Helmet of Hope.' He laughs at me, but I know it makes him feel better."

Theo had to get back to the Market Street diner and couldn't stay long. Boyle was glad he stopped to chat. When they said goodbye, he was content to sit in the back pew and wonder about many things.

A quiet feeling stole over him. Something like blessed peace. Tomorrow, he would return to Newport and find his routine again. There was a bedrock security in rote things, he thought – the predictive power of a memorized pattern. For a moment he struggled to find a quote he'd been reaching for since Thursday. When he punched his leg and gave up in frustration, it came through like a charm.

The world is a comedy to those that think; a tragedy to those that feel.

Who said it he couldn't tell you. And whether he should laugh or weep wasn't at all clear.

EPILOGUE

It was such a shining, pleasant day, Angela felt her worries subside a little. After breakfast, she walked through the garden with Sam, naming for him its flowers, trees, and shrubs as they took the gravel path along the southern side of the house.

He was a lovely young boy, she thought. So responsive, so polite.

"Auntie Angela, will Justin come back home soon?" he asked.

"Let's hope so, Sam. In the meantime, you and I and your Aunt Helena are going to get to know each other real well. Did I ever tell you Auntie Helena and I are stepsisters?"

"No. Is that anything like half-brothers?"

"Why yes, Sam," she laughed. "It is, in a way. You know, Helena and I were very close as children. I hope you and Justin will be like that."

"I hope so too, Auntie Angela," he said, gazing up at her.

A shivery mix of dread and delight took hold of her. Sam's luminous blue eyes had a look she found utterly charming. For a moment, Angela imagined she was staring into the very face of innocence.

385

Thank you for reading.
Please review this book. Reviews help others find
Absolutely Amazing eBooks and inspire us to keep
providing these marvelous tales.

If you would like to be put on our email list to receive
updates on new releases, contests, and promotions, please
go to AbsolutelyAmazingEbooks.com and sign up.

About the Author

Paul McGoran lives in Newport, Rhode Island. In his life before fiction, he was a laboratory technician, a Russian language interpreter for the U. S. Navy, a career marketing executive, a management consultant, and a day trader. As a writer in the crime genre since 2005, his inspiration comes in equal parts from spending way too much time watching black and white film noir from the forties and fifties, and from reading way too many hard-boiled detective stories.

McGoran is currently working on another novel, *Sooner or Later, Delicate Death*, which takes Stafford Boyle back to his old hometown to solve the revenge murder of the bully who terrorized his childhood.

NewPulpPress.com

www.ingramcontent.com/pod-product-compliance
Lightning Source LLC
Chambersburg PA
CBHW070357260626
47161CB00001B/168